Don't look down, a voice said inside her head.

But she did. And there he was, silhouetted by flames.

The smiling man's features were sharp, and a large, purple scar ran diagonally from the right side of his jaw to his left temple. His gaze shifted to a point behind her. He bared his teeth like an animal.

Izzy turned.

Within the arched curves of a medieval monastery, a figure scanned the horizon. It was another man, very tall, with a riot of hair that tumbled down his shoulders, like her own....

Then a voice rumbled like thunder, shaking her spine with a low, masculine timbre.

"Isabella? Je suis Jean-Marc de Devereaux des Ombres. Je vous cherche. Attendez-moi. Je vous cherche."

This time Izzy woke slowly, clutching the sheets as she whispered to the darkness, *"Oui. Je suis ici."* "Yes, I am here," in French.

Only, she didn't speak French.

I0645636

Dear Reader,

When I think of the word *heroine,* I look at two bright pink stickies clinging to my computer monitor just below a swath of my daughter's school pictures (I have a very big computer monitor!) The stickies read: "Feel the fear and do it anyway" and "I am a warrior, and I will not turn my back on the battlefield." To me, a heroine is someone who pushes through her fear and does what she must—be she a mom, a friend, a coworker, a caretaker, a wanderer, or the heiress of a magical House founded in medieval France.

For most of us, it takes an act of courage just to get up and face a busy day in an uncertain, lightning-paced world. There is magic in knowing that if we can muster the courage to step through the shadow, the sun and the moon await with light both golden and silver. I believe the universe does honor our dreams, and that there is more—much more—to each of us than meets the eye. These are the lessons I am learning, and what I hope to share in the story of Isabella "Izzy" DeMarco in THE GIFTED trilogy and hopefully, many other books to come.

Please let me know at www.nancyholder.com about your own journey.

Take heart, and be bold!

Nancy Holder

Saginaw Chippewa Indian Tribe
Tribal Library
Mt Pleasant MI 48858

NANCY HOLDER

DAUGHTER of the FLAMES

Published by Silhouette Books

America's Publisher of Contemporary Romance

If you purchased this book without a cover you should be aware
that this book is stolen property. It was reported as "unsold and
destroyed" to the publisher, and neither the author nor the
publisher has received any payment for this "stripped book."

For my strong, compassionate and courageous daughter,
Belle Claire Christine Holder,
who lives the tenets of Tae Kwon Do:
courtesy, integrity, perseverance, self-control
and indomitable spirit;
and brings honor upon herself, her family and her instructors.

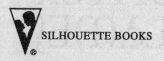 SILHOUETTE BOOKS

ISBN 0-373-51407-7

DAUGHTER OF THE FLAMES

Copyright © 2006 by Nancy Holder

All rights reserved. Except for use in any review, the reproduction
or utilization of this work in whole or in part in any form by any
electronic, mechanical or other means, now known or hereafter
invented, including xerography, photocopying and recording, or in
any information storage or retrieval system, is forbidden without
the written permission of the editorial office, Silhouette Books,
233 Broadway, New York, NY 10279 U.S.A.

All characters in this book have no existence outside the imagination of
the author and have no relation whatsoever to anyone bearing the same
name or names. They are not even distantly inspired by any individual
known or unknown to the author, and all incidents are pure invention.

This edition published by arrangement with Harlequin Books S.A.

® and TM are trademarks of Harlequin Books S.A., used under license.
Trademarks indicated with ® are registered in the United States Patent
and Trademark Office, the Canadian Trade Marks Office and in other
countries.

www.SilhouetteBombshell.com

Printed in U.S.A.

NANCY HOLDER

is the bestselling author of nearly eighty books and two hundred short stories. She has received four Bram Stoker Awards from the Horror Writers Association, and her books have been translated into two dozen languages. A former ballet dancer, she has lived all over the world and currently resides in San Diego, California, with her daughter, Belle. She would to love to hear from readers at www.nancyholder.com.

Acknowledgments:

My sincere thanks to Gillian Horvath, who first told me about
Bombshell, and to Susan Wiggs, who encouraged me to persist.
Thank you to the Bombshell team, past and present:
Natashya Wilson, Julie Barrett and Tara Parsons,
for your warm welcome and editorial vision.

Howard Morhaim, my agent and friend, you've been there through
oy and joy. And sincere thanks to Howard's assistant, Allison Keiley.
Many thanks to Pat McEwen, JoysofResearch; my San Diego
sheriff's deputy and my N.Y.P.D. contacts, both of whom have
requested anonymity so their thoughtful colleagues won't make
their lives a living hell. Thank you, Steve Perry, for the
marksmanship and ER data. My sincere gratitude to Karen Hackett
for navigating New York for me. A very big thank-you to
Special Agent Jeff Thurman, for many years of friendship,
plot parsing and all the dirt he could tell me without killing me.
Mucho mahalo to Wayne Holder, who stepped up to the plate
when my laptop ate my homework and set the whole thing
to rights despite the best efforts of all geekdom to make
computers far more complicated than they need be.

Thank you, SF-FWs, bryant street, IAMTW, and novelscribes
for various neepery and encouragement; and to my sisters in
Persephone, for the prayers and candles, and the fellowship,
especially after my laptop ate my homework. My gratitude
to Christie Holt, for teaching me to walk with purpose. To
Amy Schricker, Charlotte Fullerton, Ashley McConnell,
Debbie Viguie, Liz Cratty, Lydia Marano, Brenda Van De Ven,
Monica Elrod, Abbie Bernstein, Kym Rademacher, Terri Yates,
Lisa Morton, Leslie Jones, Sandra Morehouse, Anny Caya,
Lucy Walker and Elise Jones, for showing me that sisterhood
is powerful. A shout-out to MariAnn Palmer and Lisa Swyrs,
clothiers and cookie monsters extraordinaire. Dr. Ellen Greenfield,
thanks for the illegal loquats and the free psychological help.
Thanks to my nephew, Richard Wilkinson, for checking in
and loving us. Many thanks to Yasmine and John Palisano,
Del and Sue Howison, Art Cover and Lydia Marano,
and Paul Ruditis for inviting me to cross your thresholds.
Mr. Andrew Thompson and everyone at Family Karate, thank you
for instilling black belt principles in my family. REV, you listen
every day. And you write back. May you walk in Beauty.

Chapter 1

Isabella DeMarco was moaning in her sleep. Her fists clenched her pale blue sheets; tears and sweat trickled down her forehead as she rolled her head against her pillow.

Hustle it up, a voice urgently whispered to her. *They're dogging you!*

Izzy raced through the nightmare forest, a terrifying landscape of fleshy black trees garroted with hangman's necklaces of Spanish moss. A fiery moon blazed overhead, casting flickering shadows over rotting ferns and a matted bunting of ashy gray leaves.

Her surroundings heaved with menace and danger. The surface of a blood-colored swamp roiled as shapes glided toward the boggy earth where she ran. She saw it all with a strange clarity, as if part of her was a camera recording every moment instead of a young woman in flight for her life.

She heard herself panting in counterpoint with her over-cranked heartbeat. Her footfalls ricocheted like shell casings pinging off a tile floor. Heat seared her lungs and her ankles ached from running too long and too hard. Then the screaming of night birds swallowed up the sounds.

The voice echoed all around her. *If you don't move it, it's all over. They'll die, too. You're on point.*

Then everything shifted and the panting was inside her head, echoing in her temples. The monsters that lived in the forest were after her. They were always after her. They hunted her, night after night. She ran, night after night. She could not stop. She must not stop.

Deep in Izzy DeMarco's soul, she knew that if they caught her, she would die.

And die horribly.

She tried to remind herself it was only a dream. But it wasn't, not when she was in it. It was all so very real. Her gauzy white nightgown molded to her body as she raced barefoot over sharp rocks that sliced the soles of her feet. Slimy, shredding vines tumbled from twisted canopies of dank, dripping leaves. Skeletal branches yanked painfully at the untamed corkscrews of her sable-black hair.

As she raced past a gnarled live oak, four huge gashes in the bark warned her that *they* had been here first, crisscrossing the forest, searching for her. They were always hunting for her.

But they had never found her.

Not yet. Don't get cocky.

Refracting the beam of the burning moon's light, her mother's gold filigree crucifix flashed between her breasts. She put a hand over it to hide the gleam in case it might give her away.

A wind whipped up, twisting her nightgown around her knees. Branches slapped her arms and face; wincing, she pushed them away and tried to move on. Then the hem of her gown caught on something behind her, drawing her up short.

A wolf howled, its wail piercing the fierce rush of the wind. It was joined by another. And another…until the forest rang with eerie, inhuman cries.

Get out of here!

About fifteen feet to her right, a shadow glided through the darkness. The crazed whooping rose to a shrill shriek. The trees and vines jittered in a frenzy. Clouds raced across the moon, slicing the bloody sphere in two, fog spilling out like clots.

They're coming!

She tugged wildly at the nightgown. It wouldn't give. She tried to run, was held fast. The fabric had tangled around a tree root that looked like a gnarled hand, gripping the ruffled hem so that she couldn't get away.

When she grabbed the nearest piece of the root, it curled upward as it tried to capture her hand.

Isabella yanked back her arm in horror. The root slithered back to rejoin the main section, which was still holding on to her nightgown.

The forest is alive.

It wants to kill you.

She pulled again, and again, but it was no use.

Then she reached up to her shoulders and gathered up the gauze around the sweetheart neckline. She jerked her hands toward her shoulders, trying to tear down the front so she could strip the gown off and get away. Try as she might, it would not rip.

She balled her fist and brought it down on the finger-like root.

Another howl echoed through the forest, bold and feral and eager. Ice-water chills skittered up her spine; she looked frantically around and—

Get out of here! the nightmare voice commanded.

That was when the gun went off.

* * *

Izzy gasped and sat upright in bed, gasping for air.

Sweat trickled between her breasts and ran down her cheeks like tears. She wiped it away with a clammy hand and blotted her palm on her sheet, which was wrapped around her body like a shroud.

"Just a dream, just a dream," she chanted, her heart beating so fast it was out of rhythm. She pressed her hand against her chest, feeling the damp ivory satin ties of her nightgown against her fingertips. Touching reality.

"Where are you? In your room. In your home. You're fine," she said out loud, a technique she had learned to quell her night terrors.

She forced herself to take a deep breath in, a deep breath out, looking for her center, finding the calm place where the monsters could not go.

It was increasingly difficult to go there.

Because it wasn't just *a* dream. It was *the* dream. The blood-red moon, the swamp, the root that grabbed at her and the whispering—that insinuating, sandpapery voice—Izzy had been having the same dream ever since her mother, Anna Maria DeMarco, had died of a lingering, undiagnosable illness ten years before. Today was the tenth anniversary of her death. Izzy had been sixteen then. She was twenty-six now. For ten years, shrieking creatures had hunted her half a dozen times each year. For seventy nights or more, she had outrun them.

What if, one night, they caught her?

"Don't go there," she ordered herself. Forcing her body to stand down, she rolled her shoulders forward, made herself slump and lower her head. It was a submissive posture, a surrender, and it frightened her to perform it, even in the safety of her bedroom.

She was still on high alert. Her body was flooded with adrenaline. She glanced over at her clock. It was three in the morning. Nevertheless, she was half tempted to dress and go for a jog.

Dr. Sonnenfeld, the shrink she had finally agreed to see seven years ago, said a recurring nightmare was caused by unresolved issues. In Izzy's case, the obvious trigger was her mother's death.

Izzy fully accepted that she had been angry with Anna Maria for dying. It also made sense that she was trying to flee the pressures of her role in the family. She didn't need a stranger to point out that the dream had started the day after her mother's funeral, coinciding with the fact that her father had held her close and whispered brokenly, "You're the lady of the house, now, honey. You need to look after Gino."

And look after her father, too. He hadn't said it, but she knew that was what he was hoping for. Izzy had taken to calling him "Big Vince" when she was five—everyone called him that—and maybe there was a reason she didn't call him "Pa" the way Gino did. Her father was an excellent cop, but he was the kind of man who needed a female family member to look after him. Before his marriage, that woman had been his sister, Izzy's aunt Clara. Then Ma.

By the time of her mother's death, it had been Izzy. At sixteen, she had already been doing all the housework and cooking for years. Gino was supposed to help, but her parents had never enforced that, and she couldn't make him. Frankly, it didn't leave a lot of time for being the "lady" of the house. Despite the urgings of her schoolmates and their moms to develop some fashion sense and cultivate a little style, she had found it necessary to skip over a lot of the detail work of growing up. Makeup, hairstyles—maybe later, after Ma got better.

But Ma didn't get better.

The death had made it official—as if the closing of the coffin lid over her mother's tired but still lovely face had also signaled the end of Izzy's girlhood, such as it had been.

The dream had begun then. But Dr. Sonnenfeld kept prodding her to come up with something more than what she told him, some deeper problem between mother and daughter.

"The fact that no one could figure out why she was so sick, for example," he'd suggested. "You feel menaced by unseen shadows. They're chasing you, trying to kill you as they killed your mother."

"Okay. So now what?" she had challenged him.

"So we keep talking," he'd replied.

It did no good, did not stop the dreams. Izzy thought *he* was crazy and, besides, her insurance would only cover a finite number of sessions. Also, he took a lot of calls during her sessions and one time asked her if she was seeing anyone special.

Her father had approved of her decision to stop seeing him.

"We're Catholics," he told her, making a fist with his big, beefy hand and waving it at the crucifix on the living room wall. "Talk to our priest."

Only at that point, they were lapsed Catholics at best. They had stayed lapsed until her little brother, Gino, had been accepted by Holy Apostles Seminary in New Haven, Connecticut. After that, Big Vince had taken to attending Mass on Saturday nights or Sunday mornings if possible, as well as two or three mornings of his workweek—a schedule that varied all over the place since he was a patrol officer. Izzy often accompanied him to Mass, but she had never talked to Father Raymond about her dream. She was a very private person.

Taking another breath, Izzy unwound the damp sheet from around herself. Her hands were still trembling.

I wonder what this is doing to my life span.

She stepped into her slippers and walked to the window, pulled back the dark blue curtains and stared out onto the familiar, snow-covered street. Her parents had moved into this row house on India Street when she was three months old. Though her life had changed drastically since then, the old Brooklyn neighborhood had not. The old twin Norway maple trees still guarded the entrance to the pocket park, magical in their dustings of frosty-white.

Beside the park stood Mr. Fantone's old one-story cobbler shop with its pitted brick exterior and grimy storefront window of multiple panes crisscrossed with security bars. The neon sign in the window had been missing the "e" in "Shoe" for so long that people had nicknamed it the "sho-nuff store," all the more humorous for their nasal Brooklyn accents imitating a Southern drawl.

Russo's abutted Fantone's, the Italian deli owned by the DeMarcos' next-door neighbors. Her little brother Gino had worked at Russo's during high school part-time to pay for college. She still shopped there, and all she had to do now was to close her eyes and she could smell the garlic and dried cod, mortadella and hard salami.

The Russo family brought over a lot of "excess inventory"—cold cuts about to go past the sale date—for the cop and his kid. Izzy took them, but Big Vince cautioned her. They had to be careful not to let the Russos presume. "One day a guy is giving you free coffee, the next day he wants you to ignore that he double-parked in the alley. And the day after that, he's asking you to help him with a little scrape his nephew's gotten himself into…."

You're fine. Everything's fine, she thought as she watched snowflakes drift across the windowpane.

To her right, on her bureau, the little votive candle at the feet of her mother's statue of the Virgin Mary had burned out hours ago; but the light from the street cast a gleam on the frosted glass that made it appear to burn. It comforted her. Its warmth reminded her that Gino had blessed their home tonight. He was asleep in his old room; he'd stayed over an extra night from his weekend visit home so they could go to Mass together tomorrow morning. Surely God watched over His own.

It was chilly in the silent room; she rubbed the goose bumps on her arms as she grabbed up her pink chenille bathrobe and slid her arms through the sleeves. An embroidered French poodle sporting a pompadour of turquoise rabbit-fur "hair" beneath a black-velvet beret trotted along the hem. The robe was nothing she would have ever purchased, but her nine-year-old cousin Clarissa had given it to her last Christmas. For that reason alone she treasured it.

Izzy loved her big, noisy Italian family.

Smiling faintly, she opened her door and headed for the bathroom. As she moved into the hallway, her father's door opened at the opposite end. He poked his head out; in the darkness, it looked like a floating white balloon.

"Iz?" he said. "You okay, honey?"

"I'm fine, Big Vince." She gave him a wave. "Just need a drink of water."

"I thought I heard you talking." He paused. "You talking in your sleep again?"

She made a face that he probably couldn't see, a combination of a wince and an apologetic frown.

"Did I wake you up?" she asked.

"Nah. I was already awake. I'm just restless tonight. A little *agita*. Heartburn." He chuckled. "Maybe it's your rigatoni."

"I make fabulous rigatoni!" she protested, putting her hands on her hips and facing him squarely. "The best...okay, *second* best you ever ate! You know I got Ma's cooking genes. *And* her rigatoni recipe."

"Then it has to be the garlic bread," he said decisively. "Gino made that."

They shared a laugh. For all his having worked in Russo's Deli, Gino was famous for his pitiful ineptitude in the kitchen. He couldn't even successfully microwave a frozen entrée.

Her father added, "Let's hope he serves Mass better than he serves dinner."

It was an old joke, but it felt good to hear it. Her crazy bathrobe, her father and his gentle ribbing—she was beginning to feel reconnected with the real world. It always took her a little while to lose the feeling that the nightmare forest was real, too. She would often awaken very disoriented and confused, and check her body and feet for cuts and bruises. Tonight she could almost still feel the slap of the branches against her cheeks and hear the voice whispering in her head.

"It's late," she said gently. "Go back to bed."

The job was taking a toll on him. Sore knees, flat feet, the light in his eyes a little dimmer. He was starting to talk about taking early retirement. It was hard to accept. Her father had always been a burly, noisy, old-style Italian male, heavy on the machismo, even though he was proud of his "little baby girl" for her holding her own in a man's world—Izzy worked for the NYPD, too, although in an administrative support capacity, and as a civilian.

But there was no denying that Vincenzo "Big Vince" DeMarco was slowing down. The muscles were slackening; his helmet of black hair was shot with silver. There were wrinkles. There was a little less opera in the shower.

"Yeah, well, whatcha gonna do?" he murmured, which was what he said whenever he wasn't certain what to say next. Izzy took it as her signal to go on into the bathroom.

"Mass in the morning," he reminded her, as if she could forget.

"Of course," she replied.

"Good night, *bella mia*," he replied.

"Buona serata," she answered.

His door closed.

She clicked the light switch as she went into the bathroom, papered with Ma's vivid roses and ivy trellises. Rose-colored towels hung on ornate brass towel racks. A filigree cross twined with brass roses hung on the wall beside the turned oak medicine cabinet. Everything about her mother had been graceful, soft and feminine.

Izzy was nothing like that. Izzy was about traveling light and getting it done. No frills, no frou-frou, no time for bubble baths and very little time for herself. Not that she was complaining. It was what it was.

Leaning forward, she scrutinized herself in the mirror. She didn't know what she expected to see. She looked the same as she ever did. There was the wild tangle of ridiculously thick black curls, the kind of hair women gushed over and said they wished they had—because they had no idea how hard it was to so much as run a brush through it, much less style it in any way besides a ponytail or wrapped with a gigantic clip.

There were the large brown eyes, a little puffy from lack of sleep, with the same gold flecks in them; and lashes that were so thick some people thought she wore false eyelashes. The small, straight nose dotted over the bridge with freckles, which neither of her parents had. Ditto the lush mouth—Ma and Big Vince had thinner lips and fuller jaws. As did Gino. Everyone called her the family oddball, made jokes about the milkman. Be that as it may, her appearance this early January morning was as it should be.

Izzy took a ragged breath. Still looking at her reflection,

she turned on the water and let it run a minute. It was chilly in the bathroom; she rubbed her arms and yawned, moving her shoulders.

She tested the water; it was warm now. She began to lower her head to splash water on her face.

She stopped.

The hair on the back of her neck stood up. Fresh goose bumps sprouted along her arms and chest.

She had the strangest sensation that someone was watching her. She could feel it, like a piece of wet velvet sliding across the nape of her neck. She imagined a police flashlight clicking on, traveling up and down the walls of the bathroom, the ceiling, the floor…

…looking for her.

And if she looked into the mirror, she would see—

"Nothing," she said sharply, doing just that. Lifting her head and staring directly into the glass. Her own reflection stared directly back.

Huffing at her own melodrama, she turned off the water and left the bathroom.

She padded back into her room, shut the door, took off her slippers and got back into bed.

And Isabella Celestina DeMarco did not sleep for the rest of the night.

Chapter 2

Mass.

Gino and Big Vince flanked Izzy as the three knelt and prayed in the front pew of St. Theresa's. Beneath his heavy blue-black jacket, her father wore his NYPD uniform. She smelled his Old Spice. On her left, Gino was a handsome chick magnet in street attire: gray sweater, coat, black cords. His hair was still damp from a shower, droplets clinging to his straight, dark brown hair. She wondered how the celibacy thing was going for him. She wasn't so fond of it, herself.

Ah, well, whatcha gonna do?

Izzy had on work clothes: black wool trousers, a gray turtleneck sweater and a black jacket. Her black leather gloves were stuffed in her jacket pocket. New York at this time of year was dark clothes and darker skies. Izzy knew she looked pale, with deep smudges under her eyes. Her father and brother both had said something about her appearance, fretting over her as they'd walked three abreast through the snow to the church.

There was one other parishioner, an elderly lady sitting six pews back, all alone. Izzy had seen her a few times before. Daily morning Mass was always sparsely attended; Catholics were just as stressed out and overscheduled as anybody, trying to make a living and get the kids to soccer. Even Mass on Saturday night or Sunday morning was hard to fit in—the congregation had been steadily dwindling for years, with few new parishioners—newcomers to the neighborhood, babies—filling the pews.

It was six-thirty in the morning and chilly in St. Theresa's, the little stone parish church three blocks from their row house, on Refugio Avenue. The lacquered pews smelled of lemon oil and the dim room flickered with light from four clear-glass votives among the three dozen or so unlit ones arranged before the statue of the Virgin. The DeMarco family had lit three of them.

It was the time in the Mass for the Prayers of the Faithful, when parishioners could petition for prayers for their special needs and concerns. Izzy cleared her throat and said, "For the repose of my mother's soul, Anna Maria DeMarco, I pray to the Lord."

All present responded, "Lord, hear our prayer."

Ma, I miss you, Izzy thought, as her father sighed.

Then something shifted in the frosty air. The room sank into a deep gloom; the light from the leaded-glass windows angled in like the dull sheen of gunmetal. As she gazed upward, the arched stone ceiling seemed to sink. The sweet, young face of the Virgin became blurry and hard to see, and the votive candles at her feet flickered as if viewed through murky water.

Izzy glanced left, right, behind herself, trying to figure out what was creating the disorienting effect.

The other worshippers seemed not to notice that anything had happened. The priest continued with the Mass. In the back of the church, the elderly woman's head was bowed in prayer. Gino and Big Vince were praying, as well.

"Izzy?" Big Vince whispered as she shifted again. He opened his eyes and gazed at her.

Maybe it was her mood. Her spirits were low and she hadn't slept.

She shook her head and placed her hand over his to reassure him that nothing was wrong. Her mother's black-onyx rosary was threaded through his large fingers and the smooth beads rolled across her palm.

"It's nothing," she whispered back. "I'm just tired."

Then she jerked as a hand molded cold fingers along the small of her back. The frisson swept up her spine, cat's-paw creeping, something ready to pounce....

Anxiously she glanced behind herself again.

Her father frowned, clearly puzzled. She shook her head and pressed her hands together in prayer.

I'm fine, she told herself. But she was beginning to wonder if she was losing her mind.

"Iz?" Gino said. He raised his brows. "You bored?"

"Shut up." Brother-sister interactions; some things never changed.

Mass ended. The DeMarcos took the Five, riding the subway as a trio until Grand Central, where they got out.

"Well, I'm off to save the damned," Gino said cheerfully.

With a big hug and a kiss for both of them, he raced off to catch his train to New Haven. Izzy and Big Vince transferred to the Six.

There were no seats in the rush-hour crowd, so Big Vince and Izzy stood. He was quiet and reflective as they watched a woman with curly dark hair knit a pretty fuchsia sweater. "A decade. Hard to believe."

She nodded.

"I see an elevated white blood cell count on the streets today, I'm shooting it," he declared. "Screw Internal Affairs."

They both smiled grimly at his dark humor. Izzy saw the anger behind it, and the despair. She wondered if her father ever sensed a cold hand against his backbone. Maybe it was Death tapping her on the shoulder, reminding her that no one lived forever.

And could I be any more morose?

At the 103rd Street stop, they got off and joined the crowd going up to ground level. The noise and traffic of the day were in full force; commuters rushed everywhere and car horns blared. Bicycle messengers rang their bells.

Walking briskly together, they headed toward her Starbucks. He said, "You asking that man over tonight?"

She hesitated. "It's Ma's day—"

He waved his hand. "We talked about this, Iz. It's fine. So?"

"Okay," she replied. Then, "You know his name is Pat."

"What a name for a man." He rolled his eyes. "Well, whatcha gonna do?"

"I'ma gonna invite him," she said, giving him a lopsided smile.

He kissed her forehead. "I love you, baby," he said, and trotted off to the station house, which was located on 102nd Street between Lexington and Third, while she went to fetch her coffee drink.

Twelve minutes later, heavily fortified with a venti latte with an espresso shot, she made certain her work badge was visible as she walked through the station house, answering all "good mornings" as she sailed down the hall toward the elevator. The switchboard—actually a pair of push-button phones—chimed incessantly; the patrol officers' utility belts and leather shoes squeaked; doors slammed opened, slammed shut.

Captain Clancy was in; her frosted-glass door was half-open and Izzy heard her talking on the phone, although she couldn't make out the individual words. Detective Attebury hurried past Izzy, giving her a wave as he talked on his cell.

At the end of the hall, in front of the elevator, she swiped the first of three IDs necessary to admit her into her subterranean domain: the Twenty-Seventh Precinct Property Room. Like most NYPD Prop rooms, the Two-Seven's was located in the basement of the building, which had seen better days. It used to depress her; down in the bowels and away from the action, she felt as if she were buried alive. But now that she had a plan to get up and out, she felt a growing nostalgia for the familiar odors of dirt and old, musty furniture.

The elevator dinged and let her out. She walked the short distance to what looked like the reception area of a doctor's office and tried the door. It was locked, and she didn't see Yolanda in the cage beyond it—she had probably secured the door to use the restroom—so Izzy punched the code in the keypad beside it. It clicked open and she left it open as she walked through the area. Once she was in the Prop cage, it was all right to leave the reception door unsecured.

She glanced around to make sure everything was in order. On the wall beside the sofa, the damaged bookcase still sat; the pale orange silk flowers on the coffee table needed dusting. The aging linoleum floor smelled of lemon polish and decades of grime that couldn't be cleaned away. She glanced through the slide-open window into the Prop cage itself. It was deserted, but someone was always on duty in Property, 24/7, unless there was a lockdown. That happened twice a month at most.

She coded in the Prop room lock and swiped her badge.

The metal door clicked and she pushed her way in. The warning buzz vied with the zing of the overhead fluorescents for most annoying sound of the day.

The Property cage looked just like that—a cage, ringed with diamond-mesh lockers of various sizes, one by one by one up to longer sizes to accommodate rifles and shotguns. Metal chart holders like those on the doors of medical doctors' examination rooms held the paperwork for the property in each locker. The individual three-by-five cards told the story of the chain of custody for each item, through a series of tags with bar codes, signatures and a rainbow of tapes. Each individual who received the evidence, from collection to storage, had their own rolls of identifying tape. Prop's evidence tape was candy cane. After a few months on the job, Prop personnel could tell at a glance who had custody of what, and when.

Each person who worked in Prop had their own territory consisting of various lockers and they—and no one else in Prop—had a set of keys to their set. Izzy's were all over the place, mingled in with those who had come through Prop and moved on to something else. Aside from two retired police officers—Joe Fletcher and Steve Jones—everyone else, like Izzy, was a civilian who had two years of college and had completed the ninth-month internship program.

The Dread Machine—their computer—hummed along. The radio beside it was playing banda music—Yolanda Sanchez's choice—and Izzy turned it down low. She still needed a little time to get her work groove on.

Beside the radio was a yellow stickie from Yolanda. "Morning, Izzy, in the ladies'."

She set down her latte and logged in on the computer. She took a brief tour of the cage—both online and visual—to see what had gone on over the weekend and during Yolanda's graveyard shift. Lots of newly filled lockers. Business had been brisk.

She flipped open the logbook, the cover of which was plastered with Yankees stickers—the guys, a couple of Marc Anthony stickers—Yolanda and a Holy Apostles sticker from Gino. There, on the two-foot-long sheets of security paper printed with thermochromatic ink, were Yolanda's careful notations and the UPC codes she had generated.

Less than a minute later her first pissed-off customer of the day was blustering at her. He would not be the last, because she did her job well.

"This is ridiculous," Nick Nelson flung at her. He was tall and muscular, and very photogenic. "You are obstructing justice."

"This is procedure," she shot back. "You filled out my form wrong. Fill it out right, and you get your evidence."

Nelson scowled at her as if he wanted to reach through the reception window and throttle her. The media darling of Forensics, he was running late for court and he wanted her to hand over the murder weapon in his case, a .44 Magnum, right this very minute. That would not have been a problem if he hadn't written the incorrect case number on his Evidence Order form. He wanted to scribble it out and write over it. No could do. Big procedural sin. No write-overs, no correcting fluid. *Ever.*

She had already handed him a fresh form and suggested he hop to it...and that he do so *before* she left the cage window to retrieve the gun. No, she would not bring it out until he had complied. She was very serious about breaching chain of custody.

He was livid. She stood her ground. Yolanda had nearly gotten fired last month, and if the boys around here thought Izzy DeMarco had gone by the book before the incident, they were in for even more bad news.

On December fourth at 3:12 in the morning, a tired cop named Elario "Haha" Alcina, already on overtime, had brought in a bomber jacket from a crime scene. He could have had Prop drive it in—there were Prop van drivers on-call 24/7 for just this purpose—but he had his own reasons, which he did not share, for dropping it by himself.

He told Yolanda, who was the evidence clerk that night, that the jacket had been thoroughly checked out and was ready to be admitted into the Prop room. Yolanda had no cause to disbelieve him, so she'd processed it in and put it in one of her lockers.

Alcina went back upstairs, filed the rest of his voluminous paperwork and went home. A week later, Forensics wanted the jacket.

Her locker, her key: Yolanda had efficiently complied, fetching the jacket in the plastic bag she had closed a week before with a red paper security strap. The card with its signatures, UPC tag and evidence tapes matched the logbook: yellow from the initial collection, black dot for Alcina, candy cane from Prop.

And just as she handed the bag to the forensics tech, a loaded SIG-Sauer P-228 semiautomatic concealed in a hidden pocket discharged. The round barely missed the tech's hand and now there was a sign on the shattered remains of the bookcase in the receiving area that read Yolanda Shot Me!

The brass wanted to blame Yolanda, of course. She was a civilian and she was brand-new, twenty-two years old and still on probation. She was in the most vulnerable position; cops took care of their own first. The official argument went that the Prop Department was supposed to refuse to process any and all firearms that weren't rendered safe, and a loaded weapon had remained unaccounted for for a week because of her "negligence." Maybe Yolanda hadn't checked carefully enough, but surely this one was on someone else's shoulders—whoever collected the jacket, who maybe was or maybe wasn't Alcina—Prop was not getting a clear answer on that.

It was Christmastime and Yolanda had worked hard in Prop for sixty-four days. Her probationary period was ninety days. Besides, she had just broken up with her hideous boyfriend and moved in with her girlfriend Tria and Tria's little boy. She had enough to contend with.

"*Orale,* they're blaming me, Izzy," Yolanda had sobbed in their break room after she had had yet another meeting with the bosses. They seemed determined to fire her—despite the fact that six months before, an officer in the men's locker room had dropped his loaded weapon, caught it and almost blown his own head off—with total impunity.

Incensed, Izzy had stormed out of the cage and through reception to the elevator, with the express intention of going upstairs to their precinct captain, Lisa Clancy, and demanding justice. Thirty years her father had been on the force; is this how they treated people who worked for this woman's newer, friendlier NYPD?

Luckily—in more ways than one—she had run into Detective Pat Kittrell instead. She was not in a position to demand anything from Captain Clancy, and the last thing she'd needed was a reputation for attempting to pull rank because she was a cop's kid.

No matter, of course, that every detective in a hurry tried to pull rank on the Prop staff. NYPD figured they were doing the "real" work. So if they wanted some slack, Prop should give it to them, right?

So wrong. Especially when their own failure to follow correct procedures nearly got a sweet young woman like Yolanda canned. So…there would be no quarter given when someone wanted Izzy to leave the labyrinth of codes and procedures to save his lazy butt from a redo.

She calmly sipped her latte while the imposing cop tried again.

"If we lose this case because of *you*—"

"Talk to the form," she said, tapping the Evidence Order with a short, unadorned fingernail.

He snatched it from her and stomped off like the diva he was.

"He thinks he's all that since he got that profile on 'Court TV,'" Yolanda grumbled as she reentered the Prop cage from the bathroom. As usual, she had on so much makeup that she looked like an airbrushed *Maxim* model. Yolanda was wearing brilliant red polish that matched her lipstick. Her smooth black hair was pulled back with a red-and-silver ponytail clip. Her earrings were red-and-silver hoops. As a rule, Izzy appreciated her flamboyant style.

Despite her successful FBI background check, upstairs wasn't fully aware of some of the rough patches Yolanda had been through. They didn't need to know; Yolanda was trying hard to "overcome" her past, as she herself liked to phrase it. Izzy supported her in that, protective of the young woman and of her budding self-esteem.

So when she invited Izzy over to "fix her up"—i.e., to teach her how to trowel on a few layers of foundation and do something, *anything,* with her crazy hair—Izzy went. But Yolanda's evil boyfriend had hung around, making gibes at Yolanda and coming on to Izzy when Yolanda had to use the bathroom. It was too depressing to repeat the experience, so Izzy had found reasons not to go over to Yolanda's again. They socialized by going out for lunch during the workday and occasionally out to dinner. Because she didn't want to go to Yolanda's, Izzy didn't invite her into her own home, either. Now that Yolanda had moved, maybe they could try again.

"It doesn't matter if he's on every cable channel," Izzy said to Yolanda. "We've got rules for a reason. We do it wrong, the bad guys walk. It's that simple."

"Okay, well, I'm getting out of here," Yolanda said. Then she looked past Izzy to the window and said, "Oh, hey. Hi."

"Yo, Yo, Yo, Yolanda." John Cratty, a plainclothes from SNEU—Street Narcotics Enforcement Unit—trotted up to the window with a doughnut-size box filled with plastic Baggies. It was bagged in a very large Ziploc-style container, and a little paper-and-metal tag, like the price tag at a yard sale, was attached to the zip-tie. His signature turquoise tape was attached to the tag.

His brown hair was long and dirty, and in his jeans and Kurt Cobain T-shirt, he looked like an underachieving, very low-end drug dealer. It was a good look for him.

Yolanda said, "Yo, yo, yourself. You brought your own stuff in again?"

"Van drivers had been on sixteen hours," he explained. "I said I'd do it."

"You're so nice," Yolanda cooed. She said to Izzy, "I can get it."

Izzy glanced at the computer and said, "I already logged in. You're off the clock, girlfriend."

"No, I'll catch it. I need to show a little more effort. I, um, spent a little time in the bathroom...."

Putting on makeup, Izzy silently filled in. And perfume. Whoa, is she seeing Cratty?

Izzy read the case number off the tag and typed all the specs into the computer—case number, detective on the case, date, yada yada. The NYPD had made over four hundred thousand arrests in the prior year; fifteen hundred of the Two-Seven's arrests had been in the seven major crime categories: murder, rape, assault, robbery, burglary, grand larceny and auto theft. By contrast, the Nineteenth Precinct, which was a much nicer neighborhood, had three thousand, nine hundred and forty-two arrests, most of them for grand larceny—theft of personal property of one thousand dollars or more.

She knew all these stats because the Dread Machine took her raw data and added it to the enormous NYPD database and processed it. There were two end results: updated stats for them that cared and a set of UPC tags for her. Since this was drugs, she ordered a good dozen of the tags.

She put one strip in the logbook and began to write in all the data.

Watching her, Cratty rested his forearms on the ledge of the window.

"You look tired, Ms. Iz," he said. "You go out dancing last night without me again?"

Looking up, Izzy gave him a faint half-smile. "When have I ever done that, Justin Timberlake?"

She accidentally brushed the back of his hand with her fingertips as she picked up the bag, and remembered a time when her fingers had touched more than the evidence she was booking for him in a street bust. Not that they had gone to bed. It had ended before then. Not so much ended as fizzled out. Never started.

Which was a bit of a pity. When he wasn't working the streets, Cratty cleaned up nice, with his square jaw and his hazel eyes and his sandy-brown hair. She'd had a brief crush on him about two years ago, but she'd known even then that he didn't really think of her as a girl.

Most of the guys thought of her as one of the guys— someone to drink beer with after work, shoot some pool and ask for advice about the girls they wanted to date. Girls who *had* learned about hair and makeup back in high school, and frequently returned to the Secret School of the Feminine Arts for refresher courses.

Girls exactly like Yolanda.

Cratty whistled "Rock Your Body" to himself, grinning abstractedly at her.

"Hey, you see that Justin Timberlake special the other night?" Yolanda asked Cratty.

He gave her a look. "I'm a man," he said. "A *real* man."

"Well, you're a real *silly* man," Yolanda retorted. "Because he had these hot backup dancers."

"Bet none of them were as pretty as you two girls," Cratty replied, taking in Izzy, too.

"Yeah, but they were half-naked," Yolanda said.

"HBO naked?" Cratty asked, more interested.

They launched into the vulgar sort of repartee that police precincts are known for, no matter all the seminars and counseling sessions about how to act in public. Police work wasn't lollipops and teddy bears unless you worked in traffic safety or child abuse. It was harsh and nasty and cold. It was the front line and being on point. So personnel blew off steam, repackaging their hostility and angst in sexual innuendos and merciless teasing.

As long as it didn't get out of hand, most women in the station house dealt with it in one of three ways: recognizing it for what it was and letting it go; showing the guys the line in the sand that they'd better not cross; or giving as good as they got. It was pretty much a tap dance any way you looked at it.

The dance was more extreme if you were a female cop, because suddenly you were challenging an army of alpha males on their home turf. They were already jockeying among themselves to be leader of the pack. They didn't need any *bitches* getting in their way. Civilian women as a rule were less intimidating because their jobs were in admin support.

"You could see all *that?*" Cratty asked Yolanda incredulously as she continued to needle him about what he had missed by boycotting Justin Timberlake.

Izzy hid her grin. Yolanda was giving him the business. After Izzy put on a pair of blue latex gloves, she laid a fresh evidence bag on the scale and zeroed it out. Now the scale would not include the weight of the bag when she checked in Cratty's evidence.

She picked up her wire cutters and snicked off the zip-tie on the evidence bag.

She broke the red paper security sticker, reached in and gathered up the box.

Her stomach clenched; her skin felt too tight. Sweat broke out across her forehead. She wondered if she ought to excuse herself and head for the restroom. But she didn't feel sick, exactly. Just...very tense.

"Iz?" Yolanda asked.

"I'm okay," Izzy replied, and just as suddenly as the moment arrived, it left. "Really." She smiled to prove it.

Yolanda glanced over Izzy's shoulder and stabbed at the topmost page of the intake stack. "Where'd you go to school, J.C.? You spelled contraband wrong."

"The streets are my halls of higher education," Cratty shot back. "But give me the form back and—"

Yolanda exhaled impatiently. "By the book, Detective," she informed him. "We'll take it as is or you can redo the whole thing."

Cratty huffed. Yolanda and Izzy smiled pleasantly at him, a wall of solidarity.

Izzy put the bag on the weight scale and peered at the digital readout. She said tactfully, "It's a little light, John. I weigh the bag in at two hundred forty-eight grams."

"That's how much my earrings weigh," Yolanda said,

mocking herself as she wagged her head. "You confiscated my earrings in drugs. Good for you."

Cratty looked confused and pointed to the form. "That's what I wrote down. Two hundred forty-eight Undertaker." Undertaker was a brand name for heroin. There were all kinds of brand names, and sometimes rival dealers murdered each other for trademark infringement.

"No, you said two hundred fifty-three," Izzy replied. She was confused. "Didn't you just tell me it was two fifty-three?"

"What?" Cratty paled. He looked from her to the scale, then craned his neck to read his paperwork upside down. She glanced down at his hands, clenched so tightly that his knuckles were white.

"You said two-five-three. When you walked up," Izzy insisted. She thought back, replaying the last couple of minutes, and realized that he hadn't.

"No." He ducked forward and reached out his hand as if he were trying to yank the paperwork back from Yolanda. "I wrote—"

"Two hundred forty-eight, Izzy," Yolanda read off, pointing at the appropriate spot on the form. She held it up for Izzy to inspect. "See?"

She recognized Cratty's writing: *248 gm.*

"I'm sorry. You're right." She rubbed her eyes and shook her head as if to get rid of the cobwebs. "I don't know what's up with me."

"I never said two hundred fifty-three," Cratty insisted.

"I know. It's okay, John," Izzy replied. She understood his unease—to an extent. Drugs were a delicate subject in Property rooms. Cops were human, just like everyone else, and drugs posed a serious temptation even for saints. Skimming off a few ounces of heroin here, a line of cocaine there, whether for personal recreation or to sell on the side—drugs brought cops down.

"Hey. No big deal," he said generously.

But there were droplets of moisture on his forehead and a muscle in his cheek jumped. She wondered if he'd been written up for something. Maybe he'd been told to get it together. His love life seemed to be going okay, by the looks of Yolanda's flushed pink cheeks. But cops as a rule had a lot to contend with—usually alimony somewhere, child support…

"All right," Izzy said, lifting it off the scale. The jittery feeling was threatening to return. What the heck was up with her? She had anxious cops for breakfast.

Yolanda and Cratty continued to chat while the room whirled faster and faster. She felt as if she were standing in the middle of a whirlpool.

And then she heard a voice in her head.

He's on his way. You had better be ready.

Or he will kill you.

Chapter 3

Izzy jerked her head up.

"What?" she said out loud.

Not this one, said the voice.

Then it all faded like a strange, bad dream and she was left to wonder if it had happened at all.

The Prop elevator opened, to discharge the one guy in the precinct who didn't think of Isabella DeMarco as a semi-guy. Detective Pat Kittrell entered the reception area and ambled up to the window beside Cratty, loose and easy and minus the balled-up tension tearing at Izzy this morning.

Or maybe he was just better at hiding it. Their previous captain, Hal Schricker, had said that anyone who spent more than six years in law enforcement was certifiable, himself included. Pat had been at it a lot longer than that.

He was six-two; white-blond, including his eyebrows; sunny green eyes; no visible scars in the field of tanned skin, but she knew his history. He had a wound: his pregnant wife had been murdered by a drunk driver years ago. Maybe the tragedy had healed over into a scar by now, but she didn't know that yet. Texas born and raised, he had been with the Dallas police at the time of the murder.

Afterward, he'd bounced around; there was a stint in Arizona, one in Albuquerque and then New York. He'd put in enough time with the NYPD to become a detective, and he had transferred into the Two-Seven just before Thanksgiving.

But there was nothing New York about Pat Kittrell. He was all Southern gentleman, with plenty of time for the niceties. Courtly, old-fashioned, and in some ways as traditional as Big Vince. He talked slowly, he smiled broadly…and she was beginning to suspect that he really liked her.

They had been out a few times—coffee, a quick meal after work, cut short by a call back to the precinct for him—what to outsiders would appear to be ridiculous and short-circuited attempts to date. There were reasons so many cops were divorced and drank too much.

They were trying to go to a movie, but so far their schedules hadn't cooperated.

And I'm going to invite him over for dinner, she thought, her stomach doing a flip. *Big Vince wants to sit down with him and make sure he's good enough for me, even if he is a non-Italian.*

"Mornin', Iz," Pat said as he came up behind Cratty at the window.

She put up a hand in greeting, but shifted her attention back to Cratty as Yolanda smacked his hand. He was attempting to fish out one of the pens in Izzy's Walk for the Cure coffee cup beside their terminal.

"I want to spell 'contraband' right," he whined.

"Too late. Unless you want to do the whole page over, like Yolanda said," Izzy told him.

"You go, Iz," Yolanda said in support, pointing a red nail at Cratty. "Don't listen to him. He'll try to flirt you into it."

Cratty whined some more. "*Wrong.* That would be sexual harassment."

"Not coming from you," Yolanda teased him. "Because it has to be *sexual.*"

"God, she's mean," Cratty said, sighing as he turned hopefully back to Izzy. "C'mon. You'd let *Kittrell* here change it."

Izzy felt her cheeks go hot. She hadn't realized anyone had noticed their mutual interest.

"*Wrong,*" Izzy said sternly. "The rules are the rules."

"Woof," Yolanda said approvingly. "*Venga, mami.*"

"Okay, okay," Cratty muttered. "Let it stand."

"No one is going to care," Izzy reminded him, glad they could proceed. "The bosses are after collars, not spelling errors." Cratty was a very ambitious cop. Izzy wouldn't be at all surprised to see him make captain—unless whatever was bugging him was big enough to tarnish his sterling reputation.

With rapid-fire efficiency, she finished his paperwork and added one of her bar codes. She handed him back some dupes, his receipts for the drugs, which she would keep in one of her lockers until there was enough accumulated in the department sufficient for a pickup. Then it would go to central holding, supposedly for destruction, but no one really believed that. The Justice Department used a lot of contraband to pay for the return of CIA field personnel and other clandestine activities.

"Thank you, ladies," Cratty said, recovering his charm. "Your turn, Detective," he said to Pat.

He moved off and Pat took his place. Pat had a five o'clock shadow. His beard was light brown. There were deep dimples in his cheeks when he smiled, and he was smiling now. He was wearing a black suit and he looked sharply masculine, more like a businessman who had just tiptoed out of a date's bedroom than someone who put away bad guys for a living.

He said to her, "I pulled an all-nighter. Had an Aided I picked up in Two-Seven David. He got messed up by some At-Risks trying to loot a Bombs R Us."

An "Aided" meant he'd had to accompany someone, victim or perp, to the hospital—the Metropolitan, in this and almost all cases. That meant reams of paperwork and, usually, hours and hours of overtime. An "At-Risk" was a juvenile offender. And "Bombs R US" was any electronics store where a wise perp could buy all the components he needed to build a bomb, which had been located in the sector referred to as 27D.

She could ask for details, but it was shoptalk and she was trying to develop an other-than-work relationship with him.

"You're okay, though?" she said.

"Sure. I'm going home to sleep for a year. Or maybe until you get off work."

Her smile was frozen into place by a surprise attack of butterflies. "Ah," she croaked. "Then you'll be hungry when you wake up."

His gaze was direct, his eyes sparkling. They reminded her of the Pacific Ocean, although she had never seen it. "Yes, I will be," he said. "Starving."

"Yeah, well." She touched the tortoise shell clip restraining her insane hair. "Um, that's good, because I want to…"

"You reading your patrol manual?" he asked her. "Thought after I catch some Zs and you piss off some more law-enforcement officers, we might have dinner and I could quiz you."

Pat was helping her study the official handbook of the Department because she was getting her application together for the Police Academy. She had the sixty units of college level courses; she was still young enough—there was really nothing stopping her. Learning the manual was to give her an added boost of confidence—Pat's suggestion. He had sussed out that she was afraid she wouldn't measure up, despite being a cop's kid and the NYPD's fondness for families continuing the tradition. But because she was so anxious, Pat wanted her to have an edge. She did, too.

Her father would lose his mind if he found out. He had made it more than clear that he did not want her to become a cop. The streets were brutal. He had lost Jorge Olivera, his partner, to a bullet from Jorge's own gun, grabbed away by a suspect in a stupid convenience-store robbery attempt. He had lost his wife to an incurable disease no one could name. Izzy knew that if something happened to her, it would kill him.

And yet…what she had was not enough. What she did, not enough. She processed forms and organized evidence. She knew it was important work, that it contributed to putting away the bad guys and protecting the innocent. She understood that without clear-cut procedures, the machinery of justice, such as it was, would shatter, precisely because police officers operated under the rule of law. Chaos belonged to the street. Order, to those who wore the blue. Otherwise, it was only a matter of might making right.

She liked learning the manual with Pat, but she hadn't come clean about her real problem. She had a phobia about guns. They scared her. Badly. Every night of her recurring nightmare ended with a gunshot.

She had not even told Dr. Sonnenfeld that.

Because what if her phobia was insurmountable? The goal of becoming a cop was what made it possible for her to swipe her tag into that elevator security lock every single workday.

The tenth anniversary of her mother's death made it seem

more important that she follow her dream—also, more frustrating. She had thought her father would have moved along by now, too. Found someone to take care of him—a woman his own age.

As the years ticked by, that seemed less and less like it was going to happen.

Izzy licked her lips. "Great minds think alike," she said, "except for the 'quizzing me on the book' part." How to deliver this news? "Big Vince wants to check you out."

She went blank. This was new territory for them, and she was groggy from lack of sleep. "Because, you know, he doesn't want me to apply to the Academy. So, tonight's not good for the multiple choice..." She trailed off.

"Iz?" he asked, peering at her. "Are you asking me over for dinner at your place, darlin'?"

Darlin'? She worked overtime not to blush. For God's sake, she was twenty-six years old. She'd even had sex...twenty-six million years ago.

Trouble was, she seemed to pick men like her father—very macho on the outside, but in search of some woman to dump all the detail work on, including the housework and the day-to-day details of, well, daily life.

Or maybe that was part of the definition of macho.

Maybe this invitation was a mistake.

"Iz?" he prodded, smiling at her with all the patience and good humor a seasoned detective could muster.

"I am," she confirmed. "I am inviting you to our place for dinner. Tonight, if you'd like. Short notice, but what does it matter in our line of work?"

"That would be lovely," he drawled, pulling a smile across his exhausted features. He was the kind of man who could say words like "lovely" and drench them with masculinity. "I'd like that." He snaked his hand through the window and caught up hers. Warmth and lovely tingles. "Don't be nervous. I'll pass muster. Your father's just looking out for you. He's a cool old guy."

"Say that to his face and he'll deck you," she shot back, smiling faintly, enjoying the sensation of flesh on flesh. They'd brushed lips, hello and goodbye, not done much else. She was the one who had pulled back every time. He was the one who let her.

He flashed her a quick wink. "Let him try."

"Say that to his face and he will. Seven? That work?"

"That works. I've got the address." He chuckled when she looked slightly surprised.

She released his hand, picked up her Starbucks and sipped. "We'll be waiting. Big Vince will notice if you're late."

"Got it."

They shared another smile and he sauntered off into the day. His back was broad. His hips, not so much. Sigh.

Yolanda poked her in the ribs with her elbow.

"Snag him, *mami*," she said. "He is totally sweet."

"*You* snag him," Izzy teased her.

Yolanda closed her eyes and shook her head. "*Chavela,* I am finished with men. Never, never. Until at least next Tuesday." She opened her eyes and giggled. "It doesn't hurt to look. And that guy's looking at *you,* so you might as well return the favor."

"Whatever," Izzy said noncommittally, picking up Cratty's bag of drugs. "Meanwhile, I have evidence to stow."

"Another day, another box of junk," Yolanda said. "As if it mattered very much."

"It has to matter," Izzy said. "Doesn't it?"

Yolanda sighed. "You have stars in your eyes, *amiga.* Me, I just want to do a good job and collect my paycheck. Find a guy, marry him, become a housewife and get fat." Her eyes gleamed with predatory eagerness. "The simple life."

"Believe me, there is nothing simple about it," Izzy replied.

* * *

At five, Izzy was done for the day. She walked a few blocks in the setting sun to 110th where the Five had a stop. She went back down into the bowels of New York City and caught the train, groaning because it was packed.

As she held on to a strap in front of an old woman with a shopping bag, she reviewed her meal preparations for the evening. Cooking relaxed her, and she began to smile to herself as she envisioned the dishes she would prepare.

Serving and eating them with Pat and her father at the same table was another matter entirely.

The Five screeched to a stop and she joined the line dance as the other passengers shuffled toward the double doors and into the borough of Brooklyn. The train was steamy from riders sweating in their outerwear, rather than bothering to unpeel in the close confines of the car.

The doors opened to the underground station, letting in the stench of urine and the haunting refrain of a sax busking in the distance. Over the echoing clack of footfalls, two people argued loudly in Korean.

The escalator was broken, as usual; she took the cement steps, slowing behind a young Asian girl in a Yankees bomber jacket. Anticipating the chill outside, Izzy pulled her own jacket closer, wishing she'd worn her long coat.

Yeah, a coat like that one, she thought idly as she reached ground level and began to cross India on the same side as Russo's and Fantone's.

A man in an ankle-length black coat was standing in front of her row house. *His legs are probably toasty...*

An unexpected chill shot up her spine.

There was something about that man. Something she didn't like.

She narrowed her eyes. There was nothing odd about him,

at least when seen from the back. He was standing at the far end of the row house, closer to the Russos' than hers, which was the one in the middle. He wasn't particularly tall, and there was nothing menacing about his stance. His hands were stuffed in his pockets, his head of dark hair tipped back as if he were gazing at the stars.

Her body went rigid; adrenaline coursed through her in classic flight or fight.

Why?

She didn't have a clue. There was nothing about him to elicit her extreme reaction. But the sense of danger heightened as she reached the crosswalk and prepared to cross to her side of India.

Feeling foolish, she slunk behind the closer of the two maple trees to her right. The pocket park was padlocked after dark, and by the gleam of the streetlight, she could see that it was deserted.

Izzy peered between the branches of the tree. The man in the coat was nowhere to be seen. Snow fell where he had stood. Her heart still pounded; she was wet with sweat.

I'm insane.

She reminded herself that she knew self-defense; she also reminded herself that in the Department, the cops who trusted their instincts and knew their limitations were the ones who survived long enough to retire.

So she dialed Big Vince's number, hoping he had beaten her home. She'd ask him to step outside and wait for her. Her father always answered her summons if he could—he had programmed his Nokia to play "Donna e mobile" from an opera by Verdi when his daughter called.

But she got his voice mail, so she left a message.

"Just wondering if you're home. I'm almost there," she said. Then she disconnected, put her phone back in her small black leather hobo bag and squared her shoulders. Her gaze alternating between her path and the street, she got to the crosswalk, waited for the light and crossed the tarmac, which was shiny with ice.

Warm, cheery lights from the windows of the other homes splashed across bushes and snow.

See? It's all good, she told herself.

Then she neared the spot where the man had stood. Footprints. And a cigarette butt.

"Jerk," she muttered, bending down to retrieve it.

If she had felt a sense of dread before—upon waking, at Mass—now it was so strong that she actually recoiled, taking a step backward.

Baffled, she turned and hurried up the three stairs leading to her stoop, unlocked the door and went in, and slammed the door behind herself.

What the hell is wrong with me? she wondered as she dropped her purse on the recliner and hung her jacket on the coatrack.

She entered her private domain—the kitchen—and started dinner. She decided that she had imagined the whole thing, and let it go.

Once she got the lasagna in the oven, she changed into a long black skirt and scoop-necked black sweater. When Pat knocked on her door in his black leather coat, black turtleneck sweater, jeans and cowboy boots, he looked a little bit like the Marlboro Man. Izzy had always thought the Marlboro Man looked hot, except for the cigarette.

The cigarette reminded her of the man loitering on the street and she debated about mentioning him to Pat. But there were flowers to coo over—a big, lavish collection of roses and baby's breath. Besides, there was nothing Pat could do and he was not her knight in shining armor.

"That was delicious," Pat said three hours later as he finished drying the dessert plates with the gold borders and stacking them on the counter. He took another sip of Amaretto from an ornate hand-blown Venetian liqueur glass, then folded the kitchen towel into a neat rectangle and hung it on the hook beside her mother's collector plate of Pope John Paul II.

Izzy smiled appreciatively at the compliment. He had eaten heartily, thereby earning points with her and her father both. Big Vince had also been gratified to find out that Pat was a widower, like himself.

"Oh, I figured you for a divorced man," he'd remarked casually. He'd worn his navy-blue sweater from Gino's seminary, a Christmas present, advertising that they were Catholics and not so much fans of divorces.

"No, sir," Pat had told him. Izzy was glad he'd said "sir." Maybe he outranked Izzy's father at work, but this was the patriarch's table…and the patriarch's daughter, too.

"But you're not a Catholic," Big Vince had ventured, as if that would be hoping for too much.

"Raised a United Methodist," Pat had offered, clearly the best he could do. Izzy had winced. In her father's hierarchy of Christian denominations, United Methodists hardly counted.

"Well, *we* were lapsed for a while," Big Vince had said, dispensing religion largesse. "If you two will excuse me…"

He'd made himself scarce in his room, watching TV alone. Izzy knew this signaled his approval; had he disliked Pat, he would not have left him alone with his baby girl for one second.

Izzy poured Pat another shot of Amaretto, then gave herself one. She tipped her glass against his and said, "Cheers."

"Dinner was great, dishes are done, bodyguard has left. So you can relax," Pat said, sliding his arm around her waist and drawing her close as he leaned against the counter.

She put down her glass; he set down his own, and cupped her chin. He smiled at her. "Good?"

She nodded. He kissed her. His tongue slid between her parted lips and she tasted the sweet Amaretto, the saltiness of him. Her heart picked up speed; her body tensed. She felt his excitement. His hand moved down to the small of her back.

She put her hand around his neck and kissed him hard. He grunted as if in surprise—she usually kept their kisses short and easy—but after her victorious meal, it felt supremely right to kiss Pat Kittrell like she meant it.

When she ended the kiss, he settled his arms around her and said, "Seems I passed muster."

"Seems you did."

"It was washing the dishes, wasn't it?" He kissed her again.

"Yes," she concurred. "Think what will happen if you do the vacuuming."

He guffawed and wrapped both his arms around her waist. "Let me at your Dirt Devil."

"We both have to work tomorrow," she said. "But next time, come over a little earlier and I'll get you right on that."

"Next time." He stroked her cheek. "Nice to know there's going to be one."

"Yes. It is," Izzy agreed.

Then he was gone, and her father said grudgingly, "He's okay."

She said, "Glad you think so," and that was that. Then she added, "There was this guy outside when I came home. He was standing in front of our building, smoking."

"Yeah?" Big Vince narrowed his eyes. "He bother you?"

"Not like that," she told him. "He just seemed wrong, somehow." She gestured. "He was about six feet, long black coat, smoker."

"Hair color?"

"Mmm." She made a face. "Some kind of dark. Streetlight, couldn't tell."

"Okay." She could see the wheels of his cop brain filing it all away. "I'll mention it to Hackett." Grace Hackett was the beat cop for their neighborhood.

"I don't think it was a big deal," she continued. But she did. "Strike that."

He drew an invisible line in the air. "Done." He considered. "Maybe we ought to rethink that argument about you carrying some kind of protection. Such as a gun."

There it was, her phobia. Once she conquered that...

Tell him. Tell him that you're going to apply to the Academy.

"I think we should," she said. "Rethink it. Because..." She took a breath.

But at that precise moment, a cheer rose up from the TV and his glance ticked back toward it. He shouted, "No! Oh, damn it!"

Exhaling—she had just squeaked out of that one—she said, "Good night."

"Sleep," he ordered her, watching the set. "Oh, for crying out loud!" he shouted, raising his hands into the air. "Well, whatcha gonna do?"

Smiling faintly, she left him to his travails.

She laid out her clothes for tomorrow, got into her nightgown—a fresh one, silky and lavender—and put her hair into a sloppy bun. She knelt at her bedside for the first time in a long time and prayed.

Take care of my mother, and let her know—

And again, as in St. Theresa's, something shifted around her. Lowered, darkened.

Spooked, she crossed herself and climbed into bed.

* * *

Blood streamed down her face.

She was leaning over the lacy balcony as the creatures rushed the mansion. The trees were ablaze. The wounded were screaming.

He was gasping at her feet. If she didn't get him to safety soon, he would die.

In the beating center of the battle below, a faceless man looked up at her.

A gun went off.

Chapter 4

"Okay," Pat said to Izzy, "the movie was bad. But do you have to punish me all night for it?"

She shifted against the maroon-leatherette booth of the diner as she smiled apologetically at him. She knew she was terrible company.

They were having an after-movie snack, he a burger; she, a bowl of chicken noodle soup. She had scarcely eaten a thing since the night he had come over for dinner. Scarcely eaten and hardly slept.

That was three nights ago, when the nightmare had changed. That was an understatement—taken a quantum leap was more accurate. Maybe that helped to explain the growing feelings of unease that had been plaguing her in the waking world. The anniversary of her mom's death usually churned her up for a couple of weeks, but this was ridiculous.

"You're all het up," Pat went on, putting down his burger

and wiping his hands on his napkin. He tented his fingers as he leaned toward her. "Something happened to you. Recently."

"No." Looking down at her bowl of soup, she shook her head, fully aware that she wasn't convincing anybody, least of all a sophisticated cop who ferreted out lies for a living. She didn't know him well enough to talk to him about it. She didn't know anyone that well.

His face quirked; his dimples showed. "Well, it can't be kissing me that did this to you." He sounded so sure of himself that she had to smile back. "Forsooth, she maketh the candles to glow."

"That's nice. Shakespeare?"

"Kittrell," he answered. He took her hand and wrapped his fist around her fingers, shaking them as if to loosen her up. "A guy who cares about you. Cares if there's something eating at you. Can I help?"

"It's nothing, really."

He sighed. "Okay, I give. For now." He checked his watch. "I have to go in. I'm putting you in a cab."

"I'm fine on the subway," she insisted.

"Maybe on some other guy's watch." He cocked his head and took a breath, as if he were about to ask her a question. Maybe if there *was* another guy. But he didn't. He didn't push, and she was grateful.

He paid the check—insisting that he had to or his mama would find out and hit him upside the head. Then they put on their coats and walked outside, while Pat flagged down a cab in record time for a nonnative.

As she climbed into the back, he leaned down and kissed her. "You get some rest, you hear?"

For an answer, she kissed him back. His lips were soft and he smelled so good, like soap and limes, and she lingered, her senses tantalized.

Beaming at her, Pat shut the door and Izzy waved a bit shyly at him through the frosty window.

She got home without incident, no strange men loitering in front of her house. As she let herself in, her father looked up from the TV in the front room. When he saw her in the foyer, he said, "Hey. How was it?"

"Nice." She unwound the scarf from around her neck. "He's nice."

"He didn't walk you in." He peered around her, as if he expected Pat to appear.

"I took a cab. He had to go in to work."

Big Vince drank his beer. "Big bust coming down. They briefed us on it. Sting operation. He tell you about it?"

"We don't talk shop," she said, yawning. "I'm going to bed."

"Good." He nodded thoughtfully. "You got to take care of yourself, Iz. You're getting too thin."

She sighed. Everyone was on her case tonight.

"Night," she said.

She took the stairs, washed her face and brushed her teeth, changed into her white nightgown and crossed to her bed. For a moment she thought about pulling back the curtains. Then she ignored her impulse and pulled back the coverlet, and slid into fresh sheets and, hopefully, some rest.

Don't look down, a voice said inside her head.

But she did. And there he was, silhouetted by flames.

The smiling man's features were very sharp, and a large purple scar ran diagonally from the right side of his jaw to his left temple. His face was all angles; his almond-shaped eyes were dark and fierce beneath brows that slanted upward. He looked devilish.

She had a gun in her hand and she raised it slowly. Her

hand began to shake as she pointed it at him. His eyes widened in fear, and then his gaze shifted to a point behind her. He bared his teeth like an animal.

Izzy turned.

They are looking for you. Both of them, *a voice said.*

Within the arched curves of a Medieval monastery, a figure scanned the horizon. It was another man, very tall, with a riot of hair that tumbled down his shoulders, like her own.

A blue-tinted fog boiled up and around the long-haired man in the monastery, sharply casting him in chiaroscuro. He was holding a glowing sphere. It illuminated his fingers; on his left ring finger, something heavy and gold glittered, more like a signet ring than a wedding ring.

Then a voice rumbled like thunder, shaking her spine with a low, masculine timbre.

"Isabelle? Je suis Jean-Marc de Devereaux des Ombres. Je vous cherche. Attendez-moi. Je vous cherche."

This time Izzy woke slowly, clutching the sheets as she whispered to the darkness, *"Oui. Je suis là."* "Yes, I am here," in French.

Only, she didn't speak French.

Haggard, feeling as if she'd been run over, Izzy went down into the bowels of the Two-Seven. Yolanda was taking a personal day, but the new-hire, Julius Esposito, was there. He had had his black hair processed and she thought it looked a little silly, like he was an extra in a movie about Harlem in the thirties or something. Or maybe she was just looking to find fault. She didn't like him; there was something about the vibe he threw off that didn't sit well with her. This was only his third day, and she hoped the situation improved. On the other hand, she could use it as further incentive to get herself out of Prop. "Good morning, Isabella," he said rather formally as she entered the Property room.

"Oh, everyone calls me Izzy," she told him. There was an evidence bag beside the terminal tagged with Cratty's signature turquoise tape. She gestured to it with her head. "What did he bring in?"

"Crack," he told her.

"He's been busy lately," she said, crossing to the terminal to log herself in. Her elbow brushed the bag.

It's light. The words came to her as clearly as if someone had spoken them to her. She looked at the monitor. In the column for the weight, Julius had typed in 98 gm. *It was almost a hundred ten when he confiscated it. Cratty took some before he sealed the bag*

And there is no way for me to know that. None.

Freaked, she moved away from the terminal as casually as she could, while Julius finished his intake procedures, put the bag in one of his lockers and slammed it shut. Then he returned to the cage window and started fiddling with the radio. "Do you like smooth jazz?" he asked without looking at her.

"Sure," she said, although she hated it. Right now music was the furthest thing from her mind. A wave of vertigo made her wobbly. She felt as if she were standing under water and the air in her lungs was all the air she was going to get—so she'd better hang on to it.

Eye-level on the shelf to her left, she saw one of Yolanda's lockers. The three-by-five card in the pocket showed a strip of turquoise tape—Cratty's. She walked over to it. Touched it.

She heard his voice inside her head.

"Beating him down in the subway tunnel. Filthy skel, lowlife piece of crap, hold out on me? Me?"

Izzy jerked her hand away. She glanced at Julius, who took no notice. *I am hearing things. I'm crazy.*

She spotted another of Yolanda's locker cards marked with Cratty's turquoise tape, on the same wall but two-thirds of the way down. She stared at it for a long, hard minute.

Then she walked over and touched it.

Nothing. Nothing at all.

She touched the eye-level container for the second time.

Nothing there, either.

Hallucinations, she thought. Her heart thudded; she could feel the vein in her neck pulsing hard. *I need some sleep and maybe I need to see a shrink again. I'm in trouble.*

At a late lunch the next day, in a joint around the corner from work, Yolanda pushed a business card across the expanse of red-and-white-checked plastic tablecloth and said, "Just go see her. There is something terribly wrong with you. You look like you're dying." She grimaced. "Sorry if that's a sore subject."

"It's okay, Yolanda." Izzy reluctantly read the card. It was for Dr. Mingmei Wei, Yolanda's Oriental medicine doctor. Yolanda swore by her. She also paid her out of pocket, because their Department health insurance wouldn't cover her services.

"It's your *chi,*" Yolanda opined. "It's out of whack. What she does is like *feng shui,* only for people. Psychic chiropractic. You need to get readjusted."

"Does your priest know about this?" Izzy gibed.

"This is not funny. You are psychically ill."

She indicated Izzy's untouched barbecue-beef sandwich. "When's the last time you ate a decent meal?" She gazed hard at Izzy. "Are you pregnant?"

Izzy burst out laughing. "Please. There's only been one Immaculate Conception."

"I didn't think you were." Yolanda stabbed her finger at the card. "But—"

Flames. Heat, smoke. Lungs...searing...

The image of her father's red, sweaty face filled her mind. She heard him gasping, coughing. *"Izzy...Gino..."*

"Oh, my God!" Izzy cried. She jumped to her feet. Her chair clattered to the tile floor. "My father's in danger!"

"What?" Yolanda said, reaching out to her as she rose from her chair. "Izzy, wait!"

Izzy bolted and ran outside. A black cloud of thick, oily smoke billowed on the horizon. In her mind she *saw* her father, *saw* a hallway, *saw* rats and shapes moving in the flames.

I'm not asleep, she thought as she ran. *I'm awake, and Big Vince is in that.*

She flew toward the smoke, picking up speed until her feet were barely touching the ground. Her lungs burned but she kept going, weaving around pedestrians who yelled and jumped out of her way like missed targets in a shooting simulation. It was as if someone else was operating her body and she herself had no choice but to propel herself forward.

Images roared into her mind.

Flames...rats screeching down the halls. Shapes moving in the smoke. Officer Vincenzo DeMarco. Detective John Cratty.

And a semiauto pistol—a .9 mm Glock—in a closeup that filled her field of vision.

Pointed straight at her father's head.

A voice. "Filthy cop, you're gonna die; no one shakes me down."

"Hit the floor!" she screamed out loud.

Then abruptly and without warning, her astonishing burst of energy left her. She staggered forward, swaying wildly left, then right; she smacked against the side of a brick-faced building and slid down it, pitching painfully onto her side.

She was dimly aware of people crowding around her, asking her if she was all right. Should they call an ambulance?

"Hey!" Yolanda caught up with her. She was carrying Izzy's coat and purse. "*Hijo de puta,* did someone mug you?"

"I'm okay." Izzy ground the words out. Yolanda put her arm around her waist, helping her to her feet.

"Are you *loca?*" Yolanda said. She whistled and waved as a cab approached. The cab swerved to the curb.

"Come on, Iz," Yolanda said, helping her to the cab.

The cabbie peered at them and frowned as his window rolled down.

"Go toward 108th," Izzy told him as they got in. To Yolanda, she ordered, "Get my cell phone, and call my father. Number one on my speed dial."

The cabbie shook his head. "No way. See that smoke? The cops have got it blocked off."

"You have to go there!" Izzy yelled.

Yolanda squeezed Izzy's hand as she opened up Izzy's hobo bag with her other hand and dug around. "Easy, *mi amor.* We don't know your father is in that building."

"You need a cab or not?" the driver snapped.

Ignoring him, Yolanda found Izzy's cell phone and pressed a couple of buttons. She put the phone to Izzy's ear.

"Cratty, ten," came a raspy, hoarse voice. "Ten" was the same as saying "over" on a police radio phone.

"This is Izzy," Izzy announced, confused.

"It's John, Izzy. We're in an ambulance. Smoke inhalation. They've got him sucking some oxygen but it's just a precaution. We're going to the Metropolitan."

"He wasn't shot?" she asked, her voice shrill. "Tell me if he was shot!"

"No, Iz. No. Just smoke." He sounded a little off. "Meet us at the Met."

Located on First, it was the nearest hospital. It was where Pat had taken his Aided last night.

And her father was with the guy she had seen in visions, beating people and skimming drugs. *Why* was he with him? Had he tried to shoot him?

Izzy said neutrally, "Thanks. Tell him we'll be there."

Disconnecting, she said to the cabbie, "Take us to the Metropolitan."

"You got it." He screeched into the traffic.

She said to Yolanda. "Call in and explain. You're taking me in because I'm injured."

"Works for me, *mi'jita,*" Yolanda said, biting her lower lip as she smoothed Izzy's hair away from her wound. "Especially because it's true."

Izzy and Yolanda both knew the way to the ER entrance of the Metropolitan Medical Center. Anyone who worked for the NYPD in this part of town eventually found him or herself here, if not for a perp or a personal injury, then for someone close to them.

She half crawled out of the cab while Yolanda paid the driver. An ambulance sat in the dock as two men in scrubs burst out from the ER double doors, a gurney rattling between them.

John Cratty got out of the ambulance, appearing from behind the open back door of the rig. He was wearing kicker boots, jeans, a T-shirt, and a heavy dark brown leather jacket. His face was covered with soot, but he was walking under his own steam. He motioned to the two men, pointing back into the ambulance.

Within seconds, Izzy's father was loaded onto the gurney.

"Big Vince!" Izzy cried, hurrying toward them while Yolanda worked to stay up with her.

Izzy saw the portable O_2 bottle propped against his shoulder, the mask over his face. There were saline bags and a defib machine on the gurney with him—oh, God, had he had a heart attack?

As Izzy approached, Cratty put his arms around her, giving her a tight hug. She stiffened, but he didn't notice.

He said, "Your father's in good shape."

"The defib—"

"Wasn't used. But what the hell happened to *you?*"

"Just a fall," she said as she pushed past him and ran up to her father's gurney.

His eyes were closed.

"Daddy!" she cried. "Daddy!"

The orderlies pushed the gurney through the double doors, Izzy holding Big Vince's limp fingers. Yolanda and Cratty brought up the rear.

Inside the building, a short man in dark blue scrubs barked orders at the two men, then said to Izzy, "We're taking him in." He held up a restraining hand. "You can't go with him. Let us do our job. Besides, you look like you need help."

"No," she protested, but Cratty took her arm.

"You know the routine," he reminded her. "They need their space."

The gurney zoomed on past her as the trio hung a left and disappeared down a corridor.

"You two were in a building?" Yolanda asked him as she led Izzy to the left, through a door marked Emergency Waiting Room. "The one on fire?"

"We got the hell out of there as soon as the real firemen showed up," he concurred, puffing air out of his cheeks. "Had a couple of rough moments."

"What were you doing in there?" Izzy asked sharply. All her alarm bells were going off at once, and at full volume.

"We were on a detail," he said, locking gazes with her. "Confidential."

She didn't know what to say. They kept walking, past people sprawled in rows and rows of orange-plastic chairs, looking pale and sick and tired of waiting.

Cratty flashed his badge and the three passed through to a second security door to the curtained sections filled with ER cases. Her father was lying on his gurney with a sooty face and bloodshot eyes barely visible above an oxygen mask covering his nose and mouth. When he saw Izzy, his eyebrows met over his nose and he tried to take off the mask.

She knew he was staring at her injury. "It's nothing, Big Vince," she insisted, touching her cut.

The dark-haired nurse who had just wheeled a blood pressure monitor to the side of the gurney said, "We'll look at that."

"It's fine," Izzy repeated. But the truth was, her vision was blurring and she was dizzy. "Maybe I'll just sit down."

And then she fainted.

Chapter 5

It's the gun. They will shoot him with the gun. It will stop his heart.

Izzy woke up in a softly lit room.

Pat was bending over her, the tan lines across his forehead and at the corners of his eyes softened by the dim illumination. But the worry on his face was evident, and she was touched.

"You passed out," he said by way of greeting. He had on a sweatshirt that read Dallas Cowboys and a pair of jeans. Off-duty attire, since he wasn't undercover. He looked sexy...and worried. "They're keeping you under observation."

"My father..."

Pat chuckled softly. "He's awake, alert, and ready to leave. They want to keep him overnight, but frankly, I fear for their lives."

She smiled at that. "Where's Cratty? And Yolanda?"

"Back in the world. Yolanda's very worried about you."

"That's so sweet," she said.

An IV had been inserted into the back of her hand. Her gaze trailed up the clear plastic tubing to the bag hanging from a metal carrousel.

"Your electrolytes were out of whack." He smoothed her hair away from her forehead. His fingers were calloused, but his touch was gentle. "They're running some tests. Just as a precaution."

His voice was low and steady. She felt calmed by his air of quiet authority.

"What happened, Izzy?" he asked her, stroking her cheek with his thumb. "Yolanda said you freaked out in the restaurant."

"I…" She didn't want to try to explain it to him. It was all beginning to fade. She *had* seen her father, hadn't she? "I had a funny feeling…" She trailed off.

He urged a cup with a straw to her lips again. "It's okay, darlin'. You don't have to talk if you're too tired."

They sat in stillness for a moment—or what passed for stillness in a busy hospital. Doors opened, shut. The PA system paged a doctor. Machines beeped.

After a few moments Pat said, "I had a funny feeling like that, once."

She looked up at him. He nodded calmly, but she could see the sorrow etched in his face. She assumed he was talking about his wife. She waited for him to go on, but he didn't.

"Do you need anything?" he asked.

She said, "Is my father very upset? About me? He knows I've been admitted, right?"

He nodded. "Yes, he knows. And he's upset. Bombastic is more appropriate, I'd say. But that's because he loves you."

She sighed heavily. "If he's upset now, it'll be nothing compared to telling him I want to go the Academy." She considered. "If I can still get in. Maybe there's something wrong with me. Neurologically," she elaborated.

"Don't go looking for trouble," he chided her gently.

"Why was John Cratty partnering with him?" she asked him. She debated about telling him about all the weirdness in the Prop room. But if she was wrong, she could bring a man down for nothing.

"Can't rightly say." Pat's face was blank. She got it: private Department business, some kind of organized raid, something he wasn't at liberty to discuss.

Maybe she wasn't the only one who had felt a twinge of wrong around Cratty lately. That decided her.

"About Cratty," she said.

He gave her a little nod. "Yes?"

"Nothing firm, nothing provable."

"Same here," he said.

"Whoa." She nodded back. Their gazes locked. "I feel better."

"Me, too, Iz." He took her hand.

She took a deep breath, then said something that would humiliate Big Vince if he heard her say it. "My dad is…over fifty, Pat. He's gone through a lot. Please remind whoever's in charge of this Cratty thing. If it's dangerous…"

"Understood."

She was grateful to her core that he did understand. Suddenly it was the best thing in the world that the man she was attracted to was a cop. She was a cop's daughter, and she wanted to be a cop. It was the only world she knew—no matter how dangerous or strange.

Pat had had to go back to the station. The physician on duty refused to release Izzy until she could prove that someone was going to stay with her for the next twenty-four hours.

She thought about staying with Aunt Clara, but their place

in Queens was always pure bedlam. There would be endless calls between Clara and Big Vince, and a lot of yelling. Yes, she did love her big, noisy Italian family, but she needed some quiet tonight.

When she called Aunt Clara and the phone was busy, she took that as a sign not to pursue it. Then Yolanda arrived, telling her that her shift was over and she could take her home with her. "That okay?" Yolanda asked her excitedly. "I'd come to your house but Tria is working tonight so I need to watch Chango."

Izzy raised a brow. She was fairly certain that *chango* meant "monkey" in Spanish. She rethought her decision. Except that Clara had five children, two dogs and several very noisy finches.

One night won't kill me, she thought, making her decision.

"Okay. Thanks so much," Izzy said.

"*Bueno,*" Yolanda said, clapping her hands. "Now, let's go see your father before we go."

Finally. Izzy had been begging them for hours to take her to him.

The doctor agreed to prepare Izzy's discharge papers on condition that she sit in a wheelchair while Yolanda did the steering. Bouncing along, radiant in her helpfulness, Yolanda wheeled Izzy to an elevator.

They went up to another floor and Yolanda breezed her straight down a corridor, hung a left and paused on the threshold of a dimly lit room.

"Officer DeMarco? It's us!" Yolanda sang out.

"Izzy?" her father croaked from the nearest bed.

"Yes." Izzy began to rise from the chair. Yolanda clamped a hand on her shoulder and forced her to stay seated. She wheeled her into the room and around the side of the bed. "How are you, Daddy?" she asked softly.

"Everyone keeps asking me that. I'm fine." Big Vince sounded exasperated and hoarse.

"It's because they don't want you to sue them," Yolanda informed him. "If they let you out but you were still messed up, you'd have a case."

"That so," he said politely. He turned to Izzy. "How you doing, princess?"

Big Vince had not called Izzy "princess" in years. And she had not called him "Daddy" in years. It was as if those two softer people had been buried with her mother.

She said, "I'm okay."

Yolanda cleared her throat. "I need a Diet Dr Pepper. I'll check on you later, Izzy."

She smiled gratefully. "Thanks."

Yolanda left. Without taking his gaze from her face, Big Vince grunted. "This from falling?" he asked her, hand hovering above her temple.

Before she could answer he said in a rush, "Izzy, I have to tell you something." His eyes got watery; his mouth pulled up in a smile. "Your mother saved my life."

Izzy blinked. "What?"

He nodded eagerly, sitting up and grabbing her hands. "She looked down from heaven and warned me to hit the ground. The shooter was aiming right at us. I heard her voice in my head. If she hadn't warned me, I would be dead."

Izzy was stunned. She said slowly, "Did you really hear *her* voice? It was Ma?"

"Yes," he said, seizing a couple of sheets of tissue from the box on the end table. He wiped his three-cornered Italian eyes. "I heard her loud and clear."

His face was literally glowing.

"Your mother is still with us, baby. She hasn't left us. And she saved my life today." The tough Big Vince exterior cracked a little more. "My Anna Maria is *back*."

Izzy stared at him. "It's a miracle," he whispered.

She reeled. The nightmare…all this time, had it been in preparation for this day, this danger? Was her mother really with them? She looked up, around, joyful and a little anxious, half expecting to see her mother's ghostly apparition floating in the room.

"Did you tell Gino about all this yet?" she asked, not sure what else to say.

"His phone was turned off. Maybe he's at Mass. I left a message for him to call me back."

He held her hands and began to weep.

"Your mother," he sobbed. "Your sainted mother."

She didn't know what to say.

Upon her discharge, the doctor informed Izzy that she was anemic, gave her a prescription for iron pills and sent her home to bed.

"And have a steak," he told her.

Yolanda's roommate, Tria, picked them up at the curb in a beat-up, old, pale green Chevy station wagon. McDonald's wrappers and yellowed copies of *The Star* littered the floor. Izzy sat in front and Yolanda wrapped herself around the chubby-cheeked baby who was strapped into an infant car seat in the back.

They didn't live far away, which was to say that they lived in a bad part of town. It wasn't the projects, but it was close. They parked on the street, behind a broken-down truck and a low-rider guarded by a boy of about eleven wearing a black bandana over his hair. Tria sprang Chango—whose real name was Calvin—from car seat prison. As they walked toward the entrance of a twelve-story brick apartment building, Yolanda got quiet, as if she were embarrassed that she had brought Izzy here. Maybe in the enthusiasm of inviting Izzy to recuperate at her place, she had forgotten that her new place wasn't half as nice as her old place.

The entrance was coated with graffiti. The elevator reeked of booze, marijuana and pee. As they rode it to the ninth floor, Yolanda's perfume wafted toward Izzy and she was grateful for the sweet vanilla scent.

They entered the tiny one-bedroom apartment. Posters of movie stars had been tacked up on the cracked pale-green walls with pushpins. There was a broken-down, green corduroy couch, a pile of books, the top of which read *Medical Assistant Test Preparation*. A sliver-size kitchen was fairly clean, the counter dotted with baby food jars, bottles and a container of powdered formula.

Incongruous in the extreme, an enormous state-of-the-art high-definition TV sat about three feet from the couch. It took up over half of the entire room.

Yolanda saw Izzy looking at it and said, "Flaco gave that to me." Flaco was her evil ex-boyfriend.

"Girl, you told me you bought that thing," Tria said accusingly. "What, he give you that when you moved out? He probably stole it."

Yolanda looked stricken. Izzy said, "Well, it's a very nice TV."

"Unless it's stolen. Then it is *not* nice," Tria insisted.

Izzy really didn't want to know any more sordid details, so she excused herself, called her father from the bedroom and assured him that all was well. He sounded tired and she didn't stay on long.

Gino called and she said, "I'm okay."

"Aunt Clara's upset that you aren't staying with her," he informed her. "She wants to call you and tell you so. I told her they've got you on drugs. That may buy you some time."

"You're a saint."

"Working on it," he replied. "I'll get the boys to pray for you."

"Make sure they're getting A's in praying."

"Our permanent records are very accurate."

He hung up.

"We've got it all worked out," Yolanda told her.

It was like a teenager overnight. Izzy was supposed to take the double bed in the bedroom. The sheets, which featured angels with big eyes, were clean. Yolanda would sleep on the couch until Tria came home around five in the morning or so. Izzy wasn't sure what Tria did, and she didn't ask. When Tria got home, Yolanda would move from the couch to a pile of cushions on the floor. Izzy wanted to object, but didn't. Her head hurt and she was exhausted.

While Yolanda fussed over the baby, Tria said to Izzy, "You have whatever you want in the fridge, honey. We got some leftovers from the Roy Rogers down the street."

"Thank you," Izzy said politely. She thought with fleeting longing of the baked ziti she had made last night, with plans to microwave the leftovers tonight. At least her appetite was back.

She accepted an oversize T-shirt that read *¡Suave!* beneath a faded picture of Marc Anthony and put it on, got into bed and closed her eyes. Through the closed door, she could hear Calvin fussing and crying.

About an hour into it, she got out her cell and called her aunt's house. The phone was still busy.

Calvin keened like a banshee.

Finally she got up and walked into the living room. Yolanda was jostling the baby on her lap while she watched TV and talked on the phone. She saw Izzy and smiled.

"Hold on a sec," she said to the person on the other end.

"Hey," Izzy said. "I'm thinking of going to my house."

"Oh? No, no," Yolanda told her. "Look, I'm talking to Jax. He lives across the hall. I'll go over there with Chango. It'll get quiet." She wrinkled her nose in a moue of apology. "Okay?"

Before Izzy could reply, Yolanda disconnected, zapped the TV with the remote and said to Izzy in a motherly tone, "Now, please, *mami,* go back to bed. I'll check on you in a little bit."

Izzy complied, shuffling back into the bedroom. Her head was hurting again and she exhaled deeply as she lay down. The ticking of a clock grew louder in her ears as she settled in. She could feel herself begin to doze.

Allez! Vite!

Izzy's eyes flew open at the sound of a male voice in her room.

"Yolanda, is your friend over?" she called. Maybe he had mistaken the bedroom for the bathroom or—

Isabelle!

She knew that voice. It was the man who had appeared in her dream—the second man, the one with the wild hair tumbling over his shoulders and the golden ring. The one whom she had answered, in French.

She started fumbling for the light, but she was in a strange room and she didn't know where it was.

C'est moi, Jean-Marc de Devereàux des Ombres.

His voice was insistent, urgent. But it was inside her head. *In her mind.* Experimentally, she touched her head, feeling for headphones. Patting the pillow. "Who are you?" she demanded again, squinting into the darkness. "Where are you?"

A friend. Trust me. They're looking for you.

I've gone crazy, she thought. But as she looked around again, she said hopefully, "Ma?"

No, I'm not Marianne. But I speak for her. I speak for Maison des Flammes...the House of the Flames. They're searching for you. I'll do all I can to protect you.

Suddenly a violent pain blossomed behind her eyes. With a gasp, she pressed her fingertips against the bridge of her nose. It was so bad that she doubled over, losing her balance, and tumbled on her knees to the floor.

"Did you do that?" she yelled.

Shh. Lower your voice. They don't know where you are. But they're closing in.

Holding on to her bed, she got to her feet. Rubbing her forehead, she saw a rectangle of light around the venetian blinds. She stood to the side of it, then lifted the corner of the dark blue curtain and spied out onto the street below.

Her heart turned to ice.

The man in the long black coat stood across the street. He was smoking; she saw the glow of his cigarette against the dark outline of his head. He was not looking at her window; his gaze was focused a floor or two above it. But he was searching, scanning. She felt the familiar irrational dread at the sight of him.

She murmured, "Is that you or a friend of yours?"

Is someone outside?

"Yes," she said.

Get out! Get out immediately! Don't let him see you or you are dead!

"Okay, wait. Time out," she said. "What the hell is going on?"

Maintenant! Vite!

"I have to get dressed—"

Non! Get out! Get out now! Move!

The man outside shifted his attention to the very window she peered out of. He threw down his cigarette and began to walk across the street.

"I need to warn Yolanda—" she began.

He won't even notice anyone else! He wants no one but you! Get out of there!

Something inside her made her listen—she had saved her father's life this way—and she whipped into action, bounding across the little room to the chair where she had piled her clothes.

Get out now!

She gathered up her sweater and pants, stepped into her boots and pulled on her own long black coat over the Marc Anthony T-shirt. Her purse…she couldn't remember where it was. In the darkened bedroom? In the bathroom?

She couldn't leave without it. Her cell phone was in it. Her money, her house key—

—and then she felt the wet velvet sensation wash over her, the same as in her bathroom—was it four nights ago? She stood stock-still, feeling like a prisoner eluding the searchlight of a prison guard tower. Her heart was thudding so hard she felt dizzy again.

The sensation passed.

Where are you? the voice demanded. *Are you leaving?*

"*Oui,*" she replied, shocking herself. She was speaking in French again.

Ah, c'est bon, he replied, and rattled off a barrage of French.

She shook her head, not understanding anything more, mincing backwards out of the bedroom.

There, in the living room: her purse lay on the sofa—turned upside down. Yolanda must have let Calvin play with it.

She grabbed it up, scooping the contents in as best she could and hurried to the front door. She opened the door and went out into the hall, shutting it behind herself.

She crossed into the hall and pounded on the door. Someone—not Yolanda—bellowed an invective and loud rock music turned on. She looked left, right, having no clue where Yolanda could be.

"Where? Where should I go?" she whispered, since it didn't seem to matter how softly or how loudly she spoke. "How can you hear me? What's going on?"

Just go!

As soundlessly as she could, she crept down the hall, which was dark except for a light flickering dimly in front of the elevator. Bad move to take it, she decided.

It began to whir. It was coming up.

She looked frantically for a stairwell. She made out the shape of a door and silently made her way toward it, felt for a latch, found it and opened the door. She took a deep breath as she stepped across the threshold. It was pitch-dark.

Closing the door soundlessly behind herself, she had a moment of vertigo. It was so dark. She was scared. She fumbled in her purse for her cell phone to call 9-1-1.

Isabelle? It was the voice inside her head. She didn't dare answer.

The elevator dinged. Though she knew she had no way of knowing if he was in the elevator, she started down, hand in her purse. Her heart caught in her throat as she came up empty on her cell phone. She wondered if she had left it on the couch.

How many flights of stairs? She was wobbly. Her head hurt. Her hands were trembling and she was afraid her knees were going to buckle. She gripped the banister, which was metal…and sticky. She recoiled, rubbing her hand on the clothes cradled in her arm.

She heard the door above her open.

Isabelle? The voice—still inside her head—was frantic. *Répondez-moi! Answer me!*

There were footsteps on the stairs.

She held on to the banister again, moving as quietly as she could, wondering if speed was more important. Down she raced, each movement a cannonball to her ears; she had no idea if the other person on the stairs could hear her at all. Part of her wanted to burst into hysterical laughter; the other part remembered that her father had almost died today and either she—or her mother's angelic spirit—had saved him.

Now someone was trying to save her.

Or was he trying to flush her out so someone else could catch her?

The footsteps above her rang out, obviously not caring if she heard them.

As she turned another corner, she saw a horizontal sliver of light at an angle below her. It was light from beneath a door. It had to be coming in from somewhere—a service tunnel? A stoop?

Someone's flashlight?

She looked up and over her shoulder. Saw no one.

Looked back down at the strip of light.

The voice inside her head starting yelling her name.

Isabelle! Isabelle! Isabelle!

She pushed open the door and just as quickly shut it behind herself, feeling along the latch for a way to lock it. There was none.

She wheeled around on a square of cement and stared out on a strip of snow bounded by two privacy fences. There was a six-foot-high fence at the other end.

She stepped into the snow. It went up to her calf and the cold was a shock. She rethought her plan. She was practically naked, and every movement she made would be a roadmap to her location.

She had no other choice.

She put her other foot into the snow.

Freezing, stinging fingers raked her skin as she fought to stay upright. The moonlight gleamed down on snow-covered shapes that she hoped were bushes. Improbably, there was a statue of St. Francis near the fence.

Isabelle, are you still all right?

Panting, she gasped, "*All right?* Aren't you reading my mind?"

Non. I can't. Nor can they. But it's possible that they can hear you speaking. As I can.

Her boot came down on something hard. A rock, perhaps. Or a gun. Hard to tell in this neighborhood.

"Then it wouldn't be wise to tell you where I am or what I'm doing."

Most unwise.

"But do you have any advice for me? Survival tips?"

Stay out of sight. I'm coming to you as fast as I can.

The cold night wind whipped her cheeks and her boots squeaked against the snow like cornstarch rubbed between her fingers. Her purse batted against her hip. Her spine was rigid as she crossed to the rear of the yard, expecting the man in the long black coat to rush her at any moment.

Run. Run faster, she thought, reaching out and touching the waist-high, tonsured head of St. Francis as she brushed past him. Then she stood at the fence and stared up at it. There were no handholds. How was she going to climb over it?

To her right, she heard a sound, like the snapping of a twig. Her heart leaped into her throat. She slid her gaze in its direction, over to the right, where the side fence separated the yard from…what?

She heard a rushing sound. And then…footfalls thudded in snow.

Footfalls of someone running along the other side of the

fence. She looked back up at the tall barrier in front of her. She reached out her hands and touched the planks, searching for some way to pull herself up. She could hear herself panting. She swallowed hard, forcing herself to stop as she dropped to the ground and dug into the snow. Deep, fast; she tried to push it up over her body. Puffing with exertion, she rolled up against the base of the fence and the wood gave way like overcooked pasta. It was rotted clean through, and once she realized what that meant, she rolled hard, cupping her arms over her face and forcing her way through the wood.

She bit her lip, hard, and tasted blood as she rolled into an alley, into a pool of icy water beside a Dumpster. She almost screamed in shock.

Fighting the pain, she commando-crawled behind the large metal trash receptacle, rising unsteadily, listening hard to see if the man was following. It was difficult to hear above the chattering of her teeth.

Her bones ached; her muscles were cramping. She lurched into the alley, standing at the intersection between two two-story brick buildings. After a split-second assessment, she turned right, toward the light over the back door of what passed for a neighborhood bar. Gangsta rap pounded along with her heartbeat. *Is the bar better than nothing?* She didn't know.

And then she saw the man in the long black coat standing beneath the light with his back to her, staring down the alley in the opposite direction. That made no sense. He couldn't have gotten past her. Even if he'd taken an alternate route, he couldn't have gotten to the bar before her.

He's got an accomplice. Or maybe that other guy climbing the fence is the one who talks to me in my head.

She flattened herself against the wall. She was shivering so hard she was afraid she would knock the back of her head against the brick and injure herself again. She forced herself to stay focused, stay with it, stay…she started digging for her phone again. Where the hell was it?

Searching through her purse, she looked back the way she had come.

At the Dumpster.

No way, she thought. It would be the first place the coat man would look. But she felt drawn to it, staring at it as if it were a lifeboat bobbing on the surface of an icy sea.

Isabelle? I'm on my way, said the masculine voice inside her head. *Are you all right? Do what you must. Be clever. Trust yourself.*

That didn't sound like he was coming to her from anywhere close. She was going to have to fend for herself.

The Dumpster it was, then, though it made no sense.

She sent a prayer heavenward. *Ma, if you're here, help me.*

A burst of energy blossomed in her chest and shot throughout her body. Warmth coursed through her veins. Her muscles flexed.

Nearly out of control, she shot across the alley, grabbed the lid of the Dumpster, and lifted it with astonishing ease. She bent her knees and sprang into the air, clearing the lip of the Dumpster, then grabbing the lid as she fell back down— onto several mattresses and blankets, piled within standing height of the top of the receptacle.

Despite its weight, she was able to ease the lid shut. She fell to her knees on the teeter-totter of cushions, then onto her hands. Panic rolled over her and she shut her eyes tightly, bracing herself for discovery.

It didn't come.

She felt in the dark for her purse. Felt everywhere. Fresh panic welled but she fought it down as she moved hand over hand, coming up empty on the purse but laying hands on a soft woolly blanket. She wrapped it around herself because if she didn't, she was going to cry out from the pain of the chill. She rolled herself in more blankets, soaking in the warmth, crawling to the corner of the pitch-black Dumpster. She pulled herself into a tight ball to retain her body heat, shifting away from the frigid metal casing.

Isabelle? came the voice again.

She didn't respond. All she had now was her wits—and the voice. Maybe the men in the long coats were the good guys and the man in her head was the perp. She didn't know.

Isabelle? Answer me! Are you all right?

Shivering in the dark, she maintained her silence.

Chapter 6

Curled into a fetal position, Izzy wiped the grit from her eyes. Her head was throbbing. She was hungry and colder than she had ever been in her entire life. She had slithered off the Marc Anthony T-shirt and put on her street clothes. Like the shirt, they were soaked with ice water and no source of warmth. She was sorely tempted to get naked, but that would be foolhardy at best.

The Dumpster, which she had feared would be a trap, had become her refuge. It didn't smell. There was no garbage, and while the blankets were musty, they were not mildewed. Someone had been living here, and she guessed the sanitation workers and businesses in the alley had looked the other way, maybe even helped out.

She didn't want to leave it.

She huddled, telling herself that someone would come for her. Fleetingly, she envisioned a joyful reunion with her father. Her bed, and something hot to drink…soup…

Isabelle, for the love of all you hold dear, answer me!

He was pissed off. And a little on the melodramatic side. And if he was so damn interested in her safety, where the hell was he?

She listened for sounds of the world outside and heard none. She had no idea how long she had hidden inside the Dumpster. It was no warmer, which made her suspect the sun had not risen. If she waited long enough...

But she knew, bone-deep, that it was time to leave.

Hunched over, she got to her feet, spreading her legs and steadying herself. She raised her arms and flattened her palms against the underside of the lid, took a breath and pushed.

The lid flew back as if it were a feather, and slammed wide open with a deafening clang. Wincing, Izzy shut her eyes tight, then opened them.

The yellow-blurred ceiling of the borough nightlights il-luminated her surroundings. Across the alley, a couple of frosted windows on the second story gleamed with light. Most, however, had been broken.

Wrapped in a double thickness of blankets, she awkwardly made her way to the side, glomming onto it like a kid just learning to ice skate at a rink. She hoisted a leg over and lay along the metal lip on her stomach as she scanned her surroundings. The vista below was nothing but a vast expanse of blackness.

Swinging her other leg over, she let herself fall, remem-bering from her self-defense classes to bend her knees and stay as loose as she could for the impact.

Beside her ankle, her purse rested in a snowdrift. She grabbed it, digging inside for her cell phone. There!

The faceplate was dark. She depressed the on switch and just as quickly hit the sound control to silence it.

Nothing happened. She tried it again as she craned her head toward the fence, looking to see how obvious the damage was.

There was no sign of the hole she had created with her body.

She blinked. She was tempted to walk closer to inspect it, but there was no time.

Isabelle? It's Jean-Marc.

She didn't respond. Instead she concentrated on her non-working cell phone as she loped toward the left, where sounds of traffic held out the promise—or was it the threat?—of pedestrians. The battery should have plenty of charge, but nothing worked, not even calling the number for customer support.

Pulling her blanket around herself, using part of it to make a hood that hid her face, she stayed to the shadows, jogging easily now, as a freshet of energy warmed her. She emerged from the alley, her heart scudding. There were a few scuzzy pedestrians standing in a ring around a fire crackling in a fifty-gallon drum. All of them were men who had seen much better days.

One of them turned, saw her.

"Hey, baby," he said, "wha's happnin'?"

"I need a cell phone," she said boldly.

"Hey, I need a job," he shot back. The others laughed. "But you c'mere and I'll make you forget your troubles."

I know self-defense, she reminded herself.

And the first rule of self-defense was to run whenever you had the chance.

She darted to the right, heading away from the men, who started laughing and hooting at her. Her legs and feet were numb; she heard her boot crunch down on glass as she staggered forward. She reached out a steadying hand toward a nearby lamppost, submerging herself in a pool of watery light. As her fingers brushed the metal post, the lamp flickered and buzzed. Then it winked out, casting Izzy in darkness.

A frisson of fear crept up the back of her neck, making her hair stand on edge.

Then she saw him.

The man in the long coat was standing across the street at a bus stop and he was staring straight ahead.

She pulled the blanket more closely around her face and turned her head. The blanket's satiny edging brushed against her cheek as she backed into the next alley. Watching him, she shivered so hard it hurt to breathe.

Then…he was gone. He had disappeared as if by magic.

Frantic, she scrutinized the area around the bus stop, expecting to see the bottom of his coat as he blended into the waiting crowd of perhaps a dozen people.

Then a gloved hand snaked around her face, covering her mouth, as she was dragged backward into the alley.

She kicked, tried to bite; she pistoned her arms backward, jabbing with her elbows. She connected with a hard, flat chest; her attacker was a man. She raised her right leg up and then extended it backward, attempting to smash her boot into his leg. She only succeeded in throwing herself off balance, pitching forward; she took advantage of her momentum and drooped her torso toward the ground, tucking in her head as she executed a forward roll.

Her assailant was unprepared; he sailed over her head and flopped hard onto his back. He still had hold of her; she was facing away from him as she landed on his chest. She heard the whoosh of air as his lungs expelled all the oxygen they contained.

She tried to throw herself forward, out of his grasp, pumping her legs and arms crazily. He held on tight.

"Fire!" she shouted, because no one came if you called for help. "Fire in the alley!"

Then something shimmered in the air before her, the way

heat vibrations undulated off car hoods and cement sidewalks in the heat of summer. It looked like Fourth of July sparklers, only they were purple, buzzing and hissing as she kicked and jabbed, successfully breaking the man's grip. She flung herself forward between his legs and scrabbled away as fast as she could.

He sat up and grabbed her around the waist again. She twisted to the left, crunching her abdominal muscles as she dove at an angle, trying to rip herself out of his grasp.

"Let go of me! Let go!" she yelled at the man.

Then her leg somehow connected with his face. He grunted and released her.

She rolled over onto her butt and crab-walked away from him. He came after her, scrabbling forward like a spider; she saw with horror that he had a purple scar across his face and blank, crescent-shaped eyes. The man of her nightmares; the man who had watched her house.

Reflexively, she folded her fingers over and pressed her thumb against the first knuckle of her forefinger. She slammed her hand into his nose with a sharp Tae Kwon Do palm strike.

To her complete shock, he sailed backward, arcing into the air until he slammed hard against a row of metal trash cans. As he hit the cans, they tipped and rolled, spewing garbage into the alley. Half a dozen rats squeaked, fleeing their feast.

The man didn't move. His neck was canted at a terrible angle and his eyes stared glassily at her. Bathed in moonlight, he looked unnatural, like a toppled statue.

I barely touched him, Izzy thought, staring from the inert man to her hand.

She sucked in her breath. Her palm was *glowing*. She cried out, thinking she was on fire, and plunged her arm into the snow.

The man did not blink, did not move. His chest did not rise, did not fall.

No lights blazed. No doors opened. No one came to investigate.

I killed him.

She turned and retched into the filthy snow. Something dribbled down the side of her face; numbly, she touched it. Blood. Her bandage was gone. Her stitches had pulled open.

The man still did not move. Then snow began to fall. Crystals fluttered onto his open eye. It was the most unnerving thing she had seen so far.

Her head fell forward. She was completely drained and terribly afraid.

Without warning, making no noise of any kind, someone came up beside her and clamped a large, male-size hand on her shoulder. As she opened her mouth to scream, he leaned over and pressed his other hand over her mouth, as her first assailant had done, and said quickly into her ear, "Isabelle, I'm Jean-Marc."

Even though she recognized his voice, she began to struggle, falling to the right, and in the action, turned her face toward his. His strong, steady gaze stopped her as surely as his hand across her mouth prevented her from calling out.

Here was the man with the long hair. He wore shadows: a black coat, black sweater, black pants. His eyes gleamed with the same darkness; his hair tumbled with the same wildness; his features were harsh and his skin, somewhere between olive and light brown. He had high cheekbones, deep hollows, and heavy brows. Everything was sharp, extreme, like a hawk. Like her, he was breathing heavily, his chest rising and falling.

"Will you scream?" he asked her.

She shook her head and he released her.

Pointing to the corpse lying in the snow, she said in a rush, "I killed him!"

"You can't kill something that was never alive." At her look, he said, "I'll explain everything. But you have to get away from here."

He urged her to her feet. She stared at the body, unsure whether to approach it and check for vitals or simply to run. She said to Jean-Marc without looking at him, "Do you have a cell phone?"

"It won't work." She frowned at him, not believing him. He said, "This place is warded. Your cell phone can't penetrate the barrier I've put in place."

He swept his gaze up and down her body; defiantly, she pulled her blanket closer.

"You're freezing," he said. He took off his heavy wool coat and wrapped it around her, holding it out so that she could slip her hands into the sleeves. She didn't argue with him. She was so cold she could hardly stand it.

"We need to call 9-1-1," she insisted, ignoring his wacko spiel about why her phone wouldn't work.

He shook his head. "You know we aren't going to the police."

She scowled at him, taking a step away. "I know nothing of the kind."

"They can't be involved."

"Because?"

"Because this isn't their domain."

She raised her hand, angling her palm at his face the way she had done with the other man. The one she had killed with a glowing palm strike.

He pushed her arm down.

"You can't do it again, not for a while." He took her by the arm, studying the alley, the street behind them, the rooftops. "We have to leave," he said urgently, his attention resting on a fire escape before moving back to her. "They still don't know what you look like. But they've sensed you."

She splayed her hand over his and tried to pry his fingers off the sleeve of his coat.

"Who? How do you know that? What the hell is going on?"

"I'll show you later. We'll go this way. I don't trust the street." He started to lead her deeper into the alley, past the body that—

The body that was no longer there.

She gaped, rooted to the spot. "He's gone!"

"Later," he said, his voice rising impatiently. He frowned at her, tugging at her. *"Allons-y. Vite!"*

"I don't think so." She raised her free hand into the air, snaked it under his wrist, made a half turn in the air toward him; she made a double fist, twisted it and broke free. Then she wheeled around and sprinted away.

"There's a fire in the alley!" she yelled. "Call the fire department! Call 9-1-1!"

"Non! Isabelle!" he shouted.

She kept running, pumping her arms and legs as she put as much distance between herself and him as she could. She slipped and slid in the snow, gritting her teeth, not daring to take the time to look behind her.

"Stop now!" he bellowed.

Then something smacked into the center of her back. The force was like being hit by a sack of bricks. It propelled her forward; her head snapped back and she hit the snow.

The tunnel was beautiful, the white light glowing inside welcoming, joyous.

Izzy flew toward it, her arms outstretched, her hair stream-

ing back over her shoulders. All earthly cares dropped away;
she was buoyant and joyful, surrounded by high, sweet voices
half singing, half murmuring.

A petite figure waited at the other end; it was a feminine
shape, made of the same white light as the tunnel. Were those
wings?

"Ma?" Izzy whispered. Her heart expanded in her chest;
she could feel it beating with so much love—

"For God's sake, stop!" shrieked a feminine voice with a
thick Bronx accent. "She's freakin' back, ok?"

Coughing hard, Izzy opened her eyes. Jean-Marc's face
loomed over hers; to the left and sideways, the face of a
young woman peered down at her. She wore stark white
makeup, black eyeliner and lashes, and dark red lipstick. Her
hair was shoe-polish black streaked with indigo blue.

"Guardienne," she said reverently. "How the hell are
you?"

Dizzy, disoriented, Izzy ticked her gaze from the girl in the
white makeup to Jean-Marc. He was straddling her; still in
her sopping pants, she was naked from the waist up. His
hands were pressed together over her heart, the meat of his
hands compressing the tops of her bare breasts. He had been
performing CPR on her.

"Get off me," she said in a gravelly voice as she felt the
heat of his crotch pressed against her own.

"I had no choice," he said. It was not precisely an apology,
and she wasn't sure what it was in reference to—the attack,
her nakedness or the CPR. She felt muzzy and confused. She
had no idea where they were.

And then she remembered that he had attacked her when
she had tried to run.

She remained silent as he eased himself off her, fingertips

grazing her rib cage. He rose, standing beside the girl, who was evidently a goth. She was dressed in a blood-red bustier laced with black leather strings, a black lace skirt and black velvet lace-up ankle boots.

Sitting up slowly—the room was spinning—and covering her breasts, Izzy said to the young woman, "Call the cops *now*. This man assaulted me."

The woman grimaced. "Actually? He kind of just saved your life." Her accent was thick; she sounded like the actress Fran Drescher. She turned to Jean-Marc. "Sorry I was rude. But it's like way bad to do CPR on someone who doesn't need it."

"Indeed," Jean-Marc replied calmly, his gaze on Izzy. "Thank you."

A microwave dinged and the woman's grimace changed to a cheery smile. "Ah! That'll be your dinner."

With a strange little curtsy aimed in Izzy's direction, she swept stage left. Pulling herself together, struggling overtime to focus, Izzy watched to see where the door was, but Jean-Marc blocked her view as he gingerly reapproached, holding out a white sweater shot through with gold threads.

"If you'll take off your pants, we can give you some dry ones," he offered.

Warily she grabbed the sweater and pulled it on over her head as he averted his gaze. Amazingly, she was beginning to feel more clear-headed, her disorientation fading as the dry, soft sweater slid over her skin.

"My pants stay on. Talk," she ordered him in a steady voice, although she was terrified.

They were in what appeared to be an octagonal room, and the walls were covered floor-to-ceiling with dark wood bookcases loaded with thick, leather-bound volumes. A ladder tilted at an angle against the topmost row. A brass chandelier gleamed above their heads.

She was seated on a thick, rich carpet woven with a central design of the head of a young woman wearing a knight's helmet. Where a feather might have decorated the top of the helmet, a flaming sword stood instead.

Jean-Marc held out a hand to help her up. She refused it, crossing her arms and legs, signaling her intention to stay put. The truth was, she was too shaky to stand. But she didn't want him to know that. She wanted to show no signs of weakness in front of him.

"We can get you a robe," he said.

Determined not to let her chattering teeth embarrass her, she remained silent.

He sighed. Then he crossed his ankles and sank down to the carpet, facing her. He moved with fluid grace, and he was near enough for her to feel his body heat, smell his scent. It was faint but spicy, conjuring up the exotic fragrance of the herbs Yolanda steeped at work, following Dr. Wei's prescriptions.

His features were sharp, almost harsh. His nose long, his cheekbones very high. His eyes were black, unfathomable pools. He had a five-o'clock shadow, and his black, curly hair was all over the place, tumbling over his shoulders like some eighties pop star.

Or like *her* hair.

Everything about him, the entire quirky assemblage, merged into the most breathtakingly handsome man she had ever met. No surprise; according to Catholic tradition, Lucifer had been the fairest of God's angels. And this man, who had acted at first like an angel of mercy, was most definitely on her list of the damned. He had *attacked* her. Practically killed her.

"I'm sorry I had to do that to you," he began. "This is neutral territory and the laws don't apply."

"The laws," she said. So he was a sociopath—someone who believed the rules of civilized society didn't apply to him.

"Of magic," he concluded. "I didn't know how powerful my energy sphere would be. It was only meant to stop you, not to harm you."

Correction: not a sociopath. A wack job.

He inclined his head. "I had to get you out of there before something happened to you."

"Because stopping my heart with your...whatever...didn't fit your definition of something happening to me," she stated, deadpan.

He exhaled, and she wasn't sure if he was irritated with her or frustrated with himself. He scooted slightly toward her.

"Don't touch me." Her voice was as hard as she could make it.

"It's ready!" the young woman announced, skipping back into the room, carrying a plate with both hands. *There* was the door; it was covered by rows of books so that it blended into the rest of the room.

"Ici, merci," Jean-Marc said, beckoning her over.

The woman dimpled. With a flourish, she handed the plate down to him, making a show of displaying her ample cleavage. "It's leftovers," she told Izzy apologetically. "He does most of the cooking. It's got red meat in it. I'm a vegan."

There were several thinly sliced pieces of rare beef drizzled with what smelled like a sauce of mushrooms and wine. New potatoes and some slivers of green beans. For a single beat, Izzy thought about knocking it out of his hand, just to make a point. But she was hungry. And she had to keep up her strength.

"I'm Sauvage," the woman told Izzy. She dipped another curtsy. "Well, actually, my name is Jesse, without an 'i.' Greenfield. An 'i' in that. But I didn't think it sounded exotic enough."

Seeing Izzy hesitate, she gestured to her food and said, "It's really good. Well, I didn't try the meat, of course, but the potatoes and the beans rock."

"It's safe," Jean-Marc said, perhaps sensing the underlying reason for her hesitation. He reached forward and plucked a green bean from her plate, popping it into his mouth.

"Totally," Sauvage agreed, snatching up a potato. She nibbled on it. Her nails were black. "See? Yummy."

Izzy stabbed a piece of meat with her fork. The morsel was rich and fragrant, and her salivary glands kicked into high gear. She could feel how ravenous she was. She had to ignore the impulse to shovel all of it into her mouth.

She said quietly, "Exotic enough for what?"

Sauvage looked confused and glanced at Jean-Marc. He gestured to her food. "Eat. There's plenty of time for questions."

Izzy lowered her fork to the plate and glared at him. "Oh, you are so wrong about that."

Sauvage shifted uncomfortably. "I don't get it," she said to Jean-Marc. "It's like she doesn't *know* or something."

"Doesn't know what?" Izzy demanded. "If this is some kind of ritual kidnapping…" She glanced at Sauvage's goth clothes. "Like you need to drink someone's blood…"

Sauvage pressed her hands over her mouth. "Oh, my God! How gross!"

Jean-Marc shook his head. "It's nothing like that, I assure you." To the woman, he said, "Sauvage, would you be so kind as to bring us some wine?"

"I'll have water," Izzy cut in.

"Some water and wine," Jean-Marc said.

"Pas de problem," Sauvage said, with a lot of the Bronx thrown in. She left the room again.

Izzy shifted straightening her spine; seeing her, Jean-Marc knit his brows. "Does your back hurt?"

"Everything hurts," she replied icily. "Look, put me in a cab and no questions asked."

He regarded her with his large, sad eyes. "You know I can't do that."

"You sure as hell better do it. My father's a cop with the NYPD. As soon as he realizes that I'm missing, he'll tear this town apart until he finds me. And then he'll tear you apart. Because Big Vince DeMarco—"

"He won't," Jean-Marc interrupted her. At her confusion, he said, "He won't realize you're missing." Before she could respond, he said, "That assassin you destroyed—"

"That man I *killed*—"

"Non," Jean-Marc said emphatically. He leaned forward and took her face between his hands. She tried to free herself, but he held her tightly, bringing his face within inches of her own. His eyes blazed with intensity. As his hands cupped her, warmth spread from them into her skin and she felt her tension ebbing the smallest little bit.

"Non, you did not kill *it*. It was a created thing." He moved his hands, as if conjuring something out of thin air. "It's called a fabricant. It was created with magic. When the magic ran out, it ceased to be."

"He was flesh and bone," she argued, the chills skittering down her spine as she remembered the fight and the way she had flung him across the alley.

How did I do that?

"It was created to kill you," Jean-Marc agreed, "but magical forces go awry here. This is Borgia territory, and since they disappeared, it's neutral ground and..." He trailed off. "You have no idea what I'm talking about. You've lived among the Ungifted all your life."

"Here's the wine," Sauvage said, returning. She carried a wine bottle and two glasses. A sports bottle was tucked under her arm. "And some water for the *Guardienne*." She dimpled; she seemed about to burst with excitement. She reminded Izzy of Yolanda, so eager to take care of her.

"*Merci*," Jean-Marc said. He dropped his hands away from Izzy's face. He skillfully pulled out the cork and poured the two glasses full while Sauvage unscrewed the plastic cap on the bottle of water and ceremoniously handed it to Izzy. Izzy drank deeply. She was parched.

Holding one of the wineglasses out to her, he said, "Please."

She only stared at him; with a sigh, he set the glass back down on the carpet. He sipped his wine appreciatively. Cradling the glass against his chest, he extended his hand and held his fingers a hairbreadth away from the cut on her temple. She jerked backward; he persisted.

His lips moved but he made no sound. She felt her eyes grow heavy. She fought to keep them open; but it was a battle that she lost.

The pounding in her head lessened, then vanished altogether.

She opened her eyes again, strangely refreshed.

"I mean you no harm." His cheeks reddened, a sure sign that he was lying.

"Back to my father not missing me."

"We know he's in the hospital," Jean-Marc said.

"How do you know that?" she asked, frightened for Big Vince. Her mind jumped to the tenement fire and her hackles rose to full-alarm state. "Did you have anything to do with that fire? Or the shooter?"

"*Non*, I assure you," he said. "I swear it."

She didn't believe him. "Yolanda—"

He cut her off. "Yolanda thinks you got tired of all the noise and went home."

She was even more freaked out. "You know this because—"

"She called your home phone and left a message. She thinks you're asleep in your bed."

"You tapped my phone? Are you CIA?" A worse thought occurred to her: that this was some elaborate scheme John Cratty had set up because he was dirty and he had gleaned that she had suspicions about him.

"I'm not with the CIA," he said.

"Then how do you know all this stuff?" she demanded, her voice rising shrilly.

"I know these things from using scrying stones," he replied. He held her gaze steadily, as if mentally willing her to listen to him. "And magic mirrors."

He's crazy.

I'm dead.

"Magic mirrors," she said carefully. "Did you buy them on the Sci-Fi channel?" Bad move; she was in no position to ridicule anything he had to say.

"Don't make jokes," he said, flaring with anger. She saw a bad temper and she was even more wary of him.

"What do you expect? You kidnap me, and this…this girl from *Rocky Horror*—"

"Hey," Sauvage said, hurt. Izzy hadn't realized she was still in the room. She had moved behind Izzy, where she appeared to be reading the spines of the books in the bookcase.

"Sauvage, please," Jean-Marc said. "We need to be alone."

The girl huffed. Then she flounced out of the room.

"You kidnap me," Izzy continued, forcing her voice to stay steady.

"*No. I saved your life.*" A muscle twitched in his cheek and she could see that he was frustrated nearly beyond his ability to control himself. She tried to see things from his point of

view and decided not to. Because his point of view included
magic mirrors.

"I know too much of this is beyond your understanding.
But you have to try to listen and understand."

Standing down a little, he took another swallow of wine
as he considered how to proceed. She could practically see
the synapses firing in his brain.

She wanted to get the hell out of here.

"You think I'm lying when I say I mean you no harm," he
said. "What I mean is, that I'm sorry I have to come for you.
I wish you could stay ignorant of who you are. But it's not
possible. They know you're here."

His face was grim. "And we believe they mean to kill
you."

Chapter 7

"They," Izzy repeated slowly, as she faced Jean-Marc in the octagonal room. She kept her cool. But inside, she quaked. The room had just turned ten degrees colder, and she was scared. "They who? Kill me why?"

"We think it's the Malchances. But we're not sure." At her blank expression, he pinched the bridge of his nose, as if he had inherited her headache. "Let me try a different tack."

Staring at her, he raised his right hand in line with his chest and laid the left one over it. Squaring his shoulders, he held his head high. He began to speak in a steady monotone, like a chant, in words that sounded like Latin.

The room plunged into darkness.

A curtain of hazy light appeared between them. She looked up toward the ceiling. There was no apparent aperture from which it could have descended. She studied the floor. Nothing there, either. It seemed to have appeared out of nowhere.

Still, she was not overly impressed. She had seen a lot of high-end technology.

He whispered, "Please, watch. I'll take you home afterward."

"Right," she muttered.

"*I will.* But you have to watch."

Could it really be that simple? "Okay, it's a deal."

Shapes appeared on the screen and gradually snapped into focus. She saw a woman in a long, shapeless white dress, dark hair tumbling over her shoulders. Her eyes were bruised and she was crying.

Wrenching as the image was, Izzy knew she had to make the most of the moment. She looked away from the screen and located the door. Jean-Marc was closer to it than she was. She couldn't hope to outrun him. And who knew where Sauvage was? Maybe she was standing outside the door with a gun. Maybe after the movie was over they were going to blow her head off.

"You made a deal," Jean-Marc accused her, speaking across the barrier between them.

"You know, you're really pissing me off," she hissed.

"*Tais-toi.*"

Seething, but frightened, she looked back at the screen. The woman on the screen was wiping her eyes. Jean-Marc said, "It is Rouen, in France. In 1431. This is Joan of Arc. Do you know who she was?"

"Vaguely. I'm more certain that Columbus landed in America in 1492."

He sighed and said, "This isn't going to work."

She heard the sharp snap of his fingers and the lights in the room came back on.

His scent teased her. He was standing inches away from her, looking down on her. He gazed at her for a long moment.

She felt a spark, a connection, and there was nothing in her that wanted that.

Nothing, and everything.

He said to her, "We are descendants of noble French houses, you and I. I am de Devereaux. You are de Bouvard."

"You've got the wrong woman," she snapped. "I'm DeMarco. Italian on both sides."

He hesitated. She really didn't like that pause. It scared her even worse.

He said, "The 'de' signifies nobility. For that reason, among French speakers, we often drop the 'de' and simply use our last names. I assume that's not the case with DeMarco."

Then he continued.

"We began in France, in the early 1400s. The King of France, Charles VI, was insane, and his heir had been assassinated. The country was fragmented. Nobles were backing their own candidate for the crown. And a bloody civil war broke out. Joan of Arc fought on the side of the Armagnacs."

She shifted, but she kept listening. He was unbelievably tense; she could read it in his walk, the clench of his jaw.

"Three of the noble houses embroiled in the chaos were the Malchances, the Bouvards and the Devereaux. The Bouvards openly fought in Joan of Arc's army, and Bouvard nobles died by the score for her cause."

"The Bouvards. That would be 'my' noble house." She made air quotes.

He picked up his wineglass from the carpet. He took a long swallow and began to pace. His profile against the leather books reminded her of the paintings of warriors and kings at the Metropolitan Museum of Art. She didn't want to be fascinated by him. She didn't want any of this. She just wanted to go home and resume her normal life.

"After she was defeated in battle and delivered to the

English, Joan of Arc was burned at the stake for witchcraft," he informed her. "It was a trumped-up charge."

"Well, that goes without saying," she drawled, but her voice was not as steady as she had hoped.

He ignored her.

"The Duchess de Bouvard did everything she could to save her. I'm not certain why the Bouvards were so loyal to Joan, but they never turned their backs on her. Others did. The Malchances lobbied for her death. My own house remained neutral."

"Which means you *did* turn your back on her," she interjected. She had seen a lot of "neutrality" in her professional life—social workers who wouldn't take a stand against a foster parent when abuse was apparent. Bystanders who pretended not to hear, not to see, when a crime was committed. So they could stay uninvolved. Neutral.

He clenched his jaw for a moment before continuing.

"While all this was going on, the Malchances experimented with black magic. They raised a demon named Malfeur, and he became their patron."

Her lips parted at this further evidence of his insanity, but she maintained her silence.

"My family, the Devereaux, made a similar treaty with a powerful demon who was neither precisely evil nor precisely good. He is called *le Roi Gris.*"

"The Gray King," she ventured, not knowing how she knew that. "Shades of gray, not black, not white."

He paused again and, again, the connection zinged between them. It was like an electric current, not so much a shock as a low-level vibration. The little hairs on her neck rose; her gut told her that as pleasant as the sensation was, it was as dangerous as a live wire.

"*Oui,*" he said slowly. Did he feel it, too?

When she said nothing more, he continued. "Our families

gained magical surnames. The Malchances are the House of the Blood—*du Sang*. The Devereaux are the House of the Shadows. So, I am Jean-Marc de Devereaux des Ombres."

"*Ombres* means shadows in French."

He leaned forward. "Did you study French in school?"

"No," she said shortly. "Never. Go on."

"*Bon.* Joan of Arc was defeated and sentenced for execution. Before Joan—we call her *Jehanne*—died, the Duchess de Bouvard visited her alone. The duchess was moved by Joan's honor and courage even as she faced a horrible death, and she swore that her house would always fight to protect the weak and downtrodden, in her name.

"In return, Joan—so tradition claims—called on the angels to bestow the essence of her strength and courage on the duchess. This essence has been passed since that time through the generations, from one Bouvard female to another. So, in honor of their benefactress, the Bouvards became known in magical circles as the House of the Flames."

"Magical circles," Izzy said. "Like…Sauvage's friends down at the Anne Rice is My Goddess goth club."

"Sauvage found me through the Internet," he allowed. "She contacted me, and offered me her services in New York. I have a lot of Ungifted allies."

She ignored the urge to ask him what services those were. "Ungifted." She gestured to the shelves and shelves of books. "Where's the dictionary?"

"Let me finish, please. I know you don't want to hear this, but you have to."

She resumed her silence, realizing that rather than bait him, she should let him speak freely. She didn't believe him for a minute when he promised to take her home. But maybe if she listened to him long enough, she'd learn something that would help her formulate a plan of escape.

"There are magical groups all over the world," he said. "Some are traditional families. Some are clans. There are Asian ones, African, American. We've formed a governing body, sort of like the UN. It's called the Grand Covenate. We granted each other territories, and we agreed to keep our existence a secret."

"But something happened," she guessed.

"Yes." He regarded her steadily, his features softening. His cheeks went red again and she knew that he didn't want to tell her whatever he was going to say next. His anxiety communicated itself and she braced herself for bad news.

"Isabelle, haven't you made the connection? You are the heiress of Joan of Arc's legacy. You are the daughter of the House of the Flames."

She believed him.

For six seconds.

And then she said, "A deal is a deal. It's time to go home."

He blinked at her as if he couldn't process what he was hearing.

"I don't think you understand. I'm here to protect you, and serve as your guide, until you're ready to assume the Crown of the Flames. I have to teach you so much. You know nothing…." He sounded overwhelmed.

"Why you?" she asked bluntly.

He knelt on one knee, a quick, easy movement that while attractive, she found completely bizarre and inappropriate.

"I'm Regent for the Bouvards. It fell to me to come for you."

"Because…?"

You are the only hope of the Bouvards, Isabelle, he said inside her head.

She jerked. "You said you'd take me home."

He tilted back his face. His lips were pursed in a straight line and his thick brows drew together above his nose. There was an air of restrained power about him, as if every punch he had thrown was substantially pulled. A guy like that on her side would be awesome.

A guy like that on the other side…a nightmare.

He said, "If they sent one assassin to kill you, they can send another."

"You mentioned something about warding the area. That means protecting it, correct?"

There was a glimmer in his eyes, registering, maybe, that she might actually believe him.

"And I said something about the unpredictability of magic here in New York," he added. "I can't be certain my wards will hold."

"Of course not," she said kindly.

"It's true." He stared at her. She felt something shift in the air, as it had shifted at Mass and at the subway station. As if he were probing her. She felt naked.

"Believe me," he whispered.

"Oh, I do." She crossed her arms, cutting off all further discussion.

His face fell, but it was still the face of an angel. Wearily, he nodded. Then he got to his feet. His posture was perfect; and the way he moved telegraphed advanced knowledge of some kind of martial arts. If she had to use street smarts to get out of here, she might be in trouble.

Might be? She was already in deep, deep trouble.

He called, *"Sauvage? Viens ici."*

The goth darted into the room so fast that Izzy knew she'd been listening at the door.

Jean-Marc said to the girl, "Please get Ms. DeMarco some dry clothes."

"But…" There were no creases in Sauvage's heavy makeup as she frowned. "She's…Ms. *Bouvard.*"

Izzy tapped her fingertips against her elbow and said, "Get me something *now*. I'll give back your sweater after I get home." And call the cops and see these two in jail.

"*Vite*, Sauvage," Jean-Marc said grittily. Then, to Izzy, "The sweater was purchased for you. We'll get you a coat, as well."

"There's a whole closetful of cool clothes for you," Sauvage said wistfully. "And an awesome canopy bed. I helped him shop for it." Her smile was devilish, her red mouth a caricature against her white skin. "I tested the mattresses."

Izzy's gaze ticked from Sauvage to Jean-Marc. Jean-Marc gazed back at Sauvage impassively.

"All right," she said, sighing like a little girl forbidden to play. "I'll get her some pants."

A few minutes later Izzy was fully dressed in blessedly dry black wool pants that fit her as if they had been made for her. She also had warm black wool socks. Now Sauvage was off to get her some new boots.

Meanwhile, Jean-Marc escorted Izzy into another room. The only piece of furniture in it was a stone altar. Three brass bells, a white candle and a gray one, and a brazier wafting incense were scattered on the flat stone surface as if in no apparent order.

A white marble vase held a single lily. A white candle floated in an alabaster bowl before a Barbie-size statue of a woman dressed in battle armor. There was another figure beside St. Joan—or so she guessed it to be St. Joan, this one far more primitive, a sort of hazy male figure—and Izzy thought she saw it move as Jean-Marc knelt before it. The candle in front of it was blue.

Did not, did not, did not. Their group hysteria is not contagious.

The walls were bare except for two Medieval tapestries.

One depicted a black-haired woman wearing a halo being burned at the stake. The other showed a castle turret surrounded by clouds. A white dove was flying out of the gray arched window. A hand in a heavy gray glove was outstretched behind it—releasing it or trying to catch it?

Sauvage returned with boots and also a beautiful pair of black chandelier earrings. Those Izzy declined, but she took the boots.

Holding the earrings in her palm, Sauvage said to Jean-Marc, "What about the ring?"

"Not yet," Jean-Marc replied.

Then, while Izzy looked on, he performed a series of elaborate incantations and spells. Sauvage assisted him, picking up and ringing the bells, walking around the altar with each candle stretched before her; it was reminiscent of Mass. Izzy thought maybe Jean-Marc was speaking in an ancient form of Latin from the thick leather-bound book Sauvage held open for him, but she couldn't be sure. His voice was deep and fervent, almost vibrating inside her own chest.

She thought more than once about trying to get out of the room. But each time her gaze strayed to the door, she felt Jean-Marc's eyes on her.

The room was warm, the candlelight soft and comforting. A glow enveloped her, tugging at her to relax. She resisted with everything in her. This was certainly not the time or place to let down her guard.

"In the name of St. Joan and the Gray King," Jean-Marc concluded in English as he bowed before the altar.

Sauvage bowed, as well. Then the two said, "Amen."

Sauvage smiled at Izzy as she smoothed back her hair and tugged at her bustier, saying, "Wasn't that cool?"

Izzy made no reply. Then Jean-Marc said, "Isabelle and I need to be alone now."

"Aw." Sauvage pouted.

"No, we don't," Izzy countered, alarmed.

"We do." He ticked his head at Sauvage, who left the room and closed the door after herself.

"I am leaving this room now," Izzy said, walking toward him, since he was closer to the door.

He took a step toward her. "Wait."

She considered her options. He could tackle her if she tried to get around him. What about her palm weapon?

She raised it up, and he tensed. She closed her eyes and willed energy from it.

Nothing happened.

Damn.

She lowered her arm and said, "Okay, now what?"

He studied Izzy for a moment. Then he scratched his cheek and muttered in French, glancing over at the statue on the altar. He cocked his head as if listening to a reply.

Oh, my God, Izzy thought. *He's schizophrenic.*

He looked back at her. Then he scratched his cheek again and cocked his head appraisingly. His scent wafted toward her again; it stirred her.

She didn't want any stirring.

"I'll be blindfolded," he mused. "That might work."

"Are you talking to the space brothers, or can anyone join in?" she asked him.

He didn't react. "In many magical traditions, sex magic is the strongest form."

"Stop." She held out her hand again, forced it steady. More adrenaline drenched her nerves, igniting her fight-or-flight response. She still wasn't a hundred percent and she wasn't really much of a street fighter. A few self-defense moves did not add up to disabling a big man like him long enough to get the door open, race through the apartment, get to the front door and get out, all without knowing what Sauvage might do—and if there were other people in the apartment she hadn't yet encountered. Insanity like this usually traveled in cults.

She took a breath and added, "Sex magic? If you think that for one second, I'm buying that—"

"I won't force myself on you," he said. "If we don't have sex, the next best thing is proximity while naked."

All she could do was gape at him. Alarm bells were shrieking in her ears. If she launched a simple physical attack, would the element of surprise work in her favor? Was her palm strike sufficiently "recharged" *now?*

"Did you run this con on Sauvage? And it worked? Which is why you're imagining there's a point to even trying it out on me?" she asked him, her voice scathing, contemptuous.

"You can blindfold me," he said. "I won't see you."

"While you sit close to me, naked." She pressed her fingertips against her forehead. Her headache was pounding against her temples again. "That's a major kink you've got going, friend."

He looked as if he might smile, but he didn't. "I would offer to let you handcuff me, but frankly, I don't trust you enough. You'd probably try to choke me to death."

"Damn. There you go, reading my mind again." Folding her arms over her chest, she put some more distance between the two of them, moving toward the door. Smacking up against the altar, she unfolded her arms and flattened her palm on the stone surface for support.

"All this bravado is unnecessary," he said flatly. "Nothing will happen."

"Then why bother?" She inched her hand toward the statue of St. Joan. "You promised to take me home. Keep your promise." She closed her hand around the base of the figure.

He looked past her face to a place above her head, his gaze traveling to one side of her, moving down her body. She flushed and tightened her grip on the statue.

"You're sending out waves of magical energy," he said. "Can't you see them?"

There was no way she was going to take her eyes off him for a second. And yet, she did feel a strange warmth…and she thought she saw a white spark or two in her peripheral vision.

"We have to conceal them," he said, "or you may as well wear a bull's-eye on your chest. You're a target, pure and simple. Unless we hide what you are, they'll be after you again. And this time, they'll be able to track you better."

"They did okay tracking me to Yolanda's," she said.

"Your powers have been awakening these past few days. I don't know how else to describe it. You've been flying under everybody's magical radar for years and years. But you're going to show up now. You need help."

"And sitting naked with you will help me how?" she said.

"God, you are frustrating!" he cried, and took a step toward her.

She picked up the statue and threw it as hard as she could at him.

He raised a protective hand in front of his face, then stretched out his other hand, in a palm strike similar to the one she had used.

The statue froze in space. It hung, unmoving, midway between her and him.

He plucked the figurine out of the air, carried it to the altar and angrily set it back down in its original place. Then he grabbed her wrist as she bolted toward the door and pulled her into his arms.

He cradled her head against his chest and spoke rapidly in a low voice, in a strange language.

The connection she had felt between them before re-emerged; a tingling heat began at the crown of her head and draped over her, the antithesis of the wet-velvet sensation she had experienced in her bathroom at home. It was silky, liquid. She smelled oranges. Or was it roses? It was sweet and fragrant. Part of her sought refuge in the scent and the pleasure, and she could no more pull away than…die.

She remembered the white tunnel, and tears welled. It was like that. It was a return to something wonderful.

Her body trembled, pressed against the length of his. His chest was hard, his stomach taut and he was turned on.

Before she could muster a more reasonable reaction, he let go of her and took a step away. His forehead was shiny with perspiration. Whatever he had just done, it had taken him considerable effort.

"That's the best I can do without your cooperation," he said. He wiped his forehead with the back of his hand. "If you want to go, we'll go now."

She was weak-kneed. Her answering physical response alarmed her—she was extremely aroused. It made no sense, and she'd be damned before she let on that he had affected her. That any of this had touched her in the least.

"I want to go," she said.

"All right." He gestured for her to open the door.

As Izzy led the way out of the room, Jean-Marc said, "I've placed additional wards around this place, and us, and my car."

"Redundant systems are always best," she said evenly.

They walked to the entry of the apartment. A large plastic grocery bag contained her wet clothing. Her coat was missing.

Sauvage stood on the threshold, holding a beautiful pure-wool black coat.

"I'm really sorry about your old coat," she said. "You can

have it back if you want but it's kind of…disgusting. You fell in some dog poop or something."

"I want it back," Izzy said.

"Sauvage, go get it," Jean-Marc instructed her.

She returned with a two-handled sack, the coat folded inside it. It stank.

"I'll take that," Izzy said to Sauvage. "I'll return yours later."

"It's *yours*," Sauvage said. She looked at it wistfully, then tapped the lacings on her bustier. "It's too small for me."

Her toes pointed in slightly, Sauvage clasped her hands together, peeling back her fingers to wave goodbye as Izzy and Jean-Marc left the apartment.

"Please come back," she said sweetly.

Not a chance in hell, Izzy thought, but she said nothing except, "Thanks for the dinner."

"Oh, it was nothing." Sauvage curtsied. "It was such an honor to microwave your food."

"Sauvage, keep the door locked," Jean-Marc ordered her.

She curtsied again and shut the door behind them. Then Izzy and Jean-Marc took the elevator and went down to the parking garage.

Standing outside the elevator, Jean-Marc pulled a remote out of his pocket and punched in some numbers, and the headlights of a sexy, low-slung black Jaguar parked among other wickedly sexy cars—there was a Lotus, for God's sake—winked on. The car backed out of it parking spot and rolled toward them.

"I suppose that's magic," she murmured.

"Advanced technology," he replied, showing her the sleek black remote. "Installed at the factory. Although that's one of the topics up for debate these days. The definition of magic is 'an alteration in the status quo, for which there is no observable natural catalyst.' As technology advances, what is natural and what is supernatural? Are we simply a little ahead of the curve?"

She surreptitiously glanced down at her palm. What she had done was ahead of the curve.

They pulled out of the garage and onto the street. It was dark and snowing heavily. A bell trilled and Jean-Marc unhooked a car phone from a holster on the dash.

He put it to his ear, and she had the sense that he was unused to doing it—that he was going through the motions because she was there.

"Oui? Merci." He asked a couple more questions in French. *"D'accord."* He hung up.

She glanced at him. He said, "We've placed guards at the Metropolitan. We're sweeping your neighborhood and inserting security. We'll make the both of you as safe as we can."

"How many of you are there?" she asked, shocked.

His face softened into an ironic smile. "We have operatives throughout the city."

The car glided like a shark down Sixth. They blew past Rockefeller Center and the Hilton. Izzy wasn't certain if Jean-Marc was actually driving, or just pretending to for her sake. But why go through the motions now?

"If I…agreed to this situation, what would you need to teach me?" she asked him. "How to do magic spells like you and Sauvage?"

"As I mentioned before, Sauvage is not Gifted," he said. "She can't 'do' magic spells. But she can assist with rituals."

"Oh." That made as much sense as anything else he had told her.

"You need to learn self-defense, first and foremost. Later, strategy and politics." He warmed to the subject. "A crash course. But protective magic most of all."

"But things are off here, you said. Magic doesn't work right."

"*Oui*. It's because of the void that the Borgias left." He ticked his attention from the road to her. "Do you know who the Borgias are?"

"The name sounds vaguely familiar," she confessed. "But less familiar than Joan of Arc."

He rolled his eyes. "American public education."

"Hey. Show some respect," she said, only half teasing. "I'm your queen, after all."

He turned on the left blinker by waving his left hand over the steering wheel. "I told you, I'm not a Bouvard. I'm only acting as Regent."

"So you're my employee," she said.

He looked out the window. His shoulders were hunched. It dawned on her that all this was making him incredibly uncomfortable. He yawned, and when he realized that she'd caught him doing it, he said, "I haven't actually slept through the night in about a month. Catnapped a little."

"Because of me."

"It's my job," he said. "Tell me more about the assassin."

It seemed easier to talk to him now. Was that because of what he'd done—cast a spell on her? Could that actually be what had happened?

"I dreamed about him," she said. "I was afraid of him from the start."

"We think it sensed that you were nearby when it was in front of your home. But we don't think it had pinpointed your precise location at that point," he told her.

She considered that. "Why not?"

He made another left. "Because you're still alive."

Slowly she covered her face with her hands, rubbing her fingertips against her eyelids. Her hands shook.

"Powerful magic users give off emanations," he said. "Until recently, yours have been undetectable. We have been searching for you for a long time. It goes without saying that others have been searching, as well."

He appraised her. "But as your power awakens, so do the emanations. I can still see them—like white sparks occasionally bursting from your aura. I think that's why you felt compelled to hide in the Dumpster. To shield them from view. My spell will hide them from others, but probably only for a little while."

"Then why can you still see them?" she asked him.

He said, "I'm the one who cast the spell."

"Oh." That gave her pause. "What about the fence? It mended itself."

"You may have done it. Or I. I put wards everywhere as soon as I sensed your presence. I didn't really feel you until tonight."

The idea of his *feeling* her unnerved her.

"Why now? What changed? If I'm suddenly the *Guardienne,* that means someone else has died."

There was a beat, in which a chasm of silence fell between them.

"There's not been a death yet," he said. "But we anticipate it."

She took a breath. "Who?"

"Isabelle…" he began. Then he swerved the car across three lanes of traffic. Horns blared. Brakes squealed. Izzy held on, saying nothing.

He found an opening and pulled his Jag to the curb. He turned off the car and shifted in his seat to face her directly.

"Your *mother,* Isabelle."

Chapter 8

Izzy laughed as relief flooded through her. The snowy streets of the city were once again familiar. The man driving her home, deluded. It was all a bad dream, after all, and she could go home to the real world.

"All this trouble for nothing. Jean-Marc, my mom died ten years ago."

She saw the recurring theme of frustration on his face. Also, something she had not seen before—was it pity?

"You were adopted," he said bluntly.

"You are the missing daughter of Marianne de Bouvard des Flammes. Now that we know your identity, we're researching the records. Vincenzo and Anna Maria DeMarco adopted a baby girl just before Vincenzo left the Air Force. He was stationed in Barkdale, Louisiana."

An icy chill penetrated her relief. "No," she insisted. "I

was born there, it's true, but my mother…was my mother and Big Vince—"

He cut her off. "I wanted to do this in stages, but this is an emergency. A crisis. Your blood family is a mess. It's just like France in the 1400s. Rival factions have sprung up to claim the Crown. Some are working with enemy houses, making deals. Bad deals."

She blinked rapidly. "I was not adopted."

His dark eyes were too dark, his gaze unflinching, as he said, "When you see Vincenzo DeMarco, ask him."

Her throat closed. She tried to swallow, but she couldn't. He had to be wrong.

He pulled back into the traffic and they drove in silence. He started to speak, but she shook her head. She was overloaded.

He said quietly, "I'm sorry. I should've been more gentle. But time's running out."

She pursed her lips together, pressed her hands against her thighs. The snow tumbled from the sky, obscuring her vision. But she saw the occasional landmarks; they were only a few blocks from her house.

He said, "Meet one more time with me. I'll show you some of the things you're capable of. Then make your decision to help or to walk away. Maybe I can make some sort of announcement that you have declined the Crown and everyone will leave you alone." He sounded completely unconvincing.

"If I'm the only hope of the Rebel Alliance, you wouldn't let me go so easily," she said.

He moved his shoulders in a decidedly Gallic shrug. "I don't know what else to do. I remind you that I'm only serving as the Regent of the Bouvards. I'm a Devereaux. My family was chosen to intervene on behalf of the Flames because we're neutral."

"But you're not, are you?" she said.

"No," he agreed. "Not any longer." His brows knit. "You have magical abilities. You've used them. At least let me show you how to live as a Gifted," he urged. "Without learning how to channel your powers, you're like a wildfire. You could hurt yourself—or people you care about."

"How?" she demanded, thinking of her palm and what she had done to the assassin.

"I'll give you a demonstration." He held up his finger. "One time. Then you decide what to do next."

She blurted, "This sucks." She sounded like Sauvage, not a mature adult. She was retreating, unwilling to face how much had happened. What it meant for her life.

"In some ways, it does suck," he agreed, taking her child-like anger at face value. "In other ways…we call it the Gift for a reason. I can't imagine life without magic."

He snapped his fingers and at once she smelled the sweet rose-orange scent again. Calmed a little. She tasted wine in her mouth. It was deep, red and rich, and it was really there.

"I pity the Ungifted," he concluded. "We have terrible responsibilities, you and I. But we can also know transcendent pleasures."

And they were back to sex, of that she was certain.

"You can't know what your universe is like," he added, his voice low and deep. He sounded almost reverent. "The things you can do, *be*. The Gifted live on an entirely different plane. Some magical clans call us the Blessed." He glanced over at her. "Some Ungifted call us gods."

"Which would be rather tasteless, from my point of view."

"As a Catholic, you mean," he ventured.

"As a person," she replied. "You're implying that the Gifted are above the law."

"We have our own laws," he replied. "That's why we have

the Grand Covenate. Our governing body. To enforce them.
To keep the peace."

"And how's that working out for you people?" she asked
rhetorically. In case he didn't get her point, she underscored
it. "Since I'm apparently being hunted like a dog?"

His scowl matched hers. She saw the energy coiled in his
body and she thought again about how she never wanted to
seriously piss him off.

"Now that you have been found, we can protect you. And
I can teach you how to protect yourself."

"Magical self-defense," she muttered.

"Exactement." He held up a finger. "One session."

First one's free, she thought ruefully. But he had her at the
part about hurting people she loved. "No one else shows up,"
she said. "No Sauvage, no other crazy people, just you and me."

His startled but pleased reaction gave her pause. It was
apparent that he had assumed she would refuse.

"Agreed," he said.

I've done it now, she thought. *I should be committed.*

He drove onto her block. She glanced anxiously at the
row house, scanning for the assassin guy, wondering if her
neighbors would look at her showing up in a Jag with a guy,
when ostensibly she was in her house, asleep.

He went on. "Waiting until tomorrow night is a concession
as it is. You were *attacked,* Isabelle. Everything in me wants
you to stay at the co-op with me. But I know you aren't convinced yet, and I can't force you."

"I'm glad we're clear on that," she said, trying to sound
more certain than she felt. "The not-forcing-me part."

"You *will* be guarded, however," he said. "I already have
operatives in place." He pointed to the shadowy place beside
her door stoop, then across the street at the locked pocket park.

He parked at the curb and turned off the engine. He got out

and walked behind the car, toward her door. As she swung her legs out of the Jag, she caught sight of herself in the mirror attached to the sleek beveled side of the car. She sucked in her breath. A stranger stared back at her: she was blond, and twenty, if anything. She was wearing jeans and a Mets sweatshirt beneath a heavy forest-green jacket.

"It's a glamour," Jean-Marc said, standing behind her. "I've magically altered your appearance. It won't last long."

He stepped into view, so that his reflection was cast in the mirror, as well. Stunned, she turned to take in his new persona. He was Asian, with short, black hair, almond-shaped eyes and broad, flared cheekbones. He had on a black jacket and black jeans.

He hustled her to the trio of stairs leading to her stoop. His gaze ticked from her to somewhere behind her. She turned; a guy with gelled red hair and a goatee stepped from the darkness.

"This is David," Jean-Marc told her. "He's the leader of your protection team tonight."

"Bon soir, Guardienne," David said respectfully. He looked about nineteen. He must be a friend of Sauvage's. If there were chat rooms and IMs peppered with emoticons about the discovery of the *Guardienne.*

"We have over a dozen trained operatives watching your house," Jean-Marc informed her. "They're not Gifted, but each of them has sworn an oath to give his or her life for yours."

David inclined his head. "That's true."

"Thank you," she said, at a loss.

Without another word, David blended back into the shadows.

"I'll check your house," Jean-Marc said. "I'll go in first. Your key?"

"If my neighbors see two strangers entering my house—"

Before she could continue, he pulled her into the shadowed place beside the stoop where David had stood.

Jean-Marc's appearance changed again. He looked exactly like her father, from Big Vince's sad Italian eyes to the barely noticeable jowls that had begun to form at the corners of his mouth.

"How do you do that?" she demanded. "Is it some kind of hypnosis or—"

"You know how. Not precisely how, but you know it's not hypnosis."

He took her hand and walked her up the steps. She extracted her key and opened the door.

He gestured for her to be quiet and murmured an incantation as he crossed the threshold. Her skin prickled as she followed him in, visually scanning the entryway for signs of intrusion. She was afraid, both of what they might discover and of the man beside her.

After she shut the door, he became himself again, tall, dark, hewn from a dream. Maybe the self he presented to her wasn't the real Jean-Marc, either. Maybe he was grotesquely ugly. A monster.

"Stay here," he said. "I'll ward the house."

"No way. You're not going anywhere in this house without me."

That seemed to surprise him, but he didn't comment.

She trailed after him, detecting faint traces of garlic and olive oil—the odors of an Italian home—and feeling naked as he gazed at the photographs of her family on the walls of the living room. He paused a moment before the painted, wooden crucifix Aunt Clara had brought home from a pilgrimage to Lourdes, where she had prayed for Anna Maria to be healed of the lingering illness no one could name.

He spread his hands and murmured more words. Blue sparks flickered from his silhouette.

It was as if her house breathed a sigh of relief. She smelled oranges and roses again. It was like an animal leaving its scent, so that others would respect its territory.

Moving with the same easy grace she had witnessed in the octagonal room, he walked into the dining room. Lingering beside the chair Pat had sat in, he smiled half to himself as he touched it.

"I see," he said.

She didn't ask him what he saw. Pat was none of his business.

Then he entered the frilly kitchen and stopped at the place where she and Pat had kissed. She swallowed, feeling increasingly more violated, and muttered, "Can you hurry this up?"

"Upstairs," he told her.

Where her bedroom was.

He led the way. At the top of the stairs, he held out his hand and said, "Wait. Let me go to work up here." He looked over his shoulder, down at her. "There's a greater sense of you here than downstairs."

He squinted. "And you've suffered up here. Terribly." She saw him absorbing something she could not, reacting as if someone had dealt him a severe body blow. "You cared for all of them while your mother was sick. But who cared for you?"

He moved his gaze from her to the hallway. First door on the left was her bedroom. Across the hall, the bathroom. Beyond that, Gino's, and at the end of the hall, Big Vince's.

He held up his hand and looked at a place she could not see. His lids flickered; he was listening to something.

He said, "You have a visitor."

The doorbell rang, and Izzy jumped, startled.

"It's all right to answer the door. It's someone safe. Otherwise he wouldn't have gotten past my wards."

She hesitated. "He? He who?"

"Someone you want to see. Go ahead. I won't interfere," he said, opening the bathroom door. "I respect your privacy."

She turned and headed down the stairs; halfway down, she turned back. She experimentally touched her face. "Do I look like me?"

"Oui. Et tu es magnifique," he said in French.

Flushing, not wanting to care that he had given her a compliment, she descended, turning back to look at the stairway one more time before opening the door. Jean-Marc had made himself scarce. Whether literally, she had no idea.

Sure enough, Pat was there, wearing a black suit, his tie loosened. He smelled amazing. He looked amazing. He said, "Sorry for just dropping in, Iz. Yolanda called and said you hadn't phoned her back after you left. I tried, too."

"Hi," she said breathlessly. "I...my phone's..." She trailed off, taking a step back to let him in.

He kissed her gently but thoroughly, cupping the back of her head as she tilted upward to kiss him. This was definitely a man who knew what he was doing, and took great care to communicate that fact.

Despite her appreciation, her self-consciousness muted her response. If he noticed, he didn't indicate it. As she gently ended the kiss, he rubbed her shoulders and said, "So, for the record, are you all right?" He scrutinized her forehead. "Looks a lot better."

She smiled at him. "Better *now*."

"I'm glad." He touched her cheek. "Yolanda asked me to apologize again."

"It's okay. Too much squalling baby, is all. Care for some

wine?" She led him into the dining room and walked him toward "his" chair.

"No, thanks."

"Maybe some tea?"

He pulled out the chair and said, "I'll get it. You sit down."

She sank gratefully into the chair as he prepared the tea, carried the mugs to the table, and sat down, facing her. He sipped, exhaling with pleasure, and wrapped his hands around the mug as he leaned toward her. He had dimples on either side of his mouth and a cleft in his chin.

He said, "About Cratty. I think you need to know that we're close to something. We may have found an accomplice."

He moved his fingers from around the mug and covered her hand.

And in that moment she saw a face in her mind's eye as clearly as if Pat was showing her a mug shot. *Yolanda.*

"No," she protested, feeling ill.

"We're wondering if that potshot someone took at your father was someone looking to get rid of Cratty. A guy like that makes a lot of enemies on the street. We've heard rumors that he shakes down the dealers, makes them give him some of their merchandise in return for his looking the other way."

"You deliberately put my father in harm's way to flush someone out?" She heard herself and was mortified, both for herself and her father. That was the kind of thing cops did. It went with the job. To protest showed either incredible naiveté on her part, or a belief that her father could no longer do his job.

He gave her hand a squeeze, as if to help her through her moment of unease, saying, "We've created a Department-wide detail, putting patrol officers and SNEU together, sending them out in teams. It's a solid plan. We already got a good lead on a possible meth lab, because two guys new to partnering with each other pooled their info. Nailing Cratty—and any other dirty cops—is one of the goals, but not the only one."

"Dirty cops and dirty civilians," she said, meaning Yolanda. She debated telling about the images she had seen when she had touched Cratty's evidence. Now that she knew what she knew, they made more sense. In an insane, otherworldly kind of way.

We think Julius may be in on it, too, sharing keys with Yolanda so they can get to more of Cratty's evidence.

Her pulse quickened. His voice was as clear in her mind as Jean-Marc's had been.

I am reading his mind. I'm not human. I'm...I'm a freak.

Chapter 9

Overcoming her impulse to pull away from Pat as he leaned forward across the table, Izzy kept her fingers firmly pressed against his.

"This is all I can tell you," he said.

She heard him again: *I hate telling her shit about people she cares about. But she already knew something was up.*

God, I want her. I want to throw her down right now and just take her and—

She blinked rapidly at him and started to let go. He cocked his head and lay his other hand on top of hers, reassuringly.

I won't put her in the position of knowing we suspect Yolanda. Izzy likes her. I wish we weren't talking about this. I can't stop thinking about having sex with her. I've wanted her ever since I first saw her. Does she have any idea how much self-control I've exerted around her? I feel like an animal. I've got all this lust...damn...

She covered her mouth with her free hand. She was reeling. "Pat…"

She couldn't tell him.

"Yes?" he said.

But maybe she could tell him in a different way. She took a breath, concentrating as best she could, and thought, *Pat, Yolanda would never do anything illegal.*

She waited to see if he reacted.

Words tumbled into her mind. *I could take her right now. God, I want to. I want to do so many things with her…*

And then she saw herself as he saw her: maddeningly desirable, naked, her breasts crushed against his chest as she writhed beneath him, panting with lust. Whispering, "Yes," as he pulled himself up along her body. He wanted to take her and fill her and *God*, he wanted to do it to her like no other man had ever—

She let go of him and got to her feet.

"Pat," she said in a rush. "I—I've overdone it. I'm feeling…tired. I have to go upstairs."

"Iz?" He was all courtly concern as he reached for her. "Darlin', is there anything—"

"No," she said, folding her arms across her chest. "Let's talk tomorrow."

She faltered. He rose from his chair and steadied her. "I'm okay."

"Hell you are."

He put his arm around her shoulders and walked her out of the kitchen. He smelled good, like leather and a little bit of sweat. He smelled like a man. He felt like a man.

He thought like a man.

She probed his mind again. But this time she couldn't hear his thoughts. It was as if she'd imagined the entire episode.

"What are you doing?" she asked as they reached the entryway.

He indicated the stairs. "I just want to walk you up, make sure you make it okay."

"No." She softened the rejection by laying her hand on his chest. "Please." She took a breath and kissed him, tasting the cloves of the spiced tea. "I'll be fine. Thank you, but…I'm good."

He kissed her back, warmly, his lips a whisper against hers. "You're sure," he said.

She eased him to the front door and threw back the bolt.

He paused. "I need to ask you to hold this in confidence. Even from Yolanda."

"Of course." *Especially since you think she's a co-conspirator.*

"Call you tomorrow," he told her.

"That'd be nice."

She shut the door, throwing the dead bolt. Then she turned around and leaned against it, closing her eyes. Her heart was pounding.

I read his mind.

She heard noises on the second floor, reminding her—as if she needed any reminding—that Jean-Marc was upstairs. And that this night was too strange by half.

She moved into the hall, stalling, replaying everything she had seen and heard in Pat's mind.

She knew people lied to each other; she knew they lied to themselves. But to *hear* him lying to her. To see how he saw her sexually. She wasn't naive. She knew men were wired differently. But to be shown it, to see it firsthand. It was such a violation of his privacy. She was horribly ashamed.

I didn't try to do it. It just happened.

She looked up as she heard a door above her head open then shut. He was busy up there, whatever he was doing.

A board squeaked in the hallway. She waited for him to appear at the landing.

He did. His thumbs in his belt loops, he tilted his head. He was so different in appearance from Pat—darkness where Pat was sunny and blond. She could feel his coiled nervous energy, contrasted with Pat, who was laid back and easygoing—except in the sexual arena, and she knew that even there, Pat would go as slowly as she wanted him to.

He said, "Come up here. I want to show you a few things."

Yeah, I'll bet.

"No funny stuff," she warned. "No naked blindfolds."

"No naked blindfolds," he agreed.

She took the stairs slowly—she really was feeling a little dizzy—and he turned as she reached the landing. First he pushed open the bathroom door and walked in. She followed, glancing at herself in the mirror. She was still Izzy DeMarco, with her hair a little more mussed than usual and her cheeks rosy.

"I did some more warding while you were with that man." The fact that he didn't say Pat's name irked her. "This area reeked of violation. Someone was searching for you here. My ward should keep them at bay."

"If it holds," she pointed out. "Because we're in New York, where magic is unpredictable."

"*Oui,*" he admitted. "Which is why time is of the essence."

He walked her back into the hall. "Your brother's room is very holy," he said. His choice of words surprised her. He shrugged. "People of faith are holy."

"Please don't tell him that."

"Your father's room…he has known terrible despair. Also, he's in a lot of physical pain that he's trying to hide from you. You should make him go to the doctor."

She sighed. "It would be easier to get him to become a

United Methodist." At his blank look, she said, "Family in-joke."

"I see." Clearly he did not. "Now we come to your room." He puffed air out of his cheeks and slumped his shoulders as he splayed his fingers over the closed door. "I was defeated here. This place is tainted beyond redemption. You mustn't sleep here anymore."

Looking from his face to the door and back again, she said, "Tainted how?"

"Evil energy has crept into it from your dreams. Its aura is poisonous to you."

"My bedroom has an aura?" she asked dubiously.

"You know it does." He was impatient. "You've felt the change in the air when I've altered the aura of a space that we're both in. Your room is toxic. I could work on it, but it would take a lot of time and effort that can be better spent elsewhere."

She looked warily at her door.

"From now on, you should sleep in Gino's room. Give your father an excuse and do it. Tell him you feel closer to your mother there. That you sense her presence. Since your brother's training to be a priest, your father will buy it."

"I'm not selling my own father a bill of goods." She reached around him for the doorknob to her room.

"No!" he shouted. He raised his palm at her; a blue glow emanated from it and pushed her gently away.

"This is *my* house," she said angrily.

"You are *my* responsibility," he shot back.

She raised her palm. Concentrated. A ball of blindingly white flame sprang from her hand and crashed into the wall inches from his head. The impact shattered the plaster; chunks rained down onto the hallway floor like a miniature snowstorm.

The wall smoked; then the perimeter of the indentation the ball had created burst into flame.

"Oh, my God," she gasped.

Jean-Marc held out both hands and uttered words in another language. The fire went out. The plaster rose from the floor like a movie shown in reverse, repairing the hole until it looked as if nothing had happened.

"The only other time you used your power, you destroyed the assassin," he reminded her. "Have you forgotten how powerful you are?"

"Maybe I just don't want to know," she said honestly, staring at the wall. It was completely restored in every detail.

"This is why we need some training time," he said. "After a couple of sessions—"

"I agreed to *one*," she cut in, although she felt foolish arguing the point. She had just set her own house on fire.

He exhaled again, weary and irritated. "I'll transfer a few things to Gino's room for you. Go ahead and lie down. I'll be quick."

"But—"

"Allez, vite," he said tersely.

Combative, touchy, she did as he asked, sweeping into Gino's room and turning on the lamp at his varnished oak study desk. Football pennants and sports trophies—that was Gino.

She crossed to one of the twin beds, which were separated by a nightstand, and pulled back the navy-blue corduroy bedspread of the one furthest from the door.

Beneath the bedspread, her gauzy white nightgown lay folded on top of the blanket.

How did he do that?

As she unfolded her gown, a parade of her clothes—pants, jackets, bras, panties—glided through the air. Jean-Marc brought up the rear with her jewelry box and the votive statue of the Virgin Mary in his arms.

She took a breath, feigning nonchalance, wondering why she bothered. He knew this was unbelievably strange to her.

He murmured something and the clothes draped themselves over the twin bed closest to the door. He said, "Your father's being discharged from the hospital."

"Oh." Relief and uncertainty flooded through her. "How do you know that?"

He didn't answer her question. "David and the others are out there. And I'll wait nearby until your father is safely in the house."

"Your Jag—"

"He won't see it." He cupped her cheek, and she let him. Warmth flowed into her face. It felt good. "You're a brave woman. I know all this is overwhelming."

She nodded.

"I'll send a car for you tomorrow night. After dark. Tell your father you're going to the movies."

What about Pat? she thought; but she didn't owe Pat any explanations regarding her whereabouts.

"All right. Not too flashy," she said, referring to the car. "This is a working-class neighborhood."

He set her jewelry box down on the nightstand. The statue of the Virgin Mary he held with both hands, gazing at the face. He murmured as if he were speaking to it, and then he carried it to Gino's desk.

"I liked it better when I thought you were crazy," she said.

"Part of you still does think I'm crazy," he assured her. "But that will probably change tomorrow." He crossed his arms. "There's so much you will have to let go of."

She didn't like the sound of that.

"*Bonne nuit,*" he said. "I wish you dreamless sleep."

He walked out of the room and closed the door. She waited until she could no longer hear his footsteps, and then she wearily changed into her nightgown and puffed her pillow behind her back, determined to stay awake until her father got home.

In the nightmare forest...
She stood on the wrought-iron balcony of a three-story Southern mansion. The wounded moon bled shadows on advancing figures—capering, leathery monsters; furry creatures with glowing eyes and slashing fangs.

An army of white-faced, skeletal men shambled forward. When one collapsed, another stumbled over it, crushing a decomposing face with a bare foot of blue-tinged skin and exposed bone.

She had to stop them or he would die.

Her mother shouted, "Just let me go, Vince! I can't stand it anymore! I can't even remember anymore what it feels like not to be in pain!"

A gun went off.

He is going to take the gun. He is going to end you. And then he will end the House of the Flames.

Chapter 10

Big Vince came home from the hospital as it was turning light.

He told Izzy that while he was going back to work later in the day, she was taking some time off work. "A week. Maybe more. No arguments. You've got too much vacation time on the books anyway."

He also approved of Izzy's sleeping in Gino's room.

"It's always cold in your room," he said. "Except in summer."

Her father's shift would start at four that afternoon. He stayed in the house with her, except for a short trip across the street to Russo's Deli, bringing home a picnic of cold cuts, cheese and a loaf of fragrant, fresh bread. "I found this on the stoop," he said, showing her a large black leather glove. "Maybe it belongs to the United Methodist?"

He set the black glove down on the cherrywood table near the front door.

"Speaking of Pat," she said, and then she brought up what he had told her about Cratty as Big Vince joined her in the kitchen, father and daughter working side by side as they had for years. About the department looking into him.

"Kittrell shouldn't have told you anything," he said, carrying their plates to the table. "He should have kept my girl out of it."

"Big Vince, you're a throwback." She brought two glasses of watered-down wine and set them at each place at the dining room table.

"I'm your father." He sat down—a little slowly, she fretted. He picked up his wine. "You know me. I want you to find a nice man, preferably Catholic, who's got a good job, have my grand-kids, and cook a lot." He winked at her. "It's not so bad, eh?"

"No, Don Corleone."

"Besides, it's a violation of secrecy. For that reason alone, he shouldn't have told you."

He had a point, which irked her. She didn't want to think ill of Pat for any reason. She liked him, even if he was a sexed-up male in heat.

And what am I, then? She chuckled at herself. She was no fainting virgin. She wanted him, too.

Finally, Big Vince went to work. At a quarter to seven, she dressed in black sweats and her new coat, watching through the living room window for Jean-Marc's car to pull up to the curb. At seven exactly, a cab arrived. A familiar Asian man sat in the back. He leaned forward and gazed in her direction.

Her front door opened of its own accord. She crossed the threshold; it shut. She got in the cab; the Asian man slid over. He was wearing black sweats, too, and a thick black leather jacket. He looked like a ninja.

He said to her, "David is driving tonight."

Sure enough, he of the gelled red hair was seated behind the wheel.

"Hello, Ms. DeMarco," he said.

She liked that. She said in return, "Hey, David, thanks for watching over me." Then she looked at Jean-Marc. "Just us," she reminded him.

"Just us. David will drop us off."

The cab pulled away from the curb. Jean-Marc became Jean-Marc again, and his wildman hair was pulled back in a ponytail.

"Good evening," she said to him, feigning nonchalance.

"We're going to the Cloisters," Jean-Marc informed her. The Cloisters was a museum created out of whole sections of Medieval French monasteries and other buildings.

"What?" She had assumed they would go back to his place. "Why?"

"Have you been there?" he asked her.

"A million years ago," she confessed. "I'm a native. We don't go to the tourist spots so much."

"The Cloisters houses a collection of Medieval art from the twelfth through the fifteenth centuries," he said. "Much of it was taken from our lands. The pieces themselves are imbued with the magical essences of the Bouvards, Devereauxes and even Malchances. As well as other noble houses who failed in their attempts to become magic users. You'll sense it. Eventually you'll be able to work with it."

She stared at him. "No way."

"Wait and see."

They drove across the Brooklyn Bridge, then up through Tribeca, the Village and up to the Upper West Side. They took the next exit after the George Washington Bridge.

Snow sprinkled gently on a low-slung tiled roof overhanging arched walkways made of stone. A large, full moon glowed like a clock against a square tower. Izzy could easily picture a line of hooded monks walking to Mass, chanting in ancient Latin with their heads bowed.

David got out and opened the trunk, unloading a white leather equipment bag, which Jean-Marc slung over his shoulder. Something inside it clanked. As he walked beside Izzy, he said, "I haven't informed your family that I've found you. Until we can figure out who is loyal and who isn't, there's no reason to break your cover."

"And how will we figure that out?" she asked. She felt as if she had already had this discussion—with Pat, about the situation at the precinct.

He debated a moment and then he said, "We may not have to, if you decide to walk away."

She was impressed. "I'm glad you've accepted that as a real possibility."

"As I said before, I'm only doing a job," he replied, shrugging.

He moved his hand as they approached. Blue shimmered against the falling snowflakes, lighting up his profile. "I just disengaged the security system," he said. He snapped his fingers. "And the security guard." At her look, he said, "The guard is unharmed. He'll sleep. He won't see or hear us. Nor will we appear on the security cameras."

"Whoa. You'd make a great spy." She tried to sound light, but her voice cracked.

"I *am* a great spy," he replied seriously.

Then they were inside, moving past tapestries depicting a unicorn hunt, and for all their beauty, they were savage and cruel. From the images, she gathered that a lovely young girl was being used as bait, and that once the unicorn grew to trust her, it was slaughtered, just like any beautiful, exotic animal that was hunted for no good reason except the thrill.

There were paintings of saints, their heads surrounded by

golden halos. Haloed angels hovered in the backgrounds of many paintings, shimmering and almost pagan in their beauty.

"This place holds magical memories," he said in a hushed voice. "I can sense our ancestors. Soon you will be able to, as well."

He selected one of the enclosed quadrangles of the reassembled monasteries to take out five rainbow-colored, flat-sided oval crystals and a large, shiny, fixed-blade knife etched with a pentagram and covered with swirled writing she couldn't read. There were three moonstones in the hilt of the knife that caught the light and threw it against the walls.

Positioning the crystals on the floor, he made a semicircle above them with the knife.

"This is an athame," he said, pressing the length of his hand over the knife. "It's for magic rituals. I made it for you. When you've learned more about the Craft, you'll make your own."

She blinked as she studied the knife. "You made it for me?"

"Oui." When she started to ask him more, he picked up one of the crystals, a flat-sided oval, and said, "These are scrying stones. We can see other places with them. They're like security cameras." He waved his hand over the crystal. A soft blue glow surrounded it.

He handed it to her. It was warm in her palm. He waved his hand over it and murmured words in Latin.

The flat surface of the oval revealed a shot of Gino's bedroom about an inch square. It was focused on the bed she was using, which she had made up upon rising.

She frowned at him and said, "Have you been spying on me?"

"Yes," he replied.

She was mortified. "You had no right."

Saying nothing, he reached back into the bag and drew out a wicked black revolver with an ivory grip.

She stiffened. She set down the crystal and sat back on her haunches.

He said, "You're afraid of it." He laid the gun down carefully, watching her.

"I have a thing about guns." She rubbed her arms. "A phobia."

"That's interesting." He picked up the weapon, hefting it in his hand. "I wonder why."

He slipped it back into the equipment bag.

They wandered down a covered archway, Izzy gazing at the moon on the snow. Beyond the lacy stonework of the exterior wall, a square of snow covered what would be an elaborate herb garden come spring.

"Herbs are important," he counseled her, leading the way back into the rooms of the museum. "I collected a few books for you." He unlocked a storage closet and shifted buckets and brooms out of his way.

"Look."

There was a beautifully carved chest at the back of the closet. It was about a yard on a side, and maybe two feet deep. But when he opened it and she looked inside, there were dozens of books arranged in stacks.

She frowned, sitting back on her heels as she looked from the interior to the exterior. It made no sense. A box that size couldn't hold that many books.

She swallowed. How could she accept this? If she did, it meant that her father was not her father. Her brother, not of her blood. But with everything she had seen, how could she not believe?

Her stomach twisted; mind-numbing panic seized her and pulled her down as if she were sinking in a vast sea, with no hope of rescue. She couldn't see. She couldn't hear, or breathe, or think.

Then thoughts tumbled in, one after another, crashing over

her with a heavy weight. *I don't carry the legacy of a saint. I'm not adopted. I'm none of this. It's a horrible mistake.*

"Please," he said. "Pay attention."

Within half an hour, Izzy had examined carton-loads of books and CD-ROMS about herbs, candles, Wicca and Tarot. Jean-Marc had also printed out long lists of Web sites and even blogs written by bona fide magic users. She was utterly overwhelmed.

"You must learn everything about your family, and your Gift," he informed her. "Children in our families begin learning before they stop nursing. But you…" He let out all the air in his lungs; it rose like steam in the cold night air. *"Mon Dieu, this is really so unbelievable,"* he muttered. *"C'est impossible."*

She wanted to say something snide, like thank him for his lack of faith in her, but in truth, he was scaring her.

He began to walk. "Come here," he said, gesturing for her to follow him. Then he added, "Please."

He led her down a dark corridor. There were no artificial lights, just a faint glow of moonlight that cast silver and gold in his hair. Then even the moonlight faded as they walked deeper into the museum, so like an ancient fortress that she began to imagine other people walking past them—women in headdresses and long gowns, men in tights and sleeves that dragged on the floor. She smelled lavender, the scent of freshly turned earth….

Jean-Marc waved his hand to the right. She turned and saw a narrow, semicircular alcove cut into the stone wall. A trio of arched, leaded-glass windows revealed the snowy, black night outside.

Inside the circle stood a life-size stone statue of a figure in armor, its helmet clutched under its arm, a halo around its head. Its other hand held the staff of a banner, also made of stone. A bouquet of half a dozen lilies rested in a blue vase and a fat, alabaster-colored candle sat at its feet.

Izzy drew near, aware that Jean-Marc did not. But something about the statue called her, urged her forward.

It was a woman. The halo was a piece of separate stone secured to her head, as if it had been added later. Her short hair framed a delicate oval face and her features were soft. Her eyes held sorrow, and purpose; her mouth was firmly shut.

Joan of Arc, Izzy realized.

Without full awareness of what she was doing, she approached the statue with her hand outstretched.

Whispers surrounded her; she felt wispy fingers moving over her shoulders, down her back. She swayed. There was a lute, far off…and the crackling of flames.

She smelled smoke.

She heard distant weeping.

Then she fell to her knees.

"Jehanne, je suis là," she murmured. Tears rolled down her face as she raised her hands toward the statue. *"Je m'appelle Isabella, et je suis la jeune fille…"*

She heard herself, and froze. She cleared her throat and rasped, "Whatever you're doing, stop it."

"I'm doing nothing," Jean-Marc answered in a whisper. "You know that."

"I don't," she insisted. "I do not."

She got to her feet and backed away from the statue.

She whirled on him. He was leaning against the stone wall with his arms and legs crossed. Blue shimmered in a silhouette all around him, like a computer-graphic effect in a movie. It frightened her.

She said, "I want to leave."

He didn't respond. As she brushed past him, he grabbed her wrist, forcing her to a standstill.

"Lives depend on you," he reminded her. He jerked his head back at the statue. "As they did on her. You know that. You felt it. You felt the weight of it, and it made you cry."

She glared at him and yanked on her hand. "Let go."

He did; she walked outside into the snow and waved her arm, assuming David was somewhere, waiting for them to signal that they were finished.

Jean-Marc stomped up behind her; she heard his footfalls in the snow. She ignored him, wrapping her arms around herself as cold hands of fear squeezed her chest.

Sure enough, the taxi appeared. David popped her door open, then started to get out to assist her. Hastily she let herself in, climbing into the back seat.

Jean-Marc caught up with her.

"You're not coming with me," she said, reaching to shut the door. "I'm going home alone."

With an iron grip on the door, he kept it open. "I need to check on the wards."

"No. No more," she said. Her voice shook. Her hands were trembling. "We're done."

He scowled at her, said, "What if they come after you when your father is home? Or if that man comes to see you, and they go for him?"

That man.

"You know his name," she said.

"What if something happened to him?"

She narrowed her eyes. "Are you threatening me?"

"What purpose would that serve?" he asked evenly.

"You know what purpose." She moved around him to wrap her fingers around the armrest, in preparation for shutting the door. "You say you aren't invested in this outcome, but you know you are."

He didn't argue. The silence stretched into some kind

of conclusion between them, and he moved out of the way of the door. She slammed it shut and said to David, "Take me home, please."

Before he responded, he glanced through the window at Jean-Marc, who inclined his head, giving permission.

As the cab pulled away, Izzy looked back through the rear window. Jean-Marc stood in front of the Cloisters with his arms crossed, the lord of the ghostly manor. That was his world—crumbling ruins and phantoms, bizarre magical feuds and—

—and recurring nightmares. And things that try to kill me. And if I walk away now, those things go with me.

Jean-Marc was an iffy ally at best, but he was the only one she had in this strange new world. And he had a point: what if something *did* happen to her father or Pat?

Shoulders slumping in defeat, she said, "David, stop. Go back."

He hung a U and drove her to the entrance. She opened the door and climbed out, boots crunching in the snow. Jean-Marc had not moved since she had taken off.

They stood facing one another, she with her hands in her pockets and her head tilted up so she could look him in the eye. His arms were at his sides, faint flares of blue emanating from the crown of his head, like a halo. She thought of the halos she had seen around the heads of saints in the pictures on the walls of the Cloisters—and the head of Joan of Arc, for that matter. Were they really depictions of Gifted?

"I want more proof," she said, trembling, "that this isn't a case of mistaken identity on everybody's part. That I am the person you're looking for."

He nodded. "*D'accord.* I'll give it to you."

Then he ran his gaze over her face, to the crown of her head, and down. She felt the connection. Felt it.

"You were right to stop for the night," he observed. "You're depleted. I can't teach you anything more this evening. I'll take you home and we'll talk there awhile. I'll check the wards."

"I just said I'd stay," she protested.

"You're worn out. I can see it. Wait here while I collect the equipment." He gestured for her to get back in the cab. "David, help me," he said, heading back toward the Cloisters.

David followed, and Izzy trailed behind, quickly catching up. Jean-Marc positioned himself on her left side and David moved to her right. Were they protecting her or making sure she didn't take off again?

They reentered the museum. Izzy moved more deeply into the gloom, twisting through the labyrinthine corridors until she found herself leading them back into the alcove where the statue of Joan of Arc stood guard.

As one, the three stopped walking.

At the feet of the statue, beside the bouquet of lilies, a shaft of moonlight gleamed on the crystals, the knife and the revolver. They had been arranged inside a pentagram, which had been drawn on the stone floor in what appeared to be luminous white chalk.

The statue stared placidly, blankly, as before. But the moonlight traveled as if on scudding clouds and her halo was bathed in white light.

Jean-Marc looked questioningly at Izzy, who shook her head. In turn she looked at David, who clearly didn't grasp the significance of what he was seeing. He had not been present when Jean-Marc had showed her the objects, nor put the revolver back in his equipment bag.

Jean-Marc held out a hand for her to stay back, but she walked past him and squatted down. Folding her arms over her chest, she surveyed the layout.

She sucked in her breath.

An image had been etched into the previously blank bone-colored grip of the revolver. It was a recreation of the statue in the alcove, helmet under one arm, fist around a banner, full armor, short hair…and Izzy's face.

My face. Mine.

A sharp, visceral chill clasped her heart. It beat out of time; she heard the missed beats in her ears, in her temples.

With forced calm, she turned her attention to the knife. Rows upon rows of flames had been etched across the blade; at the hilt, a ghostly hand held an intricate rose in its palm. A scrawled "I"—for Isabella? Or was it a stake?—rose from the flames.

Jean-Marc joined her, sitting back on his haunches beside her. She whispered, "Unless you did this, someone else is in the Cloisters."

He studied the weapons. His hair brushed her arm. His exotic scent enveloped her. Then he said, "I think *you* did this."

Chapter 11

As Jean-Marc studied the weapons inside the pentagram, Izzy vigorously shook her head.

"No way," she insisted. "I didn't touch any of these…things."

He extended his hand over the pentagram and closed his eyes. "*Oui*. Your essence is on them."

"Whoa," David whispered.

"You see why I have to train you," Jean-Marc said. When she didn't respond, he continued, "*I* didn't do it, Isabelle. It's not a trick." He put a hand on her shoulder. "*Pas peur. Je suis là.*"

"*Don't be afraid?*" she asked incredulously.

Then her head exploded and pain pounded behind her eyes. She cried out loud and pressed both hands against her forehead.

"Oh, God, oh, God," she whispered, staggering to her feet. She raced to the wall of the covered walkway. She leaned over and retched.

He waited at a discreet distance. Footsteps faded, returned.

Then he brought her a paper cup of cool water. She drank it down, crumpling the cup in her fist.

He splayed his left hand across her temples, staring into her eyes. The moonlight reflected in his dark eyes seemed to swirl and dance; as she locked gazes with him, the pain lessened.

Without looking away from her, he snapped his fingers in the direction of the pentagram. At once, all the objects rose into the air.

Still gazing at her, Jean-Marc pointed to the equipment bag slung over his shoulder, holding it open. The knife gleamed as it dropped inside. The crystals plopped in next.

The gun hovered in the air. His glance ticking toward it, Jean-Marc clicked his fingers and pointed to the bag as if remonstrating a willful pet.

It remained where it was.

And as Isabelle looked at it, a strange, steadying sensation gathered inside her. She remembered this feeling: when her mother had been first diagnosed, her father had sat down next to her bed and said, "Ma is very sick, Izzy. I need you to be strong and help me with Gino. Can you do that?"

She had only been seven years old. She had wrapped her arms around Mr. Foo Foo Bunny, her bedtime buddy, and nodded. But she was so scared that she had wanted to cry and crawl into her father's arms.

Then the fake nod for her father shifted to something else—a kind of peace, acceptance. Even so little, she had known she could handle what was to come.

She had that feeling now.

Isabelle held out her hand and the gun glided over to her, descended and settled in her grip. It was warm. Its heft felt right in her hand. Felt as if it belonged to her, and it was a welcome sensation, like clasping the hand of a long-lost friend.

She said, "Where did you get this?" But she knew what he was going to say before he answered.

"It is your mother's."

And she thought maybe she finally understood why, all these years, she had been unwilling to own a gun: Jean-Marc had spoken the truth. She did have power that she didn't know how to use.

Big Vince's partner, Jorge Olivera, had his service revolver wrested away from him, and then he had been shot with it. Yolanda had nearly gotten fired when a gun had discharged. The officer in the locker room could have killed himself when his weapon fell out of his gun belt.

But a gun in *her* hand was another matter entirely.

Yes. She felt young, and strong, and filled with power. Brimming with it. Every muscle in her body, her bones…she was invincible.

She closed her hand around the handle of the knife and pulled it out of the bag. Knife in one hand, gun in the other.

Energy coursed through her. There was more, and more…it was sensuous, sexual. It made her sway. She heard thunder masquerading as her heartbeat; heard crackling currents pulsating through her body like a network of electrified veins and arteries.

Power.

She didn't know what to do with it, didn't know how to handle it.

"Now we know that one of your Gifts is psychometry," he said. "You get impressions from holding objects. You see things, or feel them. *Oui?*"

"Yes." *Now* things clicked. "There's a dirty cop at the precinct. When I touched evidence that he had bagged, I saw him stealing drugs from street dealers, beating someone." She cocked her head, remembering. "Then I tried again and nothing."

"You're adjusting to your abilities," he surmised. "Plus, you're dealing with the unevenness of the magical field in New York."

"This is really happening," she murmured. Tears welled and slid down her cheeks. "I'm...I'm not at all who I thought I was."

Agonized, she turned away.

"Isabelle..." he said softly. She could feel the heat from his hand hovering above her shoulder.

"Don't," she said. "Please."

He complied.

She took a deep breath. "Tomorrow night, I want to go to a gun range. Not the Department's. I want you to help me learn how to shoot it."

"I will." He gestured to the equipment bag. "Your revolver is called a Medusa. K-frame revolver, holds six shots. The cylinder has a unique spring system in the chambers so the thing can hold and shoot different calibers. You can fire a .380 auto round, a .38 Colt, .38 Special, 9 mm and a .357 Magnum."

Wiping her eyes, she stared down at it. "That *is* magic."

"The lines are blurring every day." He hesitated a moment, then went on. "We'll have to discuss how to transition you to the safe house. The place you woke up in. When I was, ah, reviving you. It will be a red flag if you simply disappear."

"I can't just disappear," she countered, her heart fluttering in her rib cage. "I have friends. Family. *My* family."

He said nothing, but she knew there was going to be a conversation on the subject, and soon.

She couldn't bear it.

She would have to bear it.

As before, Jean-Marc accompanied her home. Carrying the equipment back into her house, he went through each of the rooms. He was not satisfied with the condition of his wards, so he performed several rituals to reset and strengthen them.

"You may have some trouble with your phones again," he told her. "Speaking of which…"

He handed her a card. It was embossed with the same turret-clouds-dove scene she had seen on the tapestry in the altar room. The initials "J.M." stood alone on a line. The one beneath it gave a New York phone number.

"Day or night," he said.

"And if the phones don't work?"

"We'll work on our psychic connection," he replied.

She put the card in her purse, on the table in front of the front door, and looked back at him.

As he gazed at her, the same low-level current she had experienced before buzzed through her. It caressed her lower abdomen, massaged the back of her spine. Like her rush holding the weapons, there was something innately sexual about it. She was stirred, excited.

By him.

His sharp features were focused on her. His energy and power rippled in waves, merging with hers, and she found herself barely able to keep herself from raising on her tiptoes and offering her mouth to him.

The silence grew between them…speaking volumes. She felt vaguely disloyal to Pat, which didn't make sense. But there it was.

*If Jean-Marc touches me…*she thought. *If his fingers touch me…*

She broke contact. Somehow, in her mind, she shut off the connection, punctuating her effort with a step away from him.

She expected a mocking smile to cross his face, but he remained as he was, probing, seeking. She felt his energy attempting to reestablish their link.

She refused him entry.

And still the wry smile did not come.

He said in a gravelly whisper, "I fear leaving you here. I have rituals to conduct at the safe house…"

She had been wondering what he did when he wasn't with her. She said, "Can you do them here?" Then she heard what she was saying and wished she could take it back.

He shook his head. "Maybe in your brother's room, in time. The altar room in the safe house is sanctified. It's the only place in New York where I can work the spell."

"What spell?" she asked.

"To guard Alain. He's my cousin, the Devereaux I left in charge."

"His life is in danger?" she asked, shocked.

He inclined his head. "Everyone's life is in danger."

"That really makes me want to go there," she blurted. Her cheeks felt hot as she added, "I know it's not about what I *want*. I know, Jean-Marc. Please don't start."

He cupped her cheek. The contact blazed through her like a wildfire; her body seized, hard. Unbelievable pleasure shot through her.

He took his hand away. She would have protested, but her throat closed and she could do nothing but stand rooted to the spot.

"Isabelle," he murmured.

She cleared her throat and gave her head a quick shake. "Izzy. DeMarco."

"Don't leave the house," he said. "Magic is always stronger at night. Make a list of people we should be guarding. All your friends and loved ones. We'll ward the precinct as best we can. Yolanda's, your brother, places you frequent."

"Good," she said.

"And of course, your lover's home."

She bristled. "He's not my lover."

Then came the mocking smile, the amused glint. And she realized, with a start, that Jean-Marc employed it as a defense mechanism. He cared that she had a lover.

"And I have no idea where he lives," she added.

"You should find out," he informed her. He shrugged like a Frenchman. "Or we can."

As he turned to go, she reached up and tapped his shoulder. When he looked back at her, she held out her arms for the equipment bag.

"That's mine, I believe," she said.

He hesitated. "These objects are very powerful, both concretely and magically. You still don't know how to control your power."

Nevertheless, he settled the bag into her arms.

"Be careful," he said.

Why start now? she thought in reply.

He smiled warmly. "Better late than never."

After he left, she checked the voice mail, to discover that her father and Pat both had called twice.

She was settling into bed in Gino's room when the phone rang.

She felt a perverse triumph that it was working—which turned to concern as she considered if that meant that Jean-Marc's wards were no longer functional.

I hope those operatives are staying alert.

"Were you asleep?" Pat asked by way of greeting.

"No," she said softly.

"And why not?"

She smiled.

"I'm doing a four to twelve," he said.

"So is my father." She took a breath. "Is he partnering with John tonight?"

"No. I think we're winding that up," he replied.

She went on alert. "Oh? Is he going down?"

"Yes. We have an informant." A beat. "Yolanda. We had her wear a wire today." Another beat. "Iz, she was in it with him. They were skimming drugs out of her evidence lockers to sell."

Izzy felt sick. She thought about the fancy TV in Tria's apartment and how uncomfortable Yolanda had been discussing it.

She picked at the bedspread, gazing at her short nails. Thinking of all the perfume and color that swirled around the younger woman.

"Is she in protective custody?" That was customary, if she was going to provide testimony in return for immunity from prosecution. But that wouldn't save her job, of course.

"Yes. Safe house with a baby-sitter. Want the number?"

"Yes, thanks."

She got a pen and paper, and wrote it down. What a stupid, stupid thing to do. Yolanda had made it, gotten out of a tough beginning, away from a bad boyfriend…she was on her way to a great career. Now all that was gone.

"Do you know that the average street seller makes less than minimum wage?" she asked rhetorically. Because of course he did.

"This is how they played it," Pat said. "He'd bring in drugs but write the weight on his Evidence Order as lighter than it actually was. Yolanda would put some extra Property bags and sometimes even pennies on the scale before she zeroed it out. They had a precise calibration system. That would account for the phony weight on the E.O."

"Got it," she said. "The scale was jimmied, so the false reading would match the weight on the form."

"Yes. Then she would finish the intake and put the bag in one of her lockers. Later on, she'd go in and break into the bag and skim off the excess. When the drugs got checked out or taken to Central Holding, the listed weight checked out, because they were weighed on a scale that had been improperly zeroed out."

Izzy took up the thread. "So she used a new security tag when she opened the bag to skim off the excess."

"Yes. When we questioned her, she showed us the roll."

That made perfect sense. Like every Property room in North America, Prop kept out a roll of red butterfly security tags from every shipment of tags that they received. The theory was that they were used when Prop screwed up and needed to reseal a bag—when someone retrieved the wrong evidence for a case, for example. They did that rather than re-input the entire case, which would be a nightmare.

Despite the fact that the tags were sequential, as long as the tag used contained an earlier number in the sequence than a higher one, no one paid much attention. Izzy had been surprised to learn about the kluge—it clearly broke the chain of custody—but she was taught to do it when she first came on the job, as if it were part of established procedure. Still, she had never done it, nor seen it done. "Does he know that she's given him up?" Izzy asked.

"We don't think so. We're looking for him. He's not home and he's not on duty." He added, "Your father's completely out of it."

"Thank you," she said sincerely.

"We need to ask you to come in so we can open your lockers and check Cratty's bags. Everyone else in Prop will do the same. Tonight's a lockdown." Meaning no new evidence would be checked in. Deliveries would be taken to a different precinct Prop room.

"Of course. First thing tomorrow morning?"

"That'd be best. Sorry to ask. I know you're taking some time off."

"Sure, of course," she said.

"Moving on to nicer topics…you want to go to the movies again? I've got tomorrow night clear. I'll even sit through a chick flick if that makes you say yes."

The gun range. I said I'd go with Jean-Marc.

"I'm feeling kind of punk," she said, wincing at how lame that sounded.

He took it well. "That's fine." His voice softened. "This isn't a race, Iz."

"Thank you," she said feelingly, but it felt like a race. Her entire life was on fast-forward.

"Nothing to thank me for, darlin'."

She hung up and placed the call to Yolanda. A female officer answered and Izzy identified herself. The phone got handed to Yolanda.

"I'm sorry," Yolanda sniffled.

A million recriminations flashed through Izzy's brain. But all she said was, "You got out in time. You didn't end up dead. Because that's how these things usually go."

"I know," Yolanda replied, hiccupping on a sob. "Can you come to see me?" Her voice was little-girl small.

"They'll keep you sequestered for your own safety," Izzy said. "But I'll see you as soon as I can."

Yolanda dissolved into heavy weeping. The officer got back on the line and told Izzy they had to disconnect. Izzy complied, and the dial tone buzzed in her ear.

Feeling melancholy, she picked up the equipment bag and set it down on Gino's desk next to the Virgin Mary. She wondered if Yolanda had called Tria to let her know what was going on. She didn't have Tria's number; she'd used her cell while she was there and hadn't thought to ask for it. Next time she called Yolanda, she'd mention it to her. She sighed, feeling a little too involved, but not sure how to extricate herself—or if she actually wanted to. A fleeting sensation skittered across her consciousness, as if someone were tickling her nerve endings. She looked around the room. Then she wrapped her hand around the gun and pulled it out, studying the beautiful picture of Joan of Arc—wearing her face—on the ivory handle.

She said out loud, "This house is warded. I am protected from my enemies."

The feeling dissipated.

She should probably call Jean-Marc. His card was in her purse, which she'd left downstairs on the entry table, so she went downstairs to retrieve it.

The glove her father had found was lying beside her purse. She should have asked Pat if he was missing one. Idly she picked it up and—

Izzy gasped. John Cratty's face filled her mind. It was his glove.

And John Cratty's glove had a story for her.

I'm getting my share or that bitch is going down...

She saw a face, contorted in terror, a bloodshot eye, a split lip—*it was Tria!*

She heard a baby crying as Tria begged, "Please, don't hurt Calvin. Oh, my God, please...."

Izzy grabbed her cell phone and dialed 9-1-1.

It took her a moment to realize that the phone wasn't working.

Neither was the landline in the kitchen.

Did I just do that when I tried to ward the house?

"I decree that the phones work!" she shouted. "My cell phone and the landline! *In Nomini Patri, et Filii et Spiritus Sancti!*" She crossed herself.

She tried the phones again.

Nothing.

Izzy was out the front door like a shot.

Chapter 12

It was snowing, and Izzy was in a nightgown and bare feet, carrying her purse. She flew down the steps, crying, "David! People! I need help!"

No one answered. No one came out of the shadows.

She rapped on the Russos' front door. The aging, balding Italian didn't understand her torrent of words but he did comprehend that she needed a phone.

It didn't work, either. Nor did either of the Russos' cell phones.

"Something must be down, some power line or something," he said, clearly not grasping telephone technology.

She debated for two seconds about writing down Yolanda's cell phone number at the safe house. She knew she couldn't. "When they work again, call this man," she said, scribbling down Pat's cell phone number. "Tell him there's an emergency at Yolanda Sanchez's old place. The one she shares with Tria…" She didn't know Tria's last name.

"Tell him I went there," she finished, running out the front door.

She yelled, "David? David, where are you? I need you!"

There was no answer; she ran back inside her house and threw on the clothes she had worn to the Cloisters, trying her phone over and over again. No luck.

Take the gun.

She didn't have time to process the rightness—the illegality—of carrying a concealed, unlicensed weapon. She rummaged in Jean-Marc's equipment bag for ammo, found a small military-green box tucked into a side pocket and put it and the gun in her purse.

"David!" she tried again when she went back onto the stoop.

She looked in all directions before she fled down the street with her purse over her shoulder, waving her hands as she reached the main thoroughfare. An on-duty cab shot to the curb. She gave him Yolanda's—Tria's—address and his face lit up at the prospect of such a long trip.

They bolted into the snowy night. Izzy alternated between dialing Pat and the safe house, but her phone still didn't work.

Ten minutes into the cab ride, a call came through.

"Iz?" It was Pat. "A Mr. Russo called. Said you have an emergency."

She took a breath. "I think John Cratty is at Yolanda Sanchez's apartment. It's on Lexington. I think there's an attack in progress on her roommate."

"The vic call you?"

How to explain? "No. And I don't have her number. But Yolanda does."

"So you know she's in trouble because…?"

She shut her eyes tightly. "Please, Pat, just go with me on this. Please. One of us should get the number *now* and call *now*."

He hesitated. She mouthed, *Please,* and he said, "Okay. I'll get it."

"Put me on hold," she requested, afraid that if she disconnected, she might have trouble reconnecting.

"Okay. Hold on."

She heard white noise. Her heartbeat drummed against her rib cage as she waited. What was happening at Tria's? She thought about the baby. She thought about what she would do to John Cratty if he hurt either one of them.

Izzy aged a year before Pat got back on. "I've got Tria's landline, but we can't get a connection. Yolanda says she doesn't own a cell."

"Oh, God. Please, Pat. Go check it out." She clutched her phone in both her hands, speaking into the mouthpiece as if the connection depended on sheer physical effort. "Please go unofficially. Can you do that?" Was this the right thing to do? Should she tell him to take a SWAT team?

"Iz, what's going on?"

She closed her eyes. Her head was beginning to ache. She felt a coldness and then…

Ask him to trust you.

"It's one of those feelings again," she admitted. "And I can't go forward on it any further than asking you to help me. Off the record."

It was his turn to pause. And then he said, "A feeling."

"Yes. Like with my father. Like you said you had once," she reminded him. "Please."

"Iz…"

"Please."

"Okay, darlin'. I'll go over there."

"Thank you," she breathed.

"You at home?"

"No," she said. "I'm going there, too."

"Iz, I'm a cop. Let me handle it. I'll give you her number. Go home and keep calling her. Let me know if you get through."

But she couldn't turn back now. She had a…*knowing*…that she had to go, too.

Jehanne, help me, she whispered.

Then her cell phone went dead.

She punched redial. It was out. She tried Yolanda's number. Nothing. She wondered if she had just created another ward.

"I undo it," she murmured. "The phone works. Please."

But nothing happened.

The cab drove through the traffic and the snow. Still, it seemed that they were crawling along. She touched Cratty's glove again.

Fresh images blasted into her brain.

"Yolanda brought something of mine here," Cratty said as he held the baby against his chest. *"And you're going to give it to me."*

Images from the TV played across his face, cutting his handsome features into a jagged mosaic. The chubby-cheeked baby cooed and laughed, reaching out his hands to his mother.

"Calvin!" Tria cried, weeping. She was seated cross-legged on the floor beside the TV with her arms spread in front of her. Blood trailed from both nostrils, and her eyes were puffy. "I don't know who you are! I don't know what you want!"

"Move it!" Izzy shouted at the cabbie. "Oh, God, hurry up!"

"What's your problem?" the cabbie demanded. She saw his wary gaze in the mirror and realized she had to stay calm.

"No problem," she replied tersely.

They glided along, into the madhouse of Manhattan traffic. Her sense of urgency was overpowering. Several times she nearly bolted at stoplights—would have, if there had been a door handle—and each time reminded herself that she couldn't run all the way uptown.

So she stayed in the back, clutching the glove, trying the phone, willing more images to flood her mind—although the truth was, she didn't really want to see anything more. She *had* to, but nothing in her was prepared to watch a tragedy unfold.

C'mon, c'mon, Izzy begged. She squeezed the glove. She felt, sensed, nothing. It was as Jean-Marc told her—her Gift came and went.

Just like David.

Scanning the landscape, she put the glove in her coat pocket, opened up her purse and touched the gun. Moving slowly, she eased it out and slipped it out of sight—beneath her coat. She flipped open the box of ammo. There were twelve cartridges inside, maybe .9 mm. Despite her fear of guns, she had grown up in a policeman's household and she had a rudimentary knowledge about weaponry.

Still, she wasn't sure how to go about loading it. It wasn't a straightforward pistol or revolver, by any means.

She paused a moment and closed her eyes. She mouthed, *Jehanne, help me.*

The back of her head ached, as if she had drunk ice water too fast. Then the answer came to her, as clearly as if she were seeing a blueprint. Holding the revolver in her right hand, she pushed a small flange on the left side of the frame forward with her thumb. So far, so good.

Next she pushed the cylinder out of the frame with her left hand, revealing the six empty chambers. She transferred the gun to her left hand, keeping a grip on the cylinder and frame. The cartridges looked like extruded lipsticks; she loaded the first one, pressing the cartridge in nose-first. She felt rather than heard a click and glanced carefully at the cab driver. He hadn't seemed to notice.

She loaded five more cartridges. The revolver was significantly heavier. She snapped the cylinder shut.

Then she dug back into her purse and pulled Jean-Marc's card out of her wallet, completing the action that had precipitated this rescue mission. Ironically, she was no longer certain that she should call him. He would be crazed if he knew what she was doing. She put the card back in her wallet.

Finally they reached the outskirts of Two-Seven's territory. Tria's building was ten, maybe twelve blocks away.

You have to get out of the cab, a voice said inside her head. Her voice. *Now.*

But so far away?

She was having a conversation with herself. In two voices. It freaked her out. Being freaked out didn't matter right now.

"Pull over," she said. "I'll get out here."

The cabbie screamed across four lanes of traffic with amazing alacrity. She opened her purse and handed way too much money to him.

The door unlocked and as she leaped out into the night, a euphoric burst of energy sent her bounding down the street. Passersby gave her looks as she crashed through snowdrifts, seemingly unhampered by her heavy clothing and boots.

In the falling snow, she raced up four blocks, then five, as the buildings around her grew seedier, the pedestrians, less well-clothed against the elements. She smelled spicy food and sweat; she smelled cheap wine and marijuana. She kept going. She ran for blocks and blocks. She was nearly there.

Finally she hung a left.

And came face-to-face with John Cratty.

He was retrieving his overcoat out of the passenger side of the front seat of a champagne-colored Camry, and he jerked when he saw her. He turned to face her, wearing the same suit as in her vision.

"You bastard, did you find what you were looking for?" she

blurted. Then she realized that was the wrong thing to say; she had just told him way too much about what she was doing here.

He frowned, backing away from her, the coat remaining in the car.

"What?" he said calmly. But his eyes were darting left, right—possibly searching for her backup.

Or for witnesses.

Her heart skipped beats. Her face tingled.

I am facing a career police detective.

Correction—I am two feet away from a ruthless felon.

I have a gun in my pocket.

He put his hand toward the inside of his jacket. She was certain he was wearing a holster.

She dug into her pocket with her right hand and clasped the gun.

It's a revolver, she reminded herself. *It doesn't have a safety.*

I'm not licensed to carry this.

If I pull it out, I need to be willing to use it.

All her thoughts shot through her mind in a microsecond. And then she showed him the gun.

His eyes widened. "What's up?" he asked with such innocence that if she hadn't seen what she had seen, she would believe that he truly didn't know.

"I saw you. I saw what you were doing to them," she said through clenched teeth. She remembered to cup her right hand with her left to give herself as steady an aim as possible. She also remembered to let half her breath out and then to hold it. Now she was as steady as she was going to get. All she had to do was pull the trigger.

"Doing to them…?" His hand remained inside his suit. She was terrified. He could probably shoot her dead before she squeezed the trigger. He knew what he was doing. She was only going on instinct.

"I honestly don't know what you're talking about," he said.

She wondered if he had activated a pager instead of reaching for a weapon—calling for his own version of backup. She wanted to check it out, survey her surroundings, but she had already engaged the enemy. She didn't have the luxury of second thoughts now.

"You're not leaving the scene," she said, exhaling even though she knew it was ruining her aim. As it was, her hands were beginning to shake. "I'll shoot you if I have to."

"The scene of what?" His eyes focused on her revolver. "That's a Medusa. What on earth are you doing with it?"

He wasn't afraid of her. She figured that was bad news…for her.

"John," she said, trying familiarity to throw him off. "I know you just left Tria's place. I know why you were there." But she didn't know what he had done to them—if he had killed them. She prayed that Pat had already arrived and was rendering assistance. She could still hear Tria pleading, Calvin crying.

"But I didn't," he told her. "I *didn't* just leave…Tria's place." He hesitated as if he didn't know who this Tria was.

Maybe I was wrong after all, she thought, even more frightened.

And then, faster than she could react, he rushed her.

He grabbed the gun out of her hand and trained it on her, standing close. She could feel his body heat, smell his coffee breath.

He held out his free hand as he took a couple of steps away. "Drop your purse on the sidewalk."

"John, I called Kittrell," she said. Her heart picked up speed until it beat out of rhythm so hard and so fast she was afraid her head would burst. "He's on his way."

"He's not on his way *here*," he said. "I saw how shocked you looked when you ran into me."

"Pat will hunt you," she reminded him. "He'll catch you."

"Because he's your hero? Ain't gonna happen, Iz." He gave her a wink. "Drop your purse. *Now.*"

She thought about her glowing palm. Thought about the last time that she had used it, when she'd set her house on fire.

She dropped her purse on the sidewalk.

"You've seen the movies," he drawled. "Kick it toward me."

Her arms at her sides, she formed a palm strike with her right hand. Tried to concentrate as best she could.

Sent up another prayer to Jehanne of Arc.

Aiming her own revolver straight at her, Cratty bent down and grabbed up her purse. He tucked it under his arm.

"Now, just walk away, Iz," he said gently. "There is nothing in me that wants to hurt you."

Her palm began to feel warm.

Can I do it? Will I do it?

"John," she said. "Please."

"Don't try to stall me." He aimed the gun at her.

"You won't shoot me." Her voice cracked.

"I will," he replied.

She fell to the ground as she extended her palm toward him. A white sphere of flame erupted from her hand and slammed into his car.

The Camry exploded into a fireball.

In the deafening roar, Izzy screamed and rolled away, covering her head. All she felt was flame; then the sidewalk cracked as a chunk of burning metal crashed into it. More pieces of metal cannonaded at her. She propelled herself forward—hands, knees, whatever worked—trying to put as much distance as she could between herself and them.

She scrambled to her feet as the roaring blast chased her around the corner.

Onlookers were racing past her; a man grabbed her and helped her up.

It was David of the red-gelled hair.

"Where have you been?" she demanded. "Where were all your people?"

"I'm sorry. I'm so sorry." His face was ashen. "Let me get you out of here."

She shook her head. "*You* come with *me*."

David in tow, she doubled around, racing back to the scene. The car was a whirlwind of flame. People were shouting "Call 911!" as others whipped out cell phones.

She scanned the area. There was no sign of Cratty. Or of her purse.

Edging into the throng, she raised on tiptoe to look at the car. David held out his arm protectively.

"Is anyone inside?" she asked a tall man beside her.

"God I hope not," he replied, squinting into the smoke.

She shut her eyes. The heat from the oily, rank fire slapped her cheek.

I will any one inside to be saved, she thought. *I will no harm to come from this.*

She said to the tall man, "Can you let me through?"

"Ms. DeMarco, please, don't," David pleaded.

"Kid's right," the tall man said. "You don't want to go any closer."

In the distance, sirens screamed. She realized what that meant. Police. Questions.

And she was supposed to be keeping a low profile.

David said again, "Let me get you out of here. *Please.*"

"All right. Come on." She grabbed his hand and took off running, heading for Tria's building.

Chapter 13

Groups were mobbing the streets around Tria's building heading for a better view of the show. Violence was common in the hood, but car bombs were something special.

Izzy and David ran the next block together, catching each other as they lost their footing on patches of ice. As they reached the opposite side of Tria's street, Pat flew out of Tria's building. He saw Izzy and headed straight for her.

David said, "Who is that?"

"A friend," she said. "Give me some room to talk to him."

David huffed. "I have to protect you."

Like you did before?

"It will be all right," she said.

He stayed where he was while Izzy loped toward Pat.

"Is Tria all right?" she called out.

He nodded, meeting her at the corner. "She's fine. No Cratty. No attack." He gave her a crooked smile. "Guess you were wrong this time."

"That's Cratty's car," she said, gesturing to the billowing smoke, ebony against an obsidian sky. "I was coming around the corner on foot and I ran into him."

His eyes widened. "*What?* Did he hurt you?" Anger lowered his voice to a hoarse growl.

"No. I had a gun. He took it away." She hesitated. "Then the car exploded. I didn't see what happened to him. He wasn't in the car."

Approaching sirens shrieked in counterpoint to her heartbeat. Pat's cell phone rang and he pulled it out of his suit pocket, listening for a few seconds.

"On my way," he said, disconnecting. He put it back in his pocket.

"I'm going over there," he told her. "See if I can render assistance."

"I'll check on Tria," she said. At his uncertain frown, she quickly added, "That red-haired guy on the corner. He'll go with me. I'll be all right."

"Okay," he decided. "I'll try to catch up with you after I see what's up. You've got your phone?"

She shook her head. "He took my purse."

Pat stared at her. "Why?"

She shrugged. "Maybe he thought I had another gun in it." *Or some pepper spray. I never carried any weapons, yet I live in New York. Now I know why.*

"*You* call *me*, then," he told her. "From Tria's."

"I will."

He cocked his head, appraising her. She felt exposed, vulnerable. What should she tell him? What *could* she tell him?

He said, "We have to talk."

"All right," she replied.

He gave her one last look, then turned on his heel and ran

toward the smoke. A fire engine screamed down the street as if it were chasing him.

She waved a hand at David, who had been loitering about fifteen feet down the sidewalk. He sprinted to her side and she started across the street, watching the cars as they slowed to gawk at the billow of smoke that was Cratty's car.

She pointed dead-ahead and said, "We're going into that building. Do you have any weapons?"

He said calmly, "Yes, *Guardienne*. I'm heavily armed."

"Good," she told him. "And I'm not the *Guardienne*."

They came abreast of the loiterers—four older teenagers, a man in his mid-twenties, like her and one little boy who couldn't be older than ten. Sullen and hostile in gray, black and dark brown hoodies and heavy jackets, they stared in silence at Izzy and David as the two approached the entrance.

Izzy didn't know if it would be better to look at them or to just walk on by. Was staring at them showing strength or being confrontational? Avoiding their gazes—a display of weakness or a way to avoid trouble?

In the end, she glanced coolly at the man, who didn't react at all. Five faces stared at her without moving a muscle. The sixth, the little boy, muttered something under his breath and the man drew up one side of his mouth, amused.

The sharp stench of urine hit Izzy's nostrils as they entered the lobby. The floor was dirty and wet, and soggy newspapers and circulars had clumped together like snowdrifts.

The pack of guys stared back at her with narrow and predatory eyes. They reminded her of wolves. Which, she supposed, was what they were. Or what life had turned them into.

"I can protect you best in the elevator," David informed her. "It's the most direct route."

She wasn't sure about his being able to protect her

anywhere. She didn't like being back here at all. But she pushed the button, and when the elevator arrived immediately, David smiled faintly, as if he had had something to do with that. She didn't think he could perform magic.

Once inside, she said, "How did I slip past you? I shouted for you until I was hoarse."

He shook his head. "I don't know. I didn't even see you leave your house. I had a scrying stone in my pocket and I just happened to look at it just as you got in the cab." He showed it to her; it resembled the crystals Jean-Marc had shown her in the Cloisters. "I started following you but I lost you again for a while. When you used magic, I saw you right away." He rubbed his forehead. "I'm in deep shit."

"Maybe it had something to do with the wards," she said. "I think I cast one of my own." Now that she had a moment to reflect on it, she was amazed that it may have worked.

"He'll have my head," David said. "God." With a long, heavy sigh, he leaned back against the elevator wall.

And we're back to being careful not to piss off Jean-Marc, she thought.

Riding the rest of the way in silence, they made no stops other than to Tria's floor. The doors slid open into gloom and stink.

Tria's front door was vibrating with loud gangsta music. Izzy knocked hard, bellowing, "Tria? It's Izzy DeMarco."

Just in case any bad guys don't know I am around, she thought, regretting the blunder. *I'm helpful that way.*

She pounded again. The music died away and the door opened.

Tria stood before them in a pair of sweats and a sweater overlaid with an oversize Shakira T-shirt. She was fine, just as Pat had said.

I saw what could have happened. Not what did, she realized. *Just like with my father. Maybe I prevented it. Stopped Cratty before he got to her.*

Tria was wide-eyed. "Damn, girl! There was a cop just here. He told me about Yolanda!"

"What did the detective say to you?" Izzy asked.

Tria looked at David. "You another cop?" she asked suspiciously.

David shook his head. "I'm a friend of…Izzy's," he said, as if using her nickname was a form of swearing.

"He drove me here," Izzy lied.

"Okay. Well." Tria twisted the turquoise bead at the end of one of her cornrows as Chango flailed his fists at Izzy, and opened the door a little wider.

Izzy and David followed Tria into the apartment. Chango's head flopped against Tria's chest and she absently kissed the top of his head.

"He said Yo got busted for helping some guy sell drugs. They thought he might come to my place to look for them." Tria pressed her fingertips against her forehead. Her nails were very long and very fake. "I can*not* believe it!" She held her baby tightly. "What was that big boom? That man flew out of here and—"

"It's all right," Izzy said. "It's a car. No one was in it."

"Damn this neighborhood," Tria said, her brown eyes flashing with anger.

"So, do you think Yolanda was holding for him?" Izzy persisted.

Tria's mouth fell open. "Anything they find here belongs to him, not me!"

Tria was assuming there would be a search. That hadn't occurred to Izzy, and she wondered if Pat would indeed do a follow-up.

Then she realized she needed to do some follow-up of her own, face the music. She said to David, "I need to use your phone to call Jean-Marc."

David paled.

"I don't have his number," she continued. "You must have it programmed into your phone, though."

"I do." With a heavy sigh, he punched a couple of buttons and handed the phone to her.

The other end rang once and was immediately answered.

"Hello?" It was Sauvage.

"It's Izzy DeMarco," Izzy said. "I need to speak to Jean-Marc."

"Hi!" Sauvage trilled. "How are you? He's, like, doing this big ritual." She lowered her voice. *"Naked."*

"He'll want you to interrupt him," she said to Sauvage. "Perhaps with a robe."

"No way," she said. "If he stops, like, this guy in New Orleans might die. He told me not to—"

Isabelle? Jean-Marc's voice was inside Izzy's head.

Oui, she said in French, so he would know she was speaking to him.

Tell me what's going on.

She decided to go into the bathroom. There was more privacy there than anywhere else in the tiny apartment.

As she felt for the light switch and flicked it on, she began the story, filling him in on the glove and the vision. How she ran outside for help.

He interrupted her almost at once, speaking to her not in her head, but through the phone.

"Are you telling me that David didn't come when you called for him? *None* of the bodyguards came?"

"I think I had just put a new ward on the house," she replied. "It blocked him, somehow. He showed up later."

"Hostie. What precisely did you say when you set the ward?"

"I don't remember. Something about protecting myself. It interfered with the phones, too."

"Why did you do it? Set the ward?"

"I felt…something felt wrong. In the air." She cleared her throat. "But there's something else I need to tell you right away."

"If you please," he said.

"After I got in the cab, I did find John Cratty. On the street. And I pulled the gun on him. He took it away from me. I tried to retaliate, and I—I made his car explode."

"He took your gun?"

She winced as he erupted into a barrage of French. She couldn't tell if he was yelling at her or just swearing in general, or what.

"Tell me it wasn't loaded," he said.

She remained silent.

He swore some more.

"Isabelle, that gun is magical. Which caliber did you put in?"

"They looked like .9 mm cartridges," she replied. "They were the only ones I had."

More harsh, guttural French followed her disclosure.

"Why? What do they do?" she asked.

"They're a form of concentrated spell," he said. "The .9mm can stop the heart of the person who is shot with it."

She frowned even though he couldn't see her. Or so she assumed. "I don't see how that's magical. You mean, kill them, right? By shooting them?"

"Non, non, the cartridges won't pierce the skin. When you press the trigger, the cartridge dissolves and the spell is cast."

She jerked, shaken. "And just when were you going to mention this to me?"

"I knew the gun wasn't loaded, and I knew we were going to the shooting range tonight. *And I told you to stay inside your house!"*

"My God! You are so patronizing!" she shouted at him.

"I am not!" he shouted back. Then he lowered his voice. "What have you done, Isabelle?"

They both fell silent. Her heart was pounding. What if Cratty aimed that gun at her father? At Pat?

"You have to help me find him," she said.

"You can bet I'll be looking for him. But if the Malchances get hold of him first, they could attempt a psychometric search for you."

She puffed air out of her cheeks, making a corkscrew curl bounce above her right eyebrow. "How would they do that?"

"Isabelle, you forget that we are Gifted. We can do all sorts of things the Ungifted can't. If he uses the gun, they could attempt a trace on the discharge of magic. Like radar on a screen."

"Then they would find him." She took a breath. "And they'd ask him about me."

"Exactement," he said. She heard him drinking some kind of liquid. An image of him guzzling a bottle of water popped into her mind—not a real image, just a fantasy.

In which he was naked.

She leaned her forehead against the bathroom wall. "He also took my purse. Your business card was in it," she said. "If anyone finds it, they'll know I'm in contact with you."

"Go home," he ordered her. "Immediately."

"No way," she said. "I need to help look for him," she said. "I can do some footwork, search for him at his usual places. Ask around."

"Isabelle, you are the next *Guardienne*. You are not a police detective. *Vous comprenez?* There is no one in New York who is less expendable than you."

"But my father—" She checked the clock. Eleven. He was still on the job.

"The precinct house is well warded. So is your house. He's safe, at least for the moment."

"What about Pat?" she said.

"We can place guards around his home. I have an address for him now."

"Guards who will do as good a job at protecting him as they did me?" she asked. "He aimed that gun straight at me, Jean-Marc. Where were your glorious operatives then? Where were they when I was shouting for David's help?"

He said, "He won't be guarding you any longer. There are already new operatives in place where you are. I put them there to monitor that location, but I'm going to send them up to you after we disconnect."

She didn't know what to say or to do next. She was afraid for Pat, afraid for her father. Afraid for herself.

"Please, if you're on the street, it will dilute my resources," Jean-Marc continued. "I'll have to protect you and look for John Cratty and the gun at the same time."

"All right." She sighed. "But I'm not finished here. I'm not leaving until I'm sure Tria and her baby are safe."

He started to say something. She cut him off. "This is not open for discussion. I'll check back in with you in a while."

"*D'accord.*" He sounded tired. "Put David on, please."

Izzy left the bathroom. David was pacing in Tria's dark bedroom; he stopped when he saw her by the light of the bathroom.

She handed him the phone and said, "Jean-Marc wants to speak to you."

David swallowed, nodded, and shut Tria's bedroom door after Izzy went out.

She crossed into the front room and sat beside Tria on the couch. Dazed, Tria fed Calvin a bottle as she held him in her arms.

"I can't believe that bitch brought drugs into my home!"

"We don't know that for sure," Isabelle said. "But Detective Kittrell knows that Yolanda was involved in a drug scheme, and the police may conduct a search."

Tria jostled Calvin and shook her head. "I don't trust cops. They plant stuff."

"Detective Kittrell would never do that," she assured her, knowing it was true.

Next Izzy called Pat. He, too, answered on the first ring.

"Hey," she said. "You find anything?"

"It's his car. They've put the call out. We're scouring the area, knocking on doors. I'm getting a warrant for Tria's."

"Pat, if you apprehend, don't get too close to Cratty," she said urgently. "His ammo—I think he has dum-dums in his weapon." Those were a form of ammunition that exploded upon entry, creating a far larger hole than the original entry wound. They were illegal in warfare and, of course, on the street.

"I'm a careful sort," he assured her.

"I'm serious. Please. Call it another funny feeling." She cleared her throat. "My timing may be off, but you can see I'm on the right track at least."

"Okay, Izzy. I hear you."

Do you really? She felt thwarted, her hands tied.

Pat returned, and Tria consented to allow him inside. David hovered, looking worried, and she and Pat moved into the hallway with the door open, speaking in soft voices.

He said, "We were already in the process of getting a search warrant for this place. We sped it up because of the car. Roger Thurman's bringing it." Thurman was another detective in the Two-Seven. "If you don't want to get involved, you need to go before he shows up."

"Thank you," she said, moved that he would protect her like this. "You may need me as a witness. I talked to him."

"I can probably make this work without getting you in the thick of it," he said. "But if there's something you want me to know, tell me." His green eyes were hooded, probing. She knew his cases had a high conviction rate. She imagined criminals confessing all kinds of things to him.

What did she want him to know? Only everything. She wanted like anything to tell him about the gun, and Cratty, and the magic-based operatives Jean-Marc had promised would be protecting him as he slept.

"I—I saw it," she blurted. "It came into my head. Like with my father." Why did she feel like she was lying to him?

She added, "Please don't tell them. I'll never get into the Academy."

"And I'll never get another promotion," he said wryly. "This happen often, seeing things like this?"

"This is only the second time," she answered, trying to sound honest, despite knowing that trying to sound honest would make her sound guilty.

He raised his brows. "You okay?"

She swallowed hard. Her words caught in her throat, and although she planned to nod, she shook her head.

He drew her into his arms. For an instant she resisted and then let herself be comforted. Let herself feel the sheer, unvarnished terror that had not left her since Cratty pointed the gun at her. Since seeing him brutalize Tria. Since the fireball had erupted from her palm.

Pat's chest was hard and his heartbeat was steady and sure. He was a rock.

She said against his chest, "About tomorrow night. I'll check in with you after we both get some rest." She had to know he was safe. She had to be with him.

I'm in love with him.

It hit her hard.

I can't be. Not now. There's too much going on.

He pulled back, smiling gently, understanding that she was changing the dynamic between them. He leaned forward and kissed her.

"I'll be a while," he said, "but I'll get you home."

She said quickly, "I want to be there when my father gets in. His shift is almost over. My friend David will take me." She indicated David, who was seated beside Tria on her couch.

"Kind of young for you," Pat said, as if to take the edge off the fact that Izzy said nothing more, made no explanation of who David was. "He brought you here?"

"Yes," she lied, aware that it was a messy lie, made a little cleaner through repetition—first to Tria and then to Pat. But she couldn't do better at the moment.

"Maybe we should post some guys at your house," Pat considered.

"Cratty's not going to go there," Izzy argued, alarmed that they would run into Jean-Marc's operatives. And then reconsidering. What good had his people done her? What if Cratty did show?

But did she want an innocent cop to go down?

His cell phone rang. He said, "Got it." Disconnected. "It's Thurman," he said. "No sign of Cratty, but he's got the warrant. He'll be here in a few minutes."

"I'm going, then." She touched him, attempting to send him some psychic reassurance. "We'll be okay for the night. He wouldn't come to our place now."

Maybe her attempt to manipulate him worked. He sighed and said, "I don't like letting you go alone." She meant without him, and she knew it was a capitulation: he was staying to conduct the search. He glanced over his shoulder and said, "I need to stay here." He meant to keep an eye on Tria, make sure she didn't dispose of any contraband. "Call me."

She said, "All right."

Izzy said goodbye to Tria, who had made some calls of her own. A cousin was on the way to collect her and Chango.

"Thank you for stepping up," Tria said to Izzy as the two women embraced. "You had my back. I won't forget it."

Izzy stepped into the elevator with David. As they went down, David's cell phone rang.

"Nice range," she observed; seeing how white he had gone, she figured the caller was Jean-Marc.

"Yessir," he said, and handed the phone to Izzy.

"The operatives will meet you. They have talismans for you," Jean-Marc said.

Just then, they reached the lobby. The elevator doors opened, revealing the scary pack of homeys who had ogled her on the way into the building. In the dim light, their eyes seemed to gleam, their features to sharpen. The young boy with them grinned at Izzy with the look of a person twice his age.

Izzy took an involuntary step backward.

"Jean-Marc?" she asked shrilly into the phone.

"It's all right," he echoed.

"Jean-Marc sent us," the oldest one—the leader—said to Izzy. "We mean you no harm, *jolie maîtresse.*"

David looked from him to Izzy and back again. "You're on our side?"

"We *are* your side," the little boy shot back.

"*Bienvenue, Guardienne,*" the young man said. "*A votre service,* us crazy Cajuns." His face seemed to have changed again. His almond eyes peered out at her as if he was wearing a mask.

"Why didn't you just tell me who they were?" she asked David.

He shook his head as Jean-Marc said into her ear, "He didn't know."

"We were told not to break cover unless Jean-Marc told us to," he replied. "*Alors, Guardienne.* We have to go, us."

"Go with them," Jean-Marc instructed her. "The leader is Andre. I have to go. I need to conclude my ritual. If you have any problems, call."

"Sure thing," she said tersely.

The others surrounded Izzy in a block, excluding David. The leader—Andre—said to him, "Jean-Marc, he want you *à la maison.* Take your own car and go back."

David licked his lips and said to Izzy, "I'm sorry." Before she could reply, he walked ahead of them, out of the building, and jogged down the street to the right.

To Izzy's left, a black van idled at the curb, its exhaust a foggy billow that curled into the inky sky. A young woman with cornrows sat at the wheel, listening to bouncy accordion music and moving her shoulders to the beat.

Andre slid back the panel of the van and climbed in. After an inspection, he gestured for Izzy to come inside.

There were no chairs, only heaps of white satin cushions on the floor. Every inch of the ceiling and sides was covered with shiny religious symbols—crosses, Stars of David, ankhs, jeweled hands and eyes. They twinkled and jingled as she crawled onto the piles of pillows.

There was a street sign fastened to the driver's chair. It read Rue de Bourbon.

Andre shut the panel, then climbed into the passenger seat beside the driver.

None of the others got into the van. She was on alert. She said, "Where's everyone else going?"

"We're going to form a caravan, us," the woman with cornrows told her, looking at her in the rearview mirror. She grinned. "Like a Gypsy caravan, *n'est-ce pas?*"

Did her features elongate, become wolflike? Did Andre, seated beside her, let out a low howl?

The van pulled away.

Izzy said, "Who are you people?"

"Amis, chère Guardienne," the woman said. "Friends. Andre—" she gestured to the man "—and me, I am Claire." She added, "We have talismans for you."

Andre bent forward, then turned around and handed her a small white satin sack. Inside were six smaller bags about the size of a quarter and weighing just as much, each tied with a piece of ivory-colored cord.

She gathered them with both hands and said, "What are these?"

"Protective amulets," Andre told her. "Jean-Marc made them for you. Everybody 'as a set, so if we see you, we give them to you."

"What's in them?" She tried unsuccessfully to untie the cord.

"Beacoup de mojo." The woman nodded. "Things to keep you safe, *Guardienne.*"

"Do you have any for Pat or Tria? Or the baby?"

He shook his head. "No. They will only work for you."

"I see."

Suddenly she was overcome with fatigue. Her head lolled forward; she sank down, down into the satin cushions.

She thought of Pat and whispered, "Jehanne, protect him."

And then she was asleep.

In the nightmare world, Izzy saw with the eyes of a Gifted. Saw a tragedy, a sin, a vision; a voice begged her to remember.

John Cratty and Julius Esposito, the new hire in Prop with the processed hair, stood in the shadows of the fifties-era Colonial in Newton, New Jersey. The gibbous moon glowed down on them, hiding Esposito's face within a mantle of angled shadows. Around his neck, he wore a voodoo gris-gris *of chicken feet, rooster feathers and the withered fingers of dead men.*

Esposito's voice was sibilant and snakelike as he reached into a black leather pouch, extracting a handful of sleeping powder and murmured, "Yolanda Sanchez is inside. I'll get you within close range. Just aim, and pull the trigger. The gun will take care of the rest. No Yolanda, no testimony."

He flung the powder at the house. It fluffed into the night sky, dispersed by a sharp winter wind. The air smelled musty, tired, and old.

"They'll sleep now," he assured Cratty.

In a borrowed overcoat, Cratty was sweating and his hands were shaking, but he managed a grimace meant to be a smile as he said, "What is that stuff? Where did you get it?"

"A deal is a deal," Esposito replied, ignoring the questions. "I told you about her betrayal of you. I told you about the wire, and I got you here. It's payback time. Tell me where you got that unusual gun of yours."

In her sleep, Izzy moaned. A voice whispered to her, *You have more enemies than you can possibly imagine. This one came to the precinct because he detected magic. He has been searching for you just like the others. Now he knows who you are. Remember this when you wake up.*

Back in the nightmare, Cratty was just finishing up his wild story about how Izzy DeMarco had blown up his car.

Esposito said thoughtfully, "You should kill her, too."

Chapter 14

Izzy, who had successfully beat Big Vince home from his shift, had awakened with a start in Gino's bed around five in the morning, trying to remember the vestiges of the horrible dream she had had, but failing. Then she discovered the little white bags pressed around her fully clothed body. Someone had put her to bed and taken care to protect her.

Now it was 9:00 a.m., and she was coming into the precinct as Pat had requested. Her father, unaware of the events of the previous night, squinted at her and said, "This is just for today, to show your lockers to the brass. You're taking that time off. Got it?"

She nodded, aware that not having to show up at work every day would make her current situation easier.

What is *my current situation?* she wondered. *Learning to become some kind of magical ninja?*

Big Vince gazed at her, studying her face, sighing and nodding to himself as if coming to a decision. "I want us to talk to Father Raymond about the miracle. About Ma saving me from that bullet."

"Right." She nodded. "Sure, Big Vince."

He crossed himself. "I always said your mother was a saint. I just never realized…" His voice cracked and he cleared his throat.

Izzy had no idea what to say next, so she kept her own counsel. She was awash in guilt. And yet…*wasn't* it a miracle that her father had come out of that fiery building unscathed?

Two-Seven was in an uproar. Prop was still in lockdown; Cratty was still at large, Julius Esposito was missing and a search for him was being conducted. Though he was formerly not a suspect, he was one now.

Izzy spent her day making statement after statement—in interview rooms, in the break room, in the Prop room. In Captain Clancy's office, in other offices. She showed Internal Affairs the Prop logbook, booted up records on the Dread Machine, opened up her lockers. She had no idea how any of this was going to affect the ongoing cases with evidence stored in the cage.

She wished she could tell them about her visions, but she knew not to go there.

Whenever she had a moment to herself—which was not often—she called Jean-Marc to check on the search for Cratty and her Medusa.

His answer was always the same: "Nothing yet."

"How can that be, if you're so all-magical?" she demanded, then lowered her voice as Captain Clancy shouldered past her, three men in suits in tow. They had the look and feel of attorneys.

"I know you're worried about your father and…Kittrell," he said, as if speaking Pat's name cost him dearly. "I was able to make amulets for your father, but I need a sample from Kittrell."

"*What?*"

"Of his DNA."

"I say again—"

"His hair will work," Jean-Marc said.

"Did you have my hair?" she asked him.

"From the carpet. When I did your CPR," he assured her.

She remembered his hands on her breasts, the warmth of his crotch against hers. She pushed the memories out of her mind.

"What about my father?"

"I took some shavings from his razor when I warded your bathroom."

She felt invaded. "*What?* You didn't discuss that with me!"

"I didn't feel I had to," he replied. "Get some DNA from that man, so I can protect him for you."

That man.

Pat checked in with her almost as often as she checked in with Jean-Marc, to see how she was holding up.

"The SNEU detail is uncovering all kinds of graft situations," he told her as they ducked into the upstairs break room. "This place is as dirty as a pigpen." He shook his head. "Makes a man long for the far more honest corruption of my home state of Texas."

Before he could go on, one of the suits who had been walking with Captain Clancy appeared on their horizon.

"Ms. DeMarco? May I speak with you?" she inquired politely.

She started to follow, then said to Pat, "Nine tonight?"

His smile was sunlight. "That's a plan, darlin'."

One that could be altered at any moment, she understood. That was the nature of a cop's life, even when his place of business wasn't being turned upside down.

She reached for him and said, "Oh, stray hair," and soundly pulled three strands of white-blond from his head.

"Ow!" he protested.

"Sorry. I thought they were loose," she apologized.

As she walked away, she dropped them into the small manila evidence envelope she'd brought with her and placed it inside her purse.

"Samples," she murmured to herself.

The day flew by, with no word on Cratty or the gun. At a little after three, she was released, back on leave unless they needed to ask more questions. Jean-Marc arrived in a cab three blocks down from the precinct house. His glamour today was that of a dusk-hued man in a beautiful suit—an African businessman, perhaps, or an ambassador. His new driver was the laughing "Gypsy" woman with the cornrows and the unusual French accent who had driven the van last night. She scanned the area as Izzy climbed in, rolling down the window.

Did she just sniff the air?

"Well?" Izzy asked Jean-Marc as the woman smiled at her in greeting and rolled her window back up. He handed her a Starbucks venti latte as if it were part of their regular routine. In turn she handed him the envelope with Pat's hair in it.

He shook his head as he pocketed the envelope. "On Cratty? Nothing."

"At all?" Her voice rose. She lowered it. "No leads?"

"None." It was almost as if he enjoyed failing. He gestured to her drink. "It will get cold."

"How can you have no leads?" she demanded. "You found me. How come you can't find him?"

"I didn't say I can't," he corrected. "I said I haven't yet." He indicated the envelope. "I'll have six amulets for him before you leave my place tonight."

"And I'll be leaving early," she added.

He said nothing, but he didn't look happy.

They drove through the busy rush-hour traffic to the safe house. Sauvage was nowhere to be seen and the place echoed with silence.

Jean-Marc escorted her to the octagon room. He said, "Have a seat. I'll bring you some wine. Dinner's nearly ready."

He was making her dinner?

"Where's Sauvage?"

He moved his shoulders. "Boyfriend."

She was flustered by the relief she felt. *I don't care about Jean-Marc's personal life. It's Pat I want.*

When he came back with her wine, she took it, asking, "Why are your operatives so deferential to me? They work for you. For that matter, why are *you*? You're not a de Bouvard."

"You have the potential to be a *Guardienne*," he said simply, sipping from his own glass, savoring the wine in his mouth. "Guardians are held in high esteem."

"Does my family outrank yours?"

He shook his head. "We're equals."

"Who's your Guardian?"

"My father."

"Wow. You're like a prince."

He looked amused. He cradled his glass against his chest and inclined his head. "Not quite."

"Will you become the Guardian…next?"

"The magic passes from one generation to the next," he said, "but in our case, it's via a ritual, and it's voted on by our Council. I'll probably become the Guardian of the House of the Shadows, but it's not guaranteed." He looked troubled. "The longer I stay away, the weaker my position."

"So I'm holding *you* up, too," she observed. Enough for him to fabricate a crisis so she'd blindly follow him anywhere?

"To put it bluntly, yes. But that's not my concern at the moment," he replied, saluting her with his glass. "I'll be in the kitchen."

Left alone, she drank her wine, got up and wandered past the books in the bookcases. One title jumped out at her: *Gypsy Caravan: the Loupes-Garoux of New Orleans.*

She pulled it out and flipped it open. It was a history of werewolves in New Orleans. *Customs, Persecution, Susceptibility to Lunar Phases, Alliances and Wars with Vampires...*

"This has to be a joke," she said out loud, replacing the book on the shelf.

Jean-Marc said behind her, "What?"

"Nothing." She didn't want to discuss it. Didn't want to know if he believed in werewolves and vampires...and if he would tell her that she should, too.

"Dinner's ready," he said.

It was delicious. He had made *coq au vin*—chicken with wine—noodles and carrots and fresh peas. She tried very hard not to ask if cooking dinner had taken precedence over looking for Cratty and the gun.

After dinner, he brought out some cheese and fruit and two glasses of something called armagnac, in honor of the side for which Jehanne fought. It tasted like brandy.

"You should open a restaurant," she told him.

"Your family owns several of the finest restaurants in New Orleans," he told her as he nibbled on a piece of Brie. "And hotels. And dry cleaners. Nearly all of which escaped harm from Hurricane Katrina. Which is not surprising."

She was taken aback. She said, "Oh. Somehow the idea of owning businesses..."

His mouth quirked; his left brow tented. "You imagined they lived in a castle surrounded by a moat?"

She sipped her armagnac. "Something like that."

"Well, they do live in a mansion in the swamp, so you're not too far off." He tapped his napkin to his lips. "Let's train."

She thought a moment. "I have dreamed of a mansion. And...something more."

He regarded her with keen interest. "Can you tell me the details?"

She got quiet; she concentrated. Frustrated, she shook her head. "No."

"*Bon.* Maybe later, we'll investigate that," he said. "Try to bring your dreams into your conscious awareness."

"Sounds like fun," she bit off.

"It's not meant to be fun." His mercurial temper flashed. "It's meant to save lives."

"I know. All right?" she snapped at him.

"Truce," he said, flashing her a peace sign.

They changed into workout clothes, hers conveniently provided by Jean-Marc. She put on a snug sports bra under a black tank top, black tights and a pair of brand-new running shoes. Everything molded to her body and she felt nearly as naked as when Jean-Marc had straddled her, attempting to restart her heart.

He wore a pair of black sweats and a T-shirt similar to hers. He was wiry and muscular, like a dancer, with a rock-hard ass. The veins in his arms stood out in bold relief, evidence of a lot of physical training. He had big hands.

He was barefoot. She didn't know why she found that disconcerting, but she did.

Then he showed her the bedroom reserved for her, magically lighting a fire by pointing at a pyramid of logs inside an immense stone fireplace. The flames flickered across his face as he drew her into a cavern dominated by a king-size canopy bed on a dais. The hangings were ivory damask and the now-familiar portrait of Joan of Arc was scrolled into the headboard. It was matched in a mosaic on the floor. Heavy, dark furniture sat in corners barely reached by light. A large, gray-stone fireplace faced the bed. It was a stern room, and she didn't much care for it.

She said, "Why didn't you perform CPR on me in here? In a bed?"

"Sauvage was in the library," he said. "I went to her. She helped me bring you back to life."

"I need to thank her," Izzy murmured.

"That would be nice," he concurred.

First he led her through a series of stretches. Then situps, pushups. It was like being in the Academy—or so she anticipated.

Maybe I will never go, she thought, disheartened.

"Do you know tai-chi?" he asked her.

When she nodded, he began to perform the first form, and she joined in.

"Tai-chi is the basis of many of our newer, danced spells," he said as calmly as if he were discussing the merits of cardiovascular exercise. "We got the idea from a seminar with the House of Q'in."

"You're kidding." The idea of their having seminars with each other was so bizarre that she had to stifle hysterical laughter.

He gave her a look, moving his arms first to the left, then straight ahead, as he pushed his left hand toward his right wrist. "It will all seem commonplace to you sooner than you anticipate."

She moved in concert with him, aware that they were performing in perfect synchronization. The precision was exhilarating, even though she didn't want to admit it, even to herself.

Mixed with the firelight were shimmers of blue light, a deep indigo energy emanating from him. Magic. She glanced in the full-length mirror he had set at the foot of her bed, searching for the white sparks he said she was throwing off. She saw none.

As they finished, Jean-Marc lowered his arms to his sides and breathed deeply in, out. She followed suit. She assumed it was to help them become centered and relaxed, but he was coiled as tightly as a spring. She was, too. She was aware of the space he filled in the room, and it was larger than he himself. He had a presence, an aura of command, and power. She felt herself responding to it, and tried hard not to. She wanted—needed—to be her own person around him.

Seemingly oblivious of her unease, he walked to a tray placed on the nightstand beside her bed. On it were two hand towels and two sports bottles of water. He blotted his face as he handed her the other towel, following it with one of the water bottles.

He tipped back his head and drank, wiping his forehead with the back of his hand as he said, "Your House and my House are part of a great alliance among the magical families called the Grand Covenate."

"Yes, you mentioned that the first night," she reminded him.

He raised a brow. "I didn't know if you were listening to me."

"I was. Mostly so I could figure out how to get away from you."

He let that go. "What is permissible in one family may not be permissible in another. Occasionally we clash. Usually when one of the more…repressive groups does something we Europeans find distasteful."

"Like what?" Izzy asked, scoffing as she shifted her weight and drank. "Virgin sacrifice?"

"*Oui.*" He recapped the water and put it back on the tray.

Shocked, Izzy paused from drying off her chest. "Well, I'm safe there."

"I know." When she looked him, he chuckled. "The auras of virgins are different."

"You must be a laugh riot in a pickup bar."

He paused. Then he unfolded the list she had compiled of people she wanted guarded, and studied it as he slung his towel around his neck and absently wiped his fingertips on the end.

"Speaking of sex." He tapped the list. "Pat Kittrell lives in a gated apartment building. It's proving difficult for us to protect him."

Her mouth dropped open. "You promised—"

"You have a better chance at it than we do," he went on, gazing expectantly at her.

When she didn't appear to follow, he drawled, "Naked blindfolds."

"What?"

He returned his attention to the list, but something indecipherable spilled over his features. A grin?

"Please. You had a life before all this happened."

"Have. I *have* a life."

"Sex magic is the strongest magic we have," he said. "I guess you didn't hear me say *that.*"

She crossed her arms over her chest, blowing a ringlet off her forehead.

"You're telling me that sleeping with Pat will help keep him safe?"

"I thought you were already sleeping with him," he said. "When two people are sexually connected, their auras merge. Their body language complements their partner's. You two have all the signs."

"Stay out of my bedroom." She heard how that sounded, and wearily closed her eyes.

"He's on your list," Jean-Marc pointed out. "I'm trying to do as you have requested."

"We're not sleeping together," she snapped. "We barely know each other."

"Your souls know each other."

"Mind your own business."

"Everything about you is my business."

He returned his attention to the list, tapping the tip of his finger on a name. "You can tell Big Vince a little bit about what's going on. Last night he dreamed about his dead wife and she told him that you have a special bond with her."

"How do you know that?"

He faced her squarely. "Because I gave him that dream."

She uncrossed her arms.

"Like your dream about the mansion, he doesn't remember this dream," he added. "But tonight, he'll have another. And in a couple of nights, you will probably be able to confide in him."

"Wait." She walked toward him and grabbed the list out of his hand. "Is that what you did to *me?* Brainwashed me with those horrible dreams, year after year?"

"You? Never," he asserted. "We would never do such a thing."

She didn't believe him. But she said, "Could someone *else* do such a thing?"

"To you? I don't know. Usually, it's difficult to get past all the defenses a Gifted has set in place." He tilted his head. "But you're an anomaly."

"Oh, *thanks.*"

She walked past him, planning to go into the bathroom and change back into her street clothes. She had come so close to believing all this.

He grabbed her wrist as she brushed by. "You're a mystery, then."

His scent, the electric current between them.

The magic.

It was strong, too strong.

"Let go of me," she said in a deadly voice. "You lied to me about the gun, too, didn't you? It doesn't cast spells. It's just a gun."

He kept his hand wrapped around her wrist. "Why would I do that?"

"To manipulate me. To scare me. So I'd cling to you. Listen to you." As she had tried to do to Pat. And failed.

He said evenly, "My entire life, I've been aware that I will probably rule my house. It has shaped me. I think first of the House of the Shadows, and then of myself. I believe in duty and obligation. And I was sent to be the Regent of your House by the Grand Covenate itself."

He held up his hand to keep her from speaking. "I didn't want to go, but I did. As I anticipated, I began making enemies immediately. I have done all I can to govern your House as if I were the true Guardian, and I have devoted years of my life to finding you.

"My job has been thankless. You can't imagine how many Bouvards have tried to bribe me, and threaten me. There have been numerous attempts on my life. I am hated because I'm an outsider and yet, I am the titular head of your Family."

She narrowed her eyes as she tried to get away from him. "I don't ca—"

He wrapped his free hand around her bicep. She glared down at it pointedly.

"You barely know me, Isabelle. You probably don't want to know me. But I'm the closest thing to a friend you have in this. You need to listen to me. You need to learn from me."

"You've been playing me." She jerked her arm. He let her go.

"Never," he said. "I can't. You're Gifted. I can 'play' some

Ungifted, but not all. Your father is sad and lonely. A dream of his lost love is a comfort to him. The thought that she has a bond with you, a special joy. Because you are adopted and he feels guilty for not telling you."

"And you know this because you invaded his privacy, read his mind."

He pressed his fingertips against her forehead, cupping the back of her head with his other hand, forcing her to submit to his ministrations. The now-familiar warmth oozed from his fingertips like warm oil.

"Sometimes you can see things outside yourself, even from far away," he said. "Can you not? Sometimes they're dreams. Sometimes they're thoughts in another person's mind. An Ungifted mind."

He walked her to the mirror at the foot of the bed. Standing behind her as they both looked into the glass, he said, "Do you see your magic?"

She looked hard. Very faint crystalline sparkles whispered into being around her head and shoulders. They increased, until her silhouette was a neon glow of pure white light.

She covered her mouth with her hand.

"*Alors.*" Jean-Marc put his hand on her shoulder, leaning forward in his excitement. "*Bon, c'est très bon,* Isabelle. You're focusing your powers."

She shook her head. "This is crazy. All of it—"

He squeezed her shoulder. "Don't do that. Don't deny it."

The white light faded. She swallowed and moved away from him. He dropped his hand to his side, following her as she walked back toward the fireplace. She was suddenly, un-accountably, cold. She began to shiver.

"You haven't asked me about your father," he said. "For the record, we don't know who he is. Or was. We don't know a thing about him."

He was right. She hadn't asked. Of course she had wondered. *If* she believed, in the first place, that she was someone else's daughter.

I can't be. Big Vince is my father. He is, damn it.

"Why don't you shower?" he suggested. "After, I have something I need to show you."

"Show me now."

He shook his head. "It's important for you to cleanse your body of magical residue," he said. "It builds up on our skin like a toxin. It can bring on chills, malaise."

She said nothing.

He sighed.

"All right." He turned on his heel and left the room.

She sank down beside the fireplace, shivering, chilled to her bones. A sob escaped her and she covered her mouth with her hand, on emotional overload. The idea that he was manipulating Big Vince, yet denying he had anything to do with *her* dreams. His cold way of dropping bombs of information on her. The pressure he placed on her. She began to shake in earnest, holding herself, moving closer to the fire.

Jean-Marc's bare feet slapped on the stone as he returned.

He sat down beside her. On his lap he balanced an oval object that looked like a mirror, the reflective surface a shiny black. It was framed in gilt and studded with jewels.

"I promised you proof."

He handed the oval object to her. She touched it experimentally, half expecting something like an electric shock. It came, almost on cue, and she started to let go of it.

He grabbed her wrist, preventing her. Gazed at her, his dark eyes flaring with blue light. She started to pull away again. He gripped her wrist more tightly.

"Hic incipit speculum Floron," he intoned. *"Fac fieri speculum..."*

It was Latin. The room cooled, lowered, the way St. Theresa's had during Mass. His fingers around her wrist grew icy, until she felt almost as if she were being held by a frozen, dead hand.

The blue light in his eyes swirled. Then it seemed to lift out of them and rotate in front of his face. She blinked, and the swirling remained, on the backs of her eyelids, misty and blue.

It's in my eyes now, she realized, frightened.

"...Hoc peracto..."

She wanted to tell him to stop. He kept speaking, his voice rising and falling, as the strange blue light filtered her vision.

"...cum fuerit vocatus."

He gently took her chin and tipped it, indicating that she should look down.

The oval was no longer black. It was swirling with brilliance as an image flared, blurred. Then it steadied, and sharpened.

Izzy looked hard.

There was an ornate bed of gilt swirls and curlicues, dressed with satiny-white sheets. Large candleholders held ivory candles, flickering with light. Lilies hung in profusion from the ceiling.

On the bed lay...

...Izzy. The same hair, the same features. She was her twin. Unlined, unblemished. The woman's eyes were closed and her hands were folded across her chest like a dead woman.

"This is your mother," Jean-Marc said.

No. She swallowed down a rush of deep emotion.

"It is. You know it."

It's a trick. It's a lie, she thought.

"Votre mère," Jean-Marc said. *"La Guardienne, Maison des Flammes. Et vous êtes la fille..."*

"No, you liar," she croaked as other words poured into her mind. *Ma mère, ma belle mère, ah, je suis ta jeune fille...*

She began to sob.

"*Bon.*" Jean-Marc put down the mirror, and put his muscular arms around her. He cradled her head against his broad chest, but she felt no comfort in his embrace. If anything, she was more frightened, more overwhelmed. She wept harder. Perhaps he sensed that he was making it worse, and released her.

After a long time, she quieted.

"She's too young," Izzy managed. "She can't be my mother."

"She's a Gifted," Jean-Marc said. "You'll find that you age very slowly, as well. I myself am probably older than you think I am."

She barely registered what he was saying as she reached around him and picked up the mirror, staring fixedly into it.

"She's been in a coma for twenty-six years—your entire life. I have found you, and I'm training you. I think she knows that. I think she's waiting for you to come to her, so she can die. Because she is slipping away. The reports are not good."

Her scalp prickled. "Wait a minute—"

"I don't know what will happen if she dies without you there," he continued. "The Bouvards insist that it's never happened before. Many believe it is a polite fiction, and nothing more. That a male could inherit the power as easily as a female."

There was a soft knock on the bedroom door. Jean-Marc rose and went to answer it.

"*Oui?*" he said as he opened it slightly.

Someone spoke to him in French, a male voice, troubled. The sound startled Izzy out of her reverie; she had assumed they were alone.

"*Hostie,*" Jean-Marc swore.

The two spoke for another few moments and then Jean-Marc shut the door.

Izzy looked from the image of herself in the mirror to him.

Something terrible has happened. She knew it as surely as if he spoke. She saw it in his face. She felt it bone-deep; her blood froze and she shook violently. She was so cold; she was as cold as when she had run from the assassin.

She wanted to cover her ears.

She wanted to be anywhere but here.

He said somberly, "The gun has been fired." He reached down and took her hand. "Isabelle..."

It's Big Vince. It's Pat. Oh, God, no. Please, no.

"Yolanda Sanchez has had a heart attack. She's dead."

Her shock was mixed with relief. Fresh tears welled in her eyes as she shook her head.

"No. You're lying. She was in protective custody."

He squeezed her hand. "As soon as my operatives detected the discharge of magic, they converged. They clouded minds, got inside—"

She began to cry. Jean-Marc took the mirror from her and held her again. It was all too much; he was the only refuge she had, and she took it. Just as she began to sink against him, he said, "We'll get him, Isabelle. We'll get him. But you have to leave the city. It's just too dangerous for you here."

"Will you stop it!" she yelled at him, breaking out of his embrace. "Can't you let up for one damn minute!"

"No," he replied, "I can't. Even if it was Vince DeMarco, or Pat Kittrell, I can't let up."

He reached for her. She moved out of range.

"To get inside like that...we think he may have had an accomplice, someone working in the holding facility. Or...a magic user. That is far more problematic."

"I don't care, I don't care," she rasped.

"You should take a shower," he said. "The residue isn't helping you. You're shivering."

"Stop it!" she screamed at him. She made a fist and shook it at him. "Leave me the hell alone!"

"I wish I could. Believe me." He touched her cheek and then her forehead. "Let me calm you."

"Leave me!" she shrieked.

"As you wish," he said.

And then he left the room.

She showered, and it gave her so much relief that she believed him about the magical residue. With steadier hands, she redressed in the clothes she had originally worn. He gave her a dozen white satin bags, six tied with gold thread and six tied with purple.

He said, "The bags with the purple ties are for Pat. The gold ones are for your father."

Then he drove her back to her house in one of his black vans, saying, "Pat's on your porch. I'll let you out here."

It was barely seven; he was early. She hopped out and hurried toward her house. Pat, in a dark overcoat and a suit, saw her and came down the steps, reaching her and drawing her into his arms. Held her. Looked into her eyes.

"You already heard," he said. "About Yolanda."

She melted into his arms and rested her head on his chest.

"I am so sorry," he said.

She closed her eyes. *I don't ever, ever want you to die.*

"I rushed right over. I didn't want you to hear it on the news."

Then she opened her eyes and pulled away. "My father wasn't home?" She felt a burst of panic.

"I saw him at the station house," Pat said. "He said something about going to your aunt's for dinner. He figured you were going on a date with me."

"Why would he think that?" she asked.

"Because I told him you were." He trailed his fingertips down the side of her face. "Are you still up for it?"

Then and there she made her decision to sleep with him. Now. To protect him and claim him.

She laced her fingers through his and brought his knuckles to her lips.

"Come into my house, Pat."

They gazed at each other. She put her hand on his chest and felt his thundering heartbeat. He splayed his free hand over the small of her back and drew her against him.

She couldn't read his mind, but she knew what he was thinking.

He said huskily, "Not in your house."

And he was right. Jean-Marc could see into the bedroom she would take him to. Anger and embarrassment warred inside her as Pat turned and hailed a cab. Then she determinedly put those feelings aside, reaching with a gloved hand for Pat's.

She realized this was a better way anyway. This way, she could ward Pat's home.

With sex magic.

She scooted into the crook of Pat's arm. He gave her a hug and kissed the top of her head. She savored the foreplay, the anticipation. There was a desperation inside her that she wished she could ignore. She didn't want her urgency to crowd out her real desire for him.

I'm as calculating as Jean-Marc, she thought. *And I don't want to be.*

Maybe Jean-Marc doesn't want to be, either.

Pressed up against his warmth, she slipped an amulet into the pocket of his overcoat. One down, five to go.

It snowed as they crossed town. She memorized the directions; he lived in Brooklyn, too, but much closer to the bridge.

At one point, her father called on her phone.

"Hey," he said. "I think I'm going to stay at Clara's tonight. That okay?"

She hesitated, wondering if he was making it all right for her to sleep elsewhere. But maybe that would be better than his staying at their house, with Cratty at large.

"That's fine, Big Vince." Tonight he would dream of Ma...of his wife...again.

Next came Jean-Marc.

"We know your father is staying your aunt's. We will watch over him." His voice was neutral.

"Okay," she said. Her face was hot. What he was telling her was that the coast was clear for her and Pat. It was mortifying to be spied on like this. She wondered if he had a scrying stone aimed at Pat's bedroom; if guarding him meant that, like her, he had no privacy.

"Good luck," he said. She had no idea what he meant by that.

"Don't need it," she retorted, feeling like she was twelve years old. As soon as she said it, she wanted to take it back. Too late.

"I know," he replied, disconnecting.

Following Pat's instructions, the cab pulled over in front of a quaint brownstone. Pat paid the cabbie and they both got out.

He took her hand and keyed into a security door in the pleasant brick foyer. They went up in short order, to the eleventh floor. There was a vase of silk flowers in an alcove; above it a bulletin board with a few business cards for dog walkers and housecleaning services. It was so ordinary, tethering her to the world she had known all her life. The Ungifted world. Pat's world, too.

He walked her down the hall, to his front door, and put the key in the lock. Smiled and let her in.

She was surprised. Pat's interior decorating style was Southwestern, but with a warmth that she had not anticipated. Instead of whitewashed end tables and coyotes wearing bandanas and howling at the moon, there were Navajo rugs hanging on the walls, and the furniture was dark and rugged. Terra-cotta vases held dried purple and copper-colored flowers. She thought of the purple ties on the white talismans she had brought for him.

He shut the door and clicked two dead bolts. Then he walked her in with a proprietary air and led her toward the couch.

They took off their coats and he, his suit jacket. He opened a cabinet door and showed her a bottle of red wine. She nodded. When he looked away, she opened her purse and retrieved the second satin bag, hiding it beneath the cushions of his couch.

He poured two glasses and carried them to her. She saw the crotch of his tailored trousers straining against his body, and her senses flared in response.

Taking the glass, she looked up at him, put it to her lips and sipped.

He gazed down at her; he didn't sit beside her, only looked at her as he took a drink of wine.

She reached out and grasped his hand, using it to pull herself to her feet.

He took her glass and set them both on the table. Then he wrapped his arms around her and pulled her close. He sighed against her hair, inhaling her scent.

They had not spoken since they'd walked into his apartment. His thoughts were closed to her, and she was glad. She fell into the silence; she wanted to tell him everything, spill her guts. But she wanted the silence more. Wanted what was happening more.

Be my solace. Be my comfort, she thought, feeling the muscles in his biceps and the hardness of his chest. She wanted to lose herself in him.

As he breathed against her earlobe, she remembered that his wife had died. Died with his child, and he had started roaming. She felt adrift herself, unmoored and without a harbor. She didn't know what he could do for her, but she knew that she could do something for him. She had the power.

She had the magic.

I'll be more than your solace, she told him. *I will protect you from death.*

And then, sharply, it wasn't about that. It wasn't about rescue or salvation. She wanted him, pure and simple. Jean-Marc was right; the oldest magic in the universe was pure, undistilled desire. And she felt desire for this man, in every cell in her body.

And he knew it.

He held her hand and together they moved from the living room down the hall into his bedroom. There was a large oil painting of a starry desert over his bed; he leaned over and yanked the Indian-print bedspread back hard. His sheets were the color of a desert sunset.

He eased her onto the bed and pulled off her snow boots. She lifted her bottom off the bed so he could snake down her jeans. Then her sweater, over her head.

She lay in her lacy bra and a pair of sheer pale pink thigh-cut underwear. He unhooked the bra. She took off her underwear.

He drank in the sight of her nakedness. She lay still with her legs slightly parted, allowing it. His eyes flared. Excited, her body became moist and swollen. Her nipples hardened.

He was fully clothed when he eased down on top of her, kissing her. She felt his erection and rocked her pelvis gently against the heated sheath; she tugged impatiently at his shirt and he chuckled, stopping her motions, forcing her to lie naked beneath him while he kissed and teased her.

Her breathing grew ragged; she moaned softly. Then Pat let her undress him, and he was exquisite: molded shoulders and sculpted arms; a sprinkling of blond hair across a wide, muscular chest that whorled around his navel and plunged to the narrow V of his torso. And there, his penis, hard and large.

His skin was scented with limes and sunshine. He tasted of wine.

While he put on a condom, there was one moment, one discordant second, when she thought of the danger she might be bringing to him. Then all of that fell away, all the worry and the strange new world and the horror; it was gone the moment Pat entered her, moaning beneath his breath.

"Oh, honey," he murmured. "Isabella."

And as they made love, Izzy DeMarco faded into the background. Isabella took center stage; she felt herself blossoming. She was desirable and strong, and this man, who knew nothing about what was happening to her, was her man.

They moved together, and then something incredible transpired: she saw stars in his hair and all around him. Colors shifted and danced along his skin. He saw none of it.

Words tumbled into her mind.

I will you to be safe. To be protected by my magical Gift. Jehanne, stand between Patrick Kittrell and all harm.

Music played, ethereal, astonishing. When his breath caught, she heard a brush of strings. When he moaned, she heard a low, brassy chord. He was light and sound; he was a symphony. Sonorous, sensuous.

His heartbeat pulsed melodies against her ribs.

He heard none of it.

I will you to be shielded from injury. I will bullets to bend, and evildoers to burn.

And when he climaxed…there was a new universe as his release brought on her own. Her body dissolved into brilliant white light; she was energy and transcendence; it was beyond physical, mental; beyond anything she had ever known. She had no words; she knew no words. There was magic in the air. Everywhere.

Then she became herself again, a woman lying in the arms of her lover after they had both climaxed. She floated in his spent embrace.

I will you to live.

I will you to life.

"Are you all right?" he whispered afterward.

In answer, she cradled his head against her neck and drifted into the most sublime sleep of her entire life.

Into paradise.

Chapter 15

After drifting and drowsing beside Pat, Izzy jerked awake. Her body was singing. She felt colors and patterns shifting deep inside herself, and she had to close her eyes against the tide of sheer sensation.

Her head rested on Pat's chest; his strong arms were curled around in a loving, protective gesture.

Emotion rose strong in her as she whispered wordlessly, *I love you.*

She wanted to drift back to sleep, but she didn't know if staying would help protect him or draw her enemies to him. She couldn't let him be harmed. She would take that bullet for him any second of any day. But nor did she want to draw the shooter to Pat's house, to his heart.

Tell me what to do, Jehanne, she prayed.

There was no verbal reply, but her intuition told her that she should leave. Reluctantly untangling herself from him, she gathered up her clothes, tiptoed into his bathroom and dressed. She rubbed toothpaste on her teeth and rinsed with a little swish of mouthwash in a Dixie cup.

When she came back out, he had dressed, too. He had his house keys in his hand and he raised a stern brow as she began to wordlessly protest, indicating that she could leave on her own. She wanted him here, in safe harbor.

He put his hand to her lips. Still not speaking, he laced his fingers through hers and brought them to his lips. She smelled her scent on him. He kissed her and she knew he wanted to make love again.

"Coffee?" he asked. "Tea? Me?"

"I should go," she said. "I'll get some at home."

"Didn't like what you got here?" he teased.

"Loved it. It was wonderful," she told him, smiling, feeling a little shy. "But I'm going to turn into a pumpkin if I don't get home."

He released her with a heavy sigh. He returned to his nightstand and pulled out his weapon, a SIG-Sauer P-228 just like the one Yolanda had discharged in the Prop room, and a holster that he looped over his shoulder.

"I'll just be a minute," he said, going into the bathroom and shutting the door.

Moving as fast as she could, she slipped the third satin bag underneath his mattress, the fourth in his guest bathroom and the fifth in the vase near the door.

"All set," he said, joining her in the living room.

As they walked together toward the door, she surreptitiously slid the sixth amulet into his jeans' pocket with a sensuous motion that made him moan and say, "Let's go back to bed."

"We will," she replied.

They kissed.

He threw back the dead bolts and they went into the hall.

I've protected him, she told the darkness. *You can't have him.*

Oblivious of her unease, Pat pressed the elevator button. "I loved being inside you," he murmured. "I want to be inside you right now."

She was sorely tempted. Her body was ready—moist, warm, eager. But her mind had moved ahead to the concerns of her life—staying alive. Making sure he stayed alive.

The elevator arrived and she maneuvered her way in first. They descended.

She grew more anxious as they walked through the lobby and went outside. It was still dark; New York in winter.

A block down, a lone cab trundled down the street. The On Duty light was on. Pat hailed it and it pulled over.

She jerked.

Jean-Marc was driving it.

He glanced at them without a flicker of recognition. Every part of her was braced for terrible news.

Pat helped Izzy in, then shut the door. He leaned in toward the driver's window and gave Jean-Marc her address.

Jean-Marc nodded at Pat. Then he drove away.

"Tell me," she demanded, rapping on the plastic barrier that separated them, and at her touch, it disappeared.

"Your mother is worse." He spoke to her reflection in the mirror. "We have to leave."

She closed her eyes, feeling the full force of her denial as she slowly shook her head. *She can't be my mother. I don't really believe it.*

"You know I'm not ready."

Do you know what just happened to me?

"I know you have to be ready." He added, "You can call him later. Make up a story. You're on leave, so you're taking a break. He's in love with you. He'll believe you. He wants you out of here anyway, because of Cratty. It will be a relief to him."

Without missing a beat, he continued, "Your father is still at your aunt's. It's nearly six. What time does he get up?"

He drove the cab down Refugio and turned right onto India. "You can pack a few things," he said. "And then we—"

At the exact same time, both of them inhaled sharply. The cold, wet velvet sensation slithered from the crown of her head to the nape of her neck.

"Someone's in there," Jean-Marc said as he pulled to the side of the street, out of sight of Izzy's house. "Someone who doesn't belong there. Do you know who?"

She concentrated. Felt nothing beyond the horrible feeling, narrowly avoiding the probe, the search light at the guard tower. Uneasiness made her queasy. She was sweating, trembling.

"It's someone with your gun," he told her.

"Oh, my God! Is my father in there?"

"Non. He's still at your aunt's house. He's safe. I have him surrounded."

"And this house? Was it surrounded, too?" Her voice was shrill, angry. Scared.

"You're safe," he pointed out. He was quiet for a moment. "It's Cratty. He's in there with the gun."

"Does he know we're out here?" she asked.

"Non." He gestured to the cab radiophone and spoke into it, in French. Andre, the leader of the gang with the van, responded, also in French; they conversed for a minute or two, then Jean-Marc hung up the phone.

"We'll wait here," he said, pushing against the wheel and moving his shoulders, trying to loosen up, she guessed.

"For what?"

"Reinforcements."

"Are you still guarding my brother?" she asked.

"*Oui.* No one has approached him. We thought they might try kidnapping your family, but so far, nothing."

Her heart skipped beats. She stared out the window, and at the back of Jean-Marc's head. He sat unmoving, unlike her. He would make a good detective, out on a stakeout. What had he told her?

I am a good spy.

They sat in stillness until she thought she would scream. Then a flash of movement outside the cab caught her attention.

Andre and his five homeys were hugging the shadows as they dashed down her street.

"Your neighbors can't see this," Jean-Marc told her. "I've woven a barrier. The wolf brothers won't be noticed."

Wolf brothers?

The woman with the cornrows brought up the rear with a companion in tow, glancing in Izzy's direction and giving her a thumbs-up.

Her companion was David of the red-gelled hair. His face was in profile to her; she couldn't read his expression. But he seemed eager to run with the rest, ready for an assault on Izzy's house.

David? I thought he was in the doghouse. I thought—

Her eyes widened. She knew why David was here.

"He's here to take the bullet," she breathed. "If Cratty shoots the Medusa, they'll use him as a shield."

Jean-Marc said nothing, only watched in silence. The cadre reached the front of her house, four of them melting into the darkness. David joined Andre, crouching together at the bottom of the steps. The young boy skittered up behind him, his hands on David's shoulders.

Andre pointed to himself and David, and they began

crawling up the steps like crabs. The boy stayed behind, gesturing to the ones who waited in the darkness.

Izzy pushed on the passenger door. It had no handle. "You can't do that to him. You have to stop it!"

Jean-Marc turned to her. "Isabelle," he said. "Let this happen. He's a traitor. He had an accomplice who cast a spell so that the others couldn't hear you when you called for help. But *he* heard you.

"He saw you running barefoot in the snow, and he saw you confront Cratty near the apartment building. He didn't try to help you, then, either. He didn't move to help you until it was clear you were going to survive."

"That can't be," she protested. "He wouldn't be so reckless—"

He shook his head. "His masters promised he would be safe. And he believed them."

"How do you know this?"

"He is Ungifted," he said simply. "I opened his mind. But I couldn't learn who his masters are. That remained out of reach." He sounded supremely frustrated. "Perhaps Andre will have better luck."

"*Out of reach?* You messed up his mind? And you…you're letting it happen…you're just sitting here…"

He turned and looked at her over his shoulder. His face was hard, stony. "I am not 'just sitting here.' I am guarding you."

Andre had reached the stoop. He waved a hand; then he opened her front door and went in first. David followed close behind.

Swiftly, like animals, the others barreled in after them. The little boy went in last.

She braced herself, clutching her hands together in her lap. She thought she would hear something, feel something.

But she didn't.

Less than five minutes later, they emerged from her house. All of them...except David.

She began to hyperventilate. Tears slipping down her cheeks, she bit her knuckles as she tried to catch her breath.

Andre walked to the cab as the others piled back into the van. The stout one had his arm around the woman with the cornrows, whose head was lowered.

Jean-Marc pointed at the window and it rolled down of its own accord.

His eyes were narrowed, his jaw clenched, as Andre leaned forward and handed Jean-Marc Izzy's Medusa. Jean-Marc carefully set it beside himself on the seat.

Next Andre dropped some cartridges into Jean-Marc's open palm. She couldn't tell how many there were.

Andre said, "Jean-Marc, I'm sorry. I couldn't get to Cratty in time. As soon as David saw the gun, he knew. He attacked Cratty while we were transforming and Cratty took the first bullet. Then David turned the gun on himself. It happened too fast."

Izzy gasped.

Jean-Marc swore. "They had to be working for the same person."

Andre nodded. "But I don't think it was the Malchances. It might have been a *bokor.* Cratty started talking about a sleeping powder and that's when David rushed him."

Jean-Marc swore. "A *bokor* probably means *Le Fils.*"

Andre looked equally troubled. Scowling, he said, "We took care of David's body. We left Cratty for Vincenzo DeMarco to find."

Isabelle covered her mouth with her hands. "What are you talking about?"

"They disposed of David's body," Jean-Marc said as if she were hard of hearing.

"*Disposed of it?* How?"

"We'll discuss it later. *C'est bon,*" he continued, patting the back of Andre's hand. Jean-Marc's fingertips came away with blood on them.

"What does my house look like?" She pushed on the door. "Let me see my house! You've turned it into a crime scene. Possibly made suspects of me and my father!"

"You can't go in now," Jean-Marc said. "You need to stay out of there."

"All we left was Cratty, *Guardienne,*" Andre said. "No other traces. He had a heart attack."

"But David—"

"David's body is gone. By magic," Jean-Marc told her again. "It is all taken care of."

Andre continued. "I think he was in there alone because your wards held, Jean-Marc. No one using magic could get through. But my guess is that they're lurking nearby, to see if he got the job done."

"Then it's time," Jean-Marc announced. "We leave in two hours," he said to Andre. "Tell the others I'm pleased. *Allons-y.*"

"*Oui, d'accord,*" Andre replied. He drummed his fingers on the edge of the window. "Home."

"Home," Jean-Marc concurred.

Then Andre loped with a distinctive lupine grace back to the van.

Isabelle watched him go. Watched Jean-Marc point at his bloody fingertips and make the blood disappear. If only it was that easy.

He waved his hands and the cab started up.

"What just happened?" she demanded in a shaky voice. "You have to tell me now. Who are *Le Fils?* What is a *bokor?*"

"A *bokor* is a practitioner of voodoo," Jean-Marc said. He

was still being evasive, and her blood ran cold. He was usually so blunt, so direct. Whatever he wasn't telling her, it had to be even more extreme than the things he had told her.

"And?"

Jean-Marc hesitated. Then he said, "*Le Fils* is a name. More formally, *Le Fils du Diable.* The Son of the Devil."

"A voodoo practitioner."

"*Non.* He's a king vampire, and he has been terrorizing New Orleans ever since I came here to find you."

It took her perhaps a full minute to comprehend what he was saying. Then all she could manage to say was a feeble, *"What?"*

He looked at her in the rearview mirror. His jaw was set, the angles in his face harsh and unrelenting. "Blood is running in the streets. The voodoo drums are rumbling in the swamps. The mayor is threatening to end the alliance between the Ungifted and the Bouvards.

"And if he does that, your enemies will pick you off one by one, until there are no more Bouvards left."

She processed that. Or tried to. Then she raked her hands through her hair, unable—unwilling—to make rational sense of what he was telling her. "The mayor. Voodoo. Vampires."

"Mayor Gelineau, of New Orleans, Isabelle." He looked at her as if that were obvious. "Your family has been working with the state of Louisiana for centuries. The House of the Flames keep all the Gifted and the magical population in check. The vampires, the voodoo *bokors,* the *loupes garoux*—"

"Stop." She was dizzy. As they drove on, she scowled at him. "Were you just not going to mention any of this? That there are vampires? And…and *loupes*—"

"*Loupes garoux.* You know what they are. You already knew about the werewolves," he added. The cab glided down the street without his hands on the wheel. "You looked at the book in the library. You had figured out that Andre and his team are Cajun werewolves."

"No, I hadn't!" She reached for the nonexistent door handle. "You let me out, Jean-Marc. I am not going anywhere with you."

He snapped his fingers. Immediately the car filled with the sound of a ringing phone.

"Palisano." That was her boss at Prop.

"Lou? Any problem if I go out of town for a few days?" That was her voice. Her disembodied voice! *"I know the investigation is under way, but—"*

"That's all right, Iz. There's so much going on they're keeping us on lockdown. We're not going to be taking any property in for a while, looks like. You take your days. How's your head?"

"It's a little sore, but I'm pretty good."

"Lou! That's not me!" Izzy shouted. She reached for Jean-Marc, to force him to stop.

She hit a barrier as solid as the plastic one he had dissolved. She raised her palm, felt the glow.

"I'll use it," she threatened.

"I'm safe from it." He rapped against the shield. "You and Kittrell aren't the only ones to get new amulets."

"You're kidnapping me!" she shrieked at him, pummeling the barrier with both fists. She kicked at the door. At the back of his seat. "Let me out of here now!"

"Isabelle, look!" he shouted. "Look around you!"

Something hit the other side of the window. Startled, she jerked sideways, screaming. A distorted white face, all angles, hollows and bones, stared back at her. Couched in deep sockets, its eyes were two glowing coals. They sizzled and smoked, the flesh around them bubbling. Its ragged lips were drawn back in the rictus of a smile, revealing long, fanged teeth.

It opened its mouth as if it were trying to bite through the glass. Its face contorted with fury as its fangs smacked the glass. It drew back, trying again.

There was another one on the other side of the car and one smacking against the rear window.

Then a head attached to a body landed hard on the hood, spreading its arms across the windshield as it jackhammered its teeth against the glass. Taloned hands on long arms draped with leathery folds tapped crazily against the glass. It threw itself against the window, jaw working in a frenzy.

Izzy heard nothing but her own screaming. She couldn't stop.

"Do you still want me to let you out?" Jean-Marc bellowed. "Would you like me to go to New Orleans without you?"

She kept screaming. Her world was coming apart. This was insanity; these things weren't really here.

"These are vampire minions," he yelled. "Under the control of *Le Fils*. They must have been searching for you. They can smell you."

He glanced at her in the mirror. "They won't stop until they get you, or they are destroyed."

With that he moved his hands and began to speak in Latin.

"Audi ergo et time ergo…"

The creature on the hood threw back its head and shrieked. Blue flames erupted along the exterior of the windshield. The minion ignited. Its screams matched Izzy's own as it went up like a piece of kindling, the blue fire enveloping it.

He shouted more Latin; she could barely hear him. Then her screams mingled with a whooshing sound and walls of blue fire shot up around the cab.

212 Daughter of the Flames

"Call to your patroness!" he shouted.

"Jehanne!" Izzy screamed. *"Aidez-moi!"*

Shapes writhed in the firestorm. Jean-Marc kept bellowing words; Izzy cried over and over, "Jehanne! Jehanne!"

We're going to burn to death, just like her. We're going to roast!

But she felt no heat. The interior of the cab remained cool.

She had no idea how long the flames burned, but eventually they died out. To her astonishment, the cab was undamaged. The magic fire had left it unscathed.

Jean-Marc pulled the car to the curb of an unfamiliar street and opened up the passenger door. He got out and held out his hand. She wouldn't take it. She sat huddled, amazed that she could think much less move.

He wrapped his fingers around hers and eased her out, pulling her straight into his arms. He placed one hand beneath her right hip and the other beneath her head. He held her the length of his body. She had no will to pull away. She was nearly catatonic.

He murmured, *"N'ayez pas peur. Je suis là."*

Warmth moved from his body into hers; calm from his body into hers. She felt his hardness pressing against her abdomen and she realized she, too, was aroused. Which made no sense.

"It's all right. They're gone," he said inside her head.

She leaned against him. Sagged, more like. She tried very hard not to weep.

He was her only anchor. His body pressed against hers, his mind gentling hers.

"And you want me to go to New Orleans? Where blood is running in the streets?"

"I'll be there, too," he said. "I won't desert you."

"Until your family needs you," she muttered.

"Look," he said, lifting her chin and turning her to the side. They were standing catty-corner across the street from the deli near her aunt Clara's house. Through the storefront window she saw the bustling patrons, diners at the clutch of tables reading the morning paper and drinking their coffee.

"Your father's inside," he said. "He had a 'conversation' with you about having breakfast together. I've warded the restaurant heavily, and we have backup."

He gestured behind them; Andre sat behind the wheel of the black van. He gave her a wave, which she did not acknowledge.

"When did you do that?" she asked, peering at the deli. "When did you set him up?"

He didn't answer. "Go in. Tell him you're taking off for a couple of days. Tell him whatever you need to, to make him let you go."

"No," she whispered. "He's my father. *Please.* I can't leave him. I'm all he has." Tears spilled down her face.

"You know that is not true. He has a son. A son of his own blood."

His words cut deeply; even as he cupped her cheek to comfort her. But his dark eyes bored into her as if her were commanding her to face facts: she was not all he had.

"This is your destiny, Daughter of the Flames. I wish I could take it from you," he said somberly; his voice was deep, laden with urgency.

"Do take it," she whispered. "Take it from me."

"I cannot." He kept his hand on her face, his long fingers warm where they touched her, an unwelcome reminder that this was happening, this was real. "You could leave without saying goodbye. You could disappear. Or you can find a way to talk to him."

"No," she blurted.

Then he pressed the length of his body against hers again, her body that Pat had claimed so wondrously, and murmured to her in Latin. She fought for a moment and then, as a sense of calm began to infuse her, she fought harder.

"Shh, *Guardienne*," he whispered, more like a lover than a mentor. "Let me make it easy for you. It's difficult enough, *non?*"

She felt herself succumb. She felt warm and a little dizzy. She smelled oranges. She smelled Jean-Marc. Her heart skipped a beat; her stomach twisted.

She said, "I'm coming back here. To New York."

"*Oui,*" he agreed. "So, make it possible to do so. Now."

They communed a moment longer, and then she turned on her heel and went into the restaurant. The smells of coffee, fresh pastries and wet wool pulled her into the moment. The hubbub. What was in here was real. Jean-Marc and the vampire minions and the death of David...

They're real, too. She didn't want to accept that, but it was true.

The deli had six hunter-green-topped tables. Seated at the one furthest from the door, her father was dressed for work in his blues, a white coffee cup in his fist; and he waved her over to the table where he sat.

She threaded her way through the crowd and pulled out the chair across from him. He leaned across the table and kissed her cheek as she sat down. "Iz," he said. His voice was gentle. "Big doings, eh?"

She blinked at him, adrift. She had no idea which of the many big doings of late he was referring to.

"I'm glad you're getting out of the city for a few days," he said. "Wish I could, too. I just hope we find Cratty while you're gone." He clenched his teeth. "He's probably already left the city. Good riddance."

Izzy knew that there was nothing worse in Big Vince's book than a dirty cop.

"Ah, well, whatcha gonna do," he muttered. Then he offered her his coffee. "Just got it," he said. "I'll get another."

"Just had some." She thought of Cratty lying dead in their house and knew she had to be careful not to create any more complications. "At Pat's," she added.

"Ah." Her father's cheeks reddened. "Okay."

She thought to go on about that, say something to ease the awkwardness, when he rushed on. "I need...I had a talk with your aunt, last night, baby. She said it was time for me to talk to you about...things."

"Things." She held her breath. *My adoption?*

He stared down at his coffee cup, hands clenched atop the place mat. Then he gazed up at Izzy through his lashes. There were lines in his face; he looked older than he was.

"About your ma."

"Oh." Jean-Marc had fed him some lovely dream, and he must have talked to her aunt about it. She didn't want to hear the pretty illusion. She felt ashamed, even though she had done nothing to cause it.

He exhaled. "Your ma," he said softly as he picked up the cup and set it down, scrutinizing the ring of condensation on the Formica tabletop. "Your ma. Oh, Iz, she was so sick. The doctors tried all kinds of medicines, shots, pills...they just made it worse." He closed his eyes and shook his head.

"I know," she said quietly. "I remember."

He made another ring.

"One night, when you were little, she just couldn't take it anymore, know what I mean? So she..."

Her voice hitched. He set the cup down. And Izzy understood that this was not about lovely dreams and pretty illusions.

"Daddy, it's all right," she whispered. "I'm here."

"She got my gun…" His voice cracked. He shut his eyes
tight and pulled his head in toward his chest. His fists balled.
"My gun," he said again. He didn't look at her.

"And she shot herself."

Izzy jerked back her head as if he had slapped her hard
across the face.

"No," Izzy whispered.

A gun went off.

A tear rolled down his cheek. He still didn't look at her.
"It hit all kinds of organs…perforated her bowel…"

A gun went off.

Izzy reeled. She thought she was going to be sick. She went
completely numb. Her face was icy.

"She never got over it," he concluded. His head was still
down.

He blames himself, she realized.

The wounded part of her, the little girl who needed a
mother, blamed him, too.

And then she felt…something…something warm…

Jean-Marc had entered the restaurant. He moved into her
direct field of vision and stared hard at her. She felt his
strength.

Je suis là, she heard inside her head. *Pas de peur.* Have no
fear.

I am afraid, she told him. *I'm terrified.*

No need.

More strength infused her, along with a kind of detached
calm, as if she were standing beside Jean-Marc, watching
herself. It was like a drug. It was magic.

"Daddy," she said, "you couldn't have done anything."

"After I called 9-1-1, I checked on you," her father continued. He began to weep. "You didn't wake up. Gino started
crying. But you slept through the whole thing."

But she had heard it. And her subconscious had tried for years to make sense of it.

"Afterward." He slumped, wiping his chin with his hand. "Oh, *Madonna,* she was just out of surgery. She was still in the hospital. I went nuts. I told her she was the worst, most selfish mother in the world."

Izzy snaked her hand across the table and tightly clasped his hand.

I don't want to hear this. I don't want to know this.

His mouth stretched across his face, a contortion, an agony. "I said that we were Catholics. Suicide is a mortal sin. Was she going to raise her children from hell?"

She squeezed harder. Her breath was stuck in her chest. And then…more calm.

Jean-Marc was staring hard at her over Big Vince's shoulder. She stared at him as an image flashed across her mind:

A young woman in a long white gown tied to a stake. The flames are crackling. A priest raises a staff with a crucifix atop it, and she focuses on that as she is consumed…

She stared at Jean-Marc and focused on what Big Vince was saying.

"So me almost taking a bullet…and her warning me. I'm hoping it means that she forgives me for saying those things. I was just so afraid she'd try again."

Izzy tried to clear her throat. Jean-Marc was staring hard at her, his lips moving, weaving magic. Where had the magic been back when the DeMarcos had needed it?

"She's an angel now," Big Vince said. "The angels understand. And they forgive."

Jean-Marc raised his left arm and tapped on his watch. They were out of time.

She held her father's hand, silently said, *Am I your child? Tell me, Big Vince. Tell me whose child I am.*

There was nothing.

Then Big Vince said, "So. There it is. I'm glad I finally told you, baby."

But she could see that telling her had cost him. He looked wan and humiliated. She assumed he had let Aunt Clara pressure him into revealing his terrible secret. It was the wrong time to ask him to reveal another, so she closed the lid on her desperate need to discuss her adoption before she parted from him. It was the right thing to do.

"It's okay," she murmured. "I understand. Thanks for telling me."

"It's a weight lifted," he said, obviously unaware that he had transferred his burden to her. "I dreamed of her, and she told me it was all right to tell you." His face glowed. "Baby, she loves us so much."

Izzy couldn't swallow around the lump in her throat. She began to falter; Jean-Marc's gaze gave her purchase, kept her grounded.

Big Vince added almost jovially, "I'm glad you're going on a little break. Florida. Nice and sunny. Do you good, getting out of here. Pat…?"

"No," she said. When had Jean-Marc told him all this, convinced him she was going to Florida? "I'm going alone."

He fished in his pants' pocket. "Here. This is for traveling mercies."

He handed her a gold St. Christopher's medal about the size of a dime.

She held the medal tightly as anxiety prickled through her. Left to his own devices, her father would never be so sanguine about her suddenly leaving town like this. Jean-Marc was manipulating him. Just as he had manipulated her.

Jean-Marc took a step toward them; it was her cue to leave. Moving more smoothly than she would have thought possible, given the circumstances, she pushed back her chair and got to her feet.

"Call me as soon as you land. Tell me all about it." He nodded at her. "Get warm. This damn world is so cold."

"I will."

She turned to go, then stopped and turned back around. When would she see him again? When, really?

He knit his brows. "Was it right, to tell you? About Ma?"

"It was right," she said. She didn't know what possessed her—or maybe she did—as she said, "Ma speaks to me in my dreams, too, Daddy."

"It's a miracle," he said, his voice hushed with awe.

"Yes." She leaned down and kissed his cheek, smooth from his morning shave. She wanted to be his little girl again. She had not been a little girl since the night he had asked her to be brave, back when she was seven.

"Hey, you'll be back soon," he said confidently.

"Yes." She stumbled out of the restaurant, disoriented and unsteady. Jean-Marc trailed behind her; he caught up with her outside and they crossed the street side by side, but not too close. She wondered if her father was watching.

As they walked behind Andre's van, she whirled on Jean-Marc and said, "You lied to him."

"Yes." He pointed at the van door and it slid open. "Time to go."

She shook her head. "I have no clothes. No tooth-brush—"

"Of course you do."

They walked past the van. There was a gray Corolla double-parked beside the cab. Jean-Marc escorted her to the passenger's side and got behind the wheel.

He said, "We're on the run now, Isabelle."

"I'm Izzy," she said, hugging herself. Her hands shook.

They pulled into traffic.

The van followed.

Her mother had attempted suicide. The guns in her dreams, her fear of them…that jerk Dr. Sonnenfeld had been right all along. Issues.

She thought about the vampire minions and the blue fire. And David. All the woo-woo insanity.

About Pat.

She rubbed her head; it was pounding. Distanced and wary, she observed other cars and road signs, losing track, then snapping back into awareness as they made a right into a densely forested area. A landing strip stretched in front of them and, at the end of it, a small white jet that bore no markings of any kind.

"That jet belongs to you," he said.

"Not to me personally," she replied, taken aback.

"To your mother. To the *Guardienne.*"

That gave her pause. It hadn't dawned on her that her mother would be…*rich.*

He opened her car door and she climbed out, mulling over the notion of being the daughter of a millionaire.

"Look," he said, gesturing behind her. She turned around and gasped.

At least thirty cars sat fanned behind the cab. People got out of them—men and women—to stand silently, gazing at her. There were at least a hundred, maybe more. The only ones she recognized were Andre and the others from the van.

Except for one other person, who stood about twenty feet away.

Captain Clancy.

The NYPD officer, who was dressed for work in a black pantsuit, raised a hand and waved at Izzy.

Jean-Marc nodded at the captain as he said to Izzy, "She'll smooth things over at the precinct. No bridges burned."

Izzy waved back at the captain. "How? When?"

"I approached her last night," he said. "She had heard of us, but not of you specifically. I helped her ward the precinct in return for her help."

Jean-Marc beckoned Captain Clancy forward. She walked toward them, then inclined her head respectfully as she drew near.

"I'm not sure what to call you," the woman said to Izzy. "But I want you to know that I'll look after your father while you're gone."

Izzy took a breath. She said, "Pat Kittrell, too."

"Oh?" Captain Clancy smiled faintly. "All right. I will." She looked from her to Jean-Marc and back again, as if taking the measure of *their* relationship.

The police captain took a few steps back. Some of the assembled crowd knelt on one knee. Others bowed or lowered their heads. There was a scattering of applause and one brave soul who bellowed, "Yo!"

"It's time to go," Jean-Marc said.

Together they walked toward the jet.

Chapter 16

As Izzy and Jean-Marc crossed to the aircraft, the sky shifted from night to predawn. When the first hints of color tinted the blackness, Jean-Marc visibly relaxed.

"No chance of vampires," he said.

"Oh. That part's true? They can't go out in the sunlight?"

When he nodded as if he couldn't quite believe that she hadn't known that information from birth, she added savagely, "Because the part about them sticking to car windows and trying to eat through them? Missed that on 'Buffy the Vampire Slayer.'"

He huffed. She felt a surge of anger so intense that she had to consciously stop herself from hitting him. His empathy level certainly came and went. One moment he was all hugs and encouragement, the next…pretty much a bastard.

A man dressed in a long black coat emerged from the door of the jet. Izzy sucked in her breath. *Assassin?*

"It's all right," Jean Marc said. "He's your Bouvard aide-de-camp. His name is Michel. For the record, he detests me."

"How does he feel about me?" she asked, ticking her glance from the man to Jean-Marc.

"I'm not sure. You're probably better news than I am. Unless the fact that I'm your escort taints you," he reminded her somberly. "We haven't even begun to discuss all the factions and intrigues you will have to deal with."

"Madame de Bouvard, *Grâce a Jehanne* that you've been found at last," Michel gushed as he descended the stairs. With a dramatic flourish, he dropped to his knee and lowered his head. "I can't tell you how many runes I've cast, watching for this day."

Casting runes. Vampires.

"Thank you," she said.

"Monsieur de Devereaux," he said icily as he rose, not even bothering to look at Jean-Marc. He was wearing a little pin of white flames on his lapel.

"Monsieur de Bouvard," Jean-Marc replied, and it took Izzy by surprise. Were *all* the de Bouvards named de Bouvard? It hadn't even occurred to her that that might be the case.

"I am Michel," he said to her. "I'm certain Monsieur de Devereaux has already told you that." He went on, walking shoulder to shoulder with her. "I've brought you dossiers on all the most influential members of the House of the Flames. There's to be an emergency meeting as soon as we land."

"No meeting," Jean-Marc cut in. "Madame is already exhausted. We'll see what is to be done once we arrive."

Michel frowned. "They are going to want to see her. If the power transfer occurs soon—"

"They can wait."

Michel pursed his lips. "With all due respect, Monsieur de Devereaux, I know my family better than you. The tension at the *maison* is nearly unbearable. They've heard that she's coming, and they know the *Guardienne* is...fading."

"We were attacked on our way over here," Jean-Marc said. "By minions of *Le Fils*. Madame hadn't encountered vampires before and—"

"What?" Michel looked incredulous.

"One forgets," Jean-Marc said slowly, "that Madame has lived among the Ungifted all her life. Like all of us, vampires are expressly forbidden in New York."

"And yet, here you are," Michel said. His voice dripped with hostility.

"Here I am, performing my job as Regent, to locate and deliver your next *Guardienne*. Now, is the plane clear?"

Stiff-lipped, Michel nodded. "We've warded and re-warded it. I burned some white sage about a minute ago. I'll go in first. As a precaution."

As Michel reentered the plane, Jean-Marc muttered, "If the plane is clear, why does he need to take a precaution?"

She had no answer. But she had a question of her own. "If he knows I'm not married, why does he call me *madame?*"

"It's a sign of respect," he said. "It's that case in many languages."

She took a breath. "Have you had any more word about Marianne? May I see your mirror?"

"Most of my possessions are in the cargo hold," he said. "I'm sorry I couldn't take you to your home to pack. I did direct Sauvage to get you some clothes at the safe house. The plane was probably being loaded about the same time you and I were outside your house."

She thought about her French-poodle bathrobe and her black skirt. *I'll be back soon,* she reminded herself...but she knew she wasn't at all sure of that. If Marianne de Bouvard des Flammes really did die, and passed on her powers to Izzy, *could* she simply return to New York? It was too much to wrap her head around. So were vampire attacks and guns that caused heart attacks.

And Cajun werewolves and sacrificial victims with red-gelled hair.

As her boots clanged on the metal stairs, she glanced back over the crowd watching her every move. On impulse, she waved.

A cheer rose up. Most of them waved back.

"I feel like a rock star," she drawled.

Jean-Marc looked even angrier. He said, "Your departure is a covert operation."

Whoops. Not anymore.

Then she stepped into the plane. The interior was white on white—ivory walls and carpet, overstuffed white leather seats positioned with plenty of room all around them, each with an island holding a DVD player, screen and a place for refreshments. The de Bouvard signature flames logo was stamped in gold on cushion covers and on the doors of the cockpit.

"Oh, hi, *Guardienne!*" Sauvage sang out, bounding down the spacious aisle. She wore a black bolero jacket dotted with crimson satin roses over her bustier, and she had wound her hair into two little pom-pom ponytails that stuck out like antennae on either side of her head.

Her white face was wreathed in a huge smile, as if Izzy were her long-lost sister. Against her chest, she cradled a bulging black backpack with a red skull on it. She began rooting around inside it, then brightened and pulled out a necklace of silver links and pink stones, quite lovely in its craftsmanship.

"I made this for you. It's rose quartz," Sauvage announced. "It's good for…well, I'm not sure, actually. I read it in one of your books, but I forgot." She looked a little embarrassed.

"It's for healing," Jean-Marc said. He picked it up from

Sauvage's hands and held it up, admiring it. *"C'est très jolie, Sauvage."* He turned to Izzy. "It *will* help protect you."

She looked down at her simple gold crucifix. Then she turned so that Jean-Marc could put the necklace on for her.

His fingers grazed the nape of her neck and ripples of electricity fanned up her neck and across her shoulders. She wondered if he felt it, too; she ignored it as best she could by staring down at the stones. Perhaps the sensation was emanating from them.

"Oh, it looks good," Sauvage said happily.

"It was very sweet of you," Izzy said, smiling at her.

Blushing, Sauvage wheeled around. "Meet Ruthven!" She gestured at a boy of about eighteen who was sitting in one of the seats. His black hair was shot through with electric-blue dye, and he wore white makeup and eyeliner like Sauvage. He had on a T-shirt, a black vest and black leather pants.

"Um, hello, Your Majesty," he said, half rising and giving Izzy a wave.

Sauvage beamed at him. "I hope this is okay. Ruthven wants to help the cause. Michel said it was okay."

Michel cocked his head. "I said that it would be all right if it was all right with Madame."

Izzy looked to Jean-Marc, who shrugged with his trademark French insouciance.

"Oh, yay!" Sauvage cried. She galloped over to Ruthven. "You're in, baby!"

Jean-Marc murmured to Izzy, "You can be very nice when you want to be."

Her mouth dropped open. *"Me?"* she sputtered. He grinned at her and she wondered if he was teasing her. Was he even capable of humor?

The pilot and copilot introduced themselves, and Jean-Marc conferred with a man who turned out to be a steward.

Izzy realized that she hadn't eaten all day and she was ravenous.

After they took off, Michel perched across the aisle from Izzy.

"Let's go through those dossiers," he said. "If you wouldn't mind?"

"Sure," she said, fatigued and edgy, but game to do her best.

In short order, he showed her half a dozen folders of women and men who looked like her—dark eyes, crazed hair. An older woman's hair was gray.

"This is Mirielle," he announced. "She's probably your oldest relative. She's a hundred and twenty-nine." Before she could react, he opened another folder.

"This is Mayor Gelineau. Ungifted. Not in the Family. He has twin daughters named Desta and Monique. The daughters are goths who own an occult bookshop in the French Quarter. It's been closed since *Le Fils* stepped up his rampage." He looked over at Jean-Marc. "I assume you've been keeping up to date on that."

Jean-Marc stared impassively at Michel. The other man flushed and said, "Gelineau's worried. The standard protocols are no longer working. The media have gotten wind of the increase in 'criminal activity—'" he made air quotes "—and they're demanding answers."

Jean-Marc cleared his throat. "The 'standard protocols' are the procedures the law-enforcement agencies use to cover up anything the Ungifted would consider out of the ordinary— vampirism, magic use, even voodoo."

"Not all voodoo," Michel interrupted.

Jean-Marc rolled his eyes. "Voodoo is a touchy subject in New Orleans. Some *bokors* insist it's a religion. Others argue that they are Gifted and should be admitted into the Grand Covenate."

"Because they've been denied membership, they tend to ally themselves to whomever will give them the most power," Michel added.

"*Non.* They ally themselves to whomever will give them the most power because they are not a united house," Jean-Marc argued, sounding testy. "They're a ragtag bunch of *déclassé*—"

"This is a conversation for another time," Izzy said. She turned to Michel. "Tell me about *Le Fils.*"

"It's been getting worse and worse." Michel said. "Gelineau is furious. Broussand—that's the Superintendent of Police—is pressuring him to consider severing the Politesse."

"Where does Jackson stand on that?" Jean-Marc queried him. He said to Izzy, "That's the governor."

She said, "What's the Politesse?"

"That's the agreement to allow Gifted to live in your territory without persecution," Jean-Marc told her. "It was signed in 1753."

"Madame knows what her territory is?" Michel asked.

She shook her head. He looked shocked.

"The Bouvard family controls all of the American South and parts of the west," Michel explained.

Izzy's mouth dropped open. "Say that again?"

He looked at Jean-Marc as if to ask, *What have you told her?*

She couldn't comprehend what Michel had just revealed. She hadn't even realized that the Bouvards controlled all of New Orleans.

Michel cleared his throat. He said to Jean-Marc, "May I speak to you privately?"

Maybe they'll agree I'm unqualified, Izzy hoped, crossing her fingers.

They got up and walked to the back of the plane. While they muttered together, turbulence buffeted the jet. The sky outside was blue and bright; it was the first time Izzy had seen a sunny day since before Halloween.

Jean-Marc returned to his seat beside her. As if he'd been waiting, the steward brought them both plates of fragrant steak and French fries and glasses of wine.

"So, you two decided to go to the next girl on the list?" she asked Jean-Marc as she picked up her silverware.

Jean-Marc didn't crack a smile. He said, "We've agreed that only the most senior members of your family—those who are traditionalists, and believe that you must inherit your mother's Gift—should be informed of your...status."

"As someone who has no clue."

"Oui."

"You're going to BS the others."

"Oui."

"Like you BS'ed me."

His wineglass was halfway to his mouth. It stayed there as he said, "I never lied to you."

Michel returned. Jean-Marc looked over at his stack of dossiers and said, "Where's my cousin, Alain?"

"I didn't bring any Devereaux folders with me," Michel said crisply. "Since you will be handing power over to Madame de Bouvard, I am concentrating on *her* people."

"Jean-Marc is *my* Regent," she said, testing the waters a little.

Michel folded his hands one on top of the other and sniffed. "I don't suppose he mentioned the fact that nearly twenty-three percent of de Bouvards have left the Family since Jean-Marc assumed power *three years ago?*"

Jean-Marc murmured to Izzy, "I've only been serving as Regent for three years. Before that, it was Mirielle's daughter. She died in office."

"Elise was murdered," Michel said flatly.

"It was never proven," Jean-Marc replied.

"And there was that *other* girl," Michel began.

"Look," Izzy interrupted, "could you two stop the pissing contest? I only just found out that there are Gifted and Ungifted. I don't even want to be here."

Michel refolded his hands. He was unbelievably prissy. "It would be wise not to advertise that fact after we land. There are many factions who would welcome the chance to assassinate you and put their own choice forward to receive *Le Baiser du Feu* from the *Guardienne.*"

Jean-Marc turned to Izzy. "That means—"

"'The Kiss of Fire,'" Izzy translated, suddenly hooking into the French again.

"There is also the matter of your father," Michel continued. He said to Jean-Marc, "You *have* told her that we don't know who he is?"

"Oui."

Michel checked his watch. "Your existence was announced approximately three hours ago. We've already had six men come forward and insist that they're your father. They've offered to provide samples."

"Can't I just resign?" she asked Jean-Marc.

Jean-Marc said to Michel, "I explained to her that since the Guardianship is hereditary, that's probably not an option."

"Definitely. So, we're back to memorizing names and faces," Michel insisted.

They worked for another hour or so. Jean-Marc grew increasingly agitated, peering out the window, visiting the cockpit, and speaking to several men and women in black business suits, who turned out to be security.

Then he said, "It would be good to change your clothes now. There's a private room for you, with a shower. You go first and then I'll take mine."

"A...shower," she deadpanned. "Changing my clothes."

He nodded. "There is a white gown for you."

"And for you?"

He shrugged like a Frenchman. "A tux."

"You're serious."

"This is your debut with your family. They will be dressed, as well," he said.

She blew a ringlet off her forehead. She couldn't deny that a shower sounded heavenly. And it would be nice to have something fresh to wear.

He led her to a small room furnished with a bed and an altar, set up much the same as the one back in New York: a statue of Joan of Arc, a sort of human-shaped gray figure, lilies and candles. Jean-Marc genuflected before it. She did not.

He opened a door and showed her a tiny bathroom decorated with marble tiles, marble sinks and gold fixtures. There were fluffy white towels embroidered with the flames logo.

Beside the bathroom, he pointed to a wooden panel flush with the wall; as it slid open, he said, "This is for you."

She gaped at a long white dress with a boat neck and long sleeves cut on the diagonal and ending in wisp bits of cloth-like scarves. Her fingertips brushed the white-on-white embroidered flames on the bodice. The fabric was creamy silk.

As she stared at it, Jean-Marc raised the hem to reveal white high heels.

Then he hesitated and pulled from his left ring finger a heavy gold signet ring. He examined it, then showed it to Izzy. "This is the day-to-day symbol of authority in the House of Flames. It was taken off your mother's finger and given to the first Regent. It's been passed from Regent to

Regent since then. I think I should continue to wear it for the time being."

"Works for me," she said.

He nodded and put it back on his finger. "I'll leave you to your shower."

After he left, she stepped into the stall and cranked up the hot water. It was sheer pleasure; she wanted to melt. When she was finished, she toweled off and stepped into the dress. There was a shelf bra. There were no underpants, just a pair of panty hose. She slipped them on and put on the shoes, then her crucifix and Sauvage's rose quartz necklace.

She pushed on what looked to be another sliding panel and discovered a full-length mirror. Her dark eyes and hair were a stark contrast to the whiteness of her outfit and her New-York-in-winter pallor. She couldn't deny the drama of her appearance—and the fact that it was the most feminine she had ever felt in her entire life.

Jean-Marc rapped on the door as if he knew she was finished. When she opened it, his eyes flared and his lips parted. He murmured, *"Mais tu es magnifique, Isabelle."*

She flushed under his scrutiny. Then she said, "Your turn."

He nodded and she left him in the room. As she walked back down the aisle of the compartment, Sauvage blurted, "You look like a princess!"

I look like I'm about to be burned at the stake, Izzy thought. But she thanked Sauvage and took her seat.

Michel was on her within seconds with more dossiers. After complimenting her on her appearance, he flipped open the topmost one and they got back to work.

"You're doing well," he said after they'd gone through several files. "Now, here's your cousin, Jacques—"

But the rest of his words were lost as Izzy looked up and saw Jean-Marc in his tux. It was impossible not to stare at him. His dark hair glistened with shower mist. His angular face and square jaw were clean-shaven. The tux fit him perfectly, stretching across broad shoulders and narrow hips. His white shirt was elegant; his studs were simple gold.

Jean-Marc moved with fluid grace as he stepped around Michel and took his seat beside Izzy. He pressed the button for the steward and said, "Champagne."

The steward brought three flutes—one for Michel—and Jean-Marc clinked his against Izzy's.

"To a glorious reign," he said. "To long life. And a daughter."

"Whoa." She froze, her glass aloft. Was he referring to her lovemaking session with Pat? Did he think she might be pregnant? "Aren't you rushing things?"

"Not at all," he replied evenly. Then he drank. "Good champagne. We Devereaux have vineyards in the Medoc."

"Of course you do," she said.

Then she socked it back.

It seemed as if only a couple of minutes had passed when Sauvage cried out, "Ruthie! We're landing!"

Izzy leaned forward, looking past Jean-Marc, to see an airstrip that ran like an artery through the heart of a black, clotted forest. She saw nothing but trees and darkness.

She thought of Pat and his sunny home, and missed him with an ache that was real and deep and painful.

The pilot landed the plane easily and well; the security people exited first, forming a protective circle around the ramp that had been pushed up to the door. Jean-Marc descended the stairway, gesturing for Izzy to stay behind him while he took in the lay of the land.

It was brisk, autumnal weather, not the bone-chilling cold of New York. Despite the fact that it was daytime, the vista was dark and forbidding. Lush trees rustled in a cold wind.

Huge swags of Spanish moss hung from their limbs; the air smelled rotten.

Three sleek, low-slung limousines were idling beside the jet. Three limo drivers stepped from their vehicles and bowed on one knee.

Jean-Marc escorted Izzy toward the middle limo while Sauvage trailed behind with Ruthven, their heads pressed together, giggling in high spirits, as if this were a vacation. At the very least, it was a free trip to Goth Central. The security detail and the airline crew took the other two limos.

Izzy and Jean-Marc sat in the middle of the seat at the rear. Sauvage and Ruthven plopped down beside a DVD player. Ruthven reached out to press a button; Sauvage smacked his hand.

Michel sat up front with the driver, pulling a revolver from his jacket and laying it across his lap. She wondered if Jean-Marc had her Medusa, and thought about asking him for it. Then thought better of it.

Jean-Marc had words—in French—with the driver, then leaned back against the leather seat. He looked weary. There were lines around his mouth that she hadn't noticed before. She wondered how old he really was.

They drove in silence for a few minutes, Jean-Marc warily glancing through the tinted windows.

"First order of business," Jean-Marc began. "To go to your mother, of course."

She tensed. "My…"

"She's on life support inside the mansion. I thought I told you that."

"No," she said evenly. "You didn't."

Her head began to pound. She rubbed her temples and cricked her neck.

"Allow me," he said.

He touched her forehead, and his warmth seeped into her skull.

Jean-Marc's cell phone went off. He answered it, saying, *"Oui, bien. Merci."* He clicked off and looked at Izzy. "So far, so good."

"That's comforting."

They drove past silvery freshets of water dotted with cattails and large ferns. Drooping trees rose from the water, the heavy branches plunging back into the swamps. Birds took off in scattershot.

"It's so cool," Sauvage murmured.

They went deeper into the darkness. Izzy called her father on her cell phone and reported in.

"Florida's so nice," she said, wincing. Why hadn't Jean-Marc told him she was going to New Orleans?

"Iz, I have to tell you something. John Cratty was found in our house. Dead."

She closed her eyes and tried to sound surprised. "What? How?"

"Heart attack. Like that girl, Yolanda. Isn't that just nuts? They're thinking drugs. They were in on it together, so maybe they sampled the same bad batch. No autopsy results yet. Pat said he'd let me know. I'm staying at Clara's since our home is a crime scene."

"Are you okay?" she asked.

"It wasn't fun finding him. Captain Clancy came down to the briefing room, asked if I was okay."

"Do you think she'll go down?" Izzy asked, grateful that the captain had kept her word to watch over her father.

"I hate to say it, but yeah, I do. They'll scapegoat her. It's a shame, but it's the Job, you know?"

"I was wrong. You're not a throwback," she murmured, moved by his compassion for his female commanding officer.

"Maybe not. But I'm still glad you're out of here. Now, listen, I have the number for your hotel. You just relax and have some fun."

She shut her eyes. Jean-Marc had explained that it was a simple matter to forward her calls from the fake hotel number to the mansion.

"Okay," she said.

They hung up, and next she called Gino.

"Jeez, Iz, did you hear about the dead cop in our house?"

"It's so weird, Gino."

"You dated him, didn't you?"

"Only a couple of times."

"I'm thinking you should become a nun."

She made a face, even though he couldn't see her. "You and me both."

"I can't become a nun. Big Vince says you stayed out all night with some guy."

"*Mea maxima culpa.* Are you shocked?"

"Not about that. It goes with the territory. You're young and filled with sin. But what does shock me is that Big Vince is in raptures about some bond he is having with Ma."

"Well, we *are* Catholics," she said. "We're supposed to believe in stuff like that or the whole system is shot to hell."

"He was never like this until I started seminary. Don't say hell so much."

"Yes, his embracing his faith is your fault. Tell your father superior you want extra credit."

"There's a thought. Listen, I gotta go. It's time to pray."

"It's always time to pray with you people."

"Yeah, well," he said. "Whatcha gonna do. Love you, Iz."

"Gino, wait," she said in a rush. "Gino…" She took a breath. "Are you still there?"

"Yeah. What's up?"

"Am I…" She decided to come straight out with it. "Did our parents adopt me?" There. It was out. Jean-Marc was staring at her intently. Sauvage stopped chattering and fell silent.

Gino said, *"What?"*

Izzy was not going to back down. "I need to know. Has anyone ever said anything to you?"

There was silence on the other end. She tried to translate it. Then Gino said, "Oh, my God. Aunt Clara said something just the other day. About how strange it was that you were following in Dad's footsteps, much more so than me, his 'real son' she said. I thought it was weird. But I didn't think that it meant you were adopted. Who told you that? That's just…that can't be."

"Oh," she said faintly, feeling dizzy. Jean-Marc caught her gaze, held it. Steadied her.

"Did you talk to Big Vince about it?" Gino asked her.

She almost said, *I never found the right time.* But that was a dodge. She hadn't asked because she hadn't wanted to know.

"When you get back from your vacation, maybe we three should have a sit-down," Gino suggested.

"He wants to see Father Raymond," Izzy told him, trying to keep her voice steady. "To talk about Ma. That would be a good time."

"Pffft. That guy has no social skills. Better we should keep it in the family. And it is our family, Iz, no matter how it got that way." His voice was gentle and concerned. Her throat closed up.

"Iz?" he said. "You still there?"

"Yeah. I'm…okay," she assured him. "You go on to prayer class."

"I love you," he replied. "You're my sister, Iz. You *are.*"

"Yeah. Same here. I'm stuck with you, too, Gino." It was difficult to speak.

After she hung up, Jean-Marc tentatively extended his hand, as if to comfort her. She resolutely ignored him and dialed Pat.

"Hey." Her voice was still tight; she discreetly cleared her throat.

"Iz. You just…took off."

"I'm sorry. I just…things…"

"*Are* you sorry?" he asked, and she realized he was referring to their lovemaking.

"Not at all," she promised. "I'll…I'll be back before you know it."

"You…" He took a breath. "What's wrong, Iz?"

She ticked her gaze to Jean-Marc, who was watching her closely. Perhaps too closely. A frisson of anxiety trilled up her spine. Had she walked into some kind of trap? Was she his prisoner?

"Is it John Cratty?" he asked.

She answered a question with another question. "Was it really a heart attack?"

"Yes. Like Yolanda's." He paused. "I found this little white bag under my mattress."

"Oh." She flushed. "Ah."

"Good-luck charm?" he asked her.

"Yes," she said.

"Well, it worked. I got lucky."

She loved how bright he was, how quick. "Keep rolling the dice," she said. "Your number's sure to come up again."

"That won't be everything that comes up."

She smiled wanly, missing him, wanting to come clean, wanting to be with him.

"When are you coming home?" he asked.

"Soon. You won't have time to miss me."

"Too late for that," Pat replied.

Pensively she hung up. Sauvage leaned forward, goggle-eyed, and said, "Was that your boyfriend?"

Izzy avoided Jean-Marc's gaze as she said, "Yes."

"That's nice." Sauvage snuggled against Ruthven, who clasped her upper thigh with a lustful grimace. "Having a boyfriend is cool."

After about an hour, the car rolled through an alley of perhaps fifty live oaks on each side of the road, up to an exquisite three-storied, Southern-style mansion. The roof was pointed and there were carvings in the triangular frieze of stone.

Seven enormous columns fronted the house, which was perched on a sweep of steps, bisected by a large, flowing fountain.

Wrought-iron balconies encircled the middle and top floors. They were crowded with dozens of people waving and applauding as the limo drove toward them. Many of them were holding lilies; trellises of small white flowers ringed the ground floor of the mansion.

"Everyone has gathered to greet you," Jean-Marc said. "Not all of them are happy that you're here. We have a lot of security. You'll be heavily protected."

"Okay, so why are they still around if they don't like her?" Sauvage piped up. "Why don't you just boot them?"

"Jesse, they're magic users," Ruthven said. "You don't want to piss people like that off. No offense to you guys," he added. "But seriously, they can, like, make your head explode."

"They can not. You are so clueless about the Gifted," Sauvage snapped, and the two began bickering.

"The political situation is complicated," Jean-Marc explained in an undervoice to Izzy. "Think of yourself as the long-lost oldest daughter of a large dysfunctional family."

She frowned. "How large? How many Bouvards are there?"

"In New Orleans, about three hundred. But all over your territory? Ten times that."

Three thousand people with magical powers? And they expected her to be their next fearless leader?

"That's a joke, right?"

He shook his head.

The limo rolled to a stop. At once men and women dressed in black suits poured from the front door and gathered in a line between the limo and the crowd. They were heavily armed.

Jean-Marc pointed and said, "Those are state-of-the-art submachine guns. Each operative who is holding one is also a seventh-degree Bouvard magic user."

"What degree am I?"

His expression never changed. "That's not a meaningful measurement for you quite yet."

From the front seat, Michel cocked his head and pressed his fingertips against his ear. He was wearing an earphone. He announced, "The governor and the mayor have both arrived. They're in your private briefing room."

"My private briefing room," she echoed. *The governor. The mayor.*

Then the limo stopped and the operatives grouped around the door. Jean-Marc got out of the way and took from the closest security detail what appeared to be a shield. He held it above her head and said, "Please, welcome to your family home. *Bienvenue à la Maison des Flammes.*"

Bodies pressed around her. She couldn't see anything, and she could barely breathe. Jean-Marc walked in front of her, taking her hand in a protective gesture.

"We're moving you in through a side door," Jean-Marc said as everyone turned en masse to the right.

The cheers and boos began to coalesce and form a rhythm, like a chant. The words were muffled by the footsteps surrounding her, but the intensity of the emotion—whether welcoming or hostile—unnerved her.

"What are they saying?" she asked Jean-Marc, but her attention was diverted as the operatives parted into two lines, one on either side of her. She looked down the corridor they made to see a heavily armed guard standing in front of a door the color of a gloomy Manhattan winter afternoon.

"Madame," the guard said, snapping to attention. With military precision, he took a step to the right, pulled a swipe card from around his neck, and held it out to her.

Jean-Marc intercepted it. He placed it in his palm and waved his other palm over it. It glowed; he turned it over, inspecting it.

"It's all right." He handed it to her and stepped aside.

It was fairly obvious that she was supposed to unlock the door. She walked toward it and saw a keypad with a swipe strip beside it, exactly as they appeared at the entrance to the Prop cage at work.

She walked up to it and swiped the card along the strip. The door rose vertically, like a panel.

Two figures stood shoulder-to-shoulder on the other side of the door. They were dressed in blindingly shiny Medieval armor just as she had seen at the Cloisters, with closed helmets over their faces topped with miniature swords encrusted with moonstones and bits of black, so that they looked like white-hot flames.

As one, they knelt on one knee and lowered their heads.

She heard Jean-Marc's voice in her head. *"Merci bien, mes chevaliers. Je suis Isabelle Bouvard."*

She repeated it out loud. Flawlessly. She heard herself and marveled. Magic was afoot. Her body thrummed with it.

The knights stood at attention, their armor clinking. Then they wheeled smartly around, in an about-face, and glided forward. They did not walk. They made no sound at all as they moved.

"Freaky-deaky," Ruthven muttered.

"Shh," Sauvage snapped at him.

As the entourage progressed, Izzy's feet left the floor as well. She was *floating*.

Jean-Marc took her hand again.

The heady scent of oranges wafted around her. She was buoyed higher and a white mist surrounded Jean-Marc, the two knights and her.

She looked over her shoulder, but she could see nothing through the fog.

A rectangle of light formed in front of the knights. They glided toward it and then through it and disappeared.

Jean-Marc said, "You know this will change everything."

She said, "No, I don't know that."

He nodded slowly. "Cautious to the last. I admire your tenacity."

"You're doing nothing to reassure me. You know that," she said.

They exchanged a long look. She focused on his dark, compelling eyes. She wanted him to reassure her. She wanted him to comfort her and to tell her everything was going to be fine.

Instead he said, "I have not lied to you, ever. I won't start now."

Then he tightened his grip on her hand, as if to ensure that she would not bolt, and urged her across the threshold.

Chapter 17

End of the road. I'm here, Izzy thought. *And there's a lot more here than was in Jean-Marc's magic mirror.*

The white mist wafted around her as she stood at the end of a long corridor lined on either side by dozens of women seated on graceful wooden benches with white satin padded backs and cushioned seats. The women were wearing long white gowns like hers, the hems so long they bunched over their feet. White veils concealed their heads and faces. Each one held the hand of the one beside her—some young and unlined, others wizened and veined. The two on Izzy's end each held a glowing white sphere in her free hand.

Behind and above the women, mosaics in shades of ivory depicted flames and hearts glowing and shifting like kaleidoscopes. Overhead, circular chandeliers of platinum glowed with multifaceted white stones.

The room seemed to stretch forever, a trick of the light, perhaps...or a bit of magic. Something gleamed at the opposite end, but it was so far away she couldn't make out what it was.

The two knights flanked Izzy as their disembodied voices announced in English, "The Daughter of the Flames."

As one, the veiled faces turned toward her. She couldn't see their faces, but Izzy felt their scrutiny, and her chest tightened.

"Why are they dressed like that?" she asked him. "For that matter, why am I?"

"Tradition, ritual, magic. A blend. White gowns echo the white robe Jehanne wore when she was burned at the stake. More practically, the veils help them concentrate their magical currents. Or so they say." He made a face. "Me, it would drive me crazy."

"Me, too," she said. It seemed repressive; it made her uneasy. Was she expected to do something like this?

Not going to happen.

"They are *les Femmes Blanches*. The White Women. They're renowned throughout the Grand Covenate as healers," he went on. "They've been specially trained to share their *magical essence* with her."

She gave her head a little shake. "I don't understand."

He continued. "The Ungifted have accepted the mind-body connection—that how and what they think can directly affect their physical health. We Gifted have a third component—our magical bodies. *Les Femmes Blanches* work to keep your mother's magical body from failing."

She still wasn't grasping it. "So...are they in contact with her? They talk to her, the way you and I talk in our heads?"

"*Non.* No one has been able to reach her."

Except me, maybe, Izzy thought, thinking of her premonitions, the voice that on occasion guided her. Jehanne or Marianne?

"Then how do they know it's working?"

"I don't know," he said bluntly. "I'm not a Bouvard, and I can't pretend to fully understand it. I'm not sure they do."

His mouth quirked, but there was no humor in his expression. "No *Guardienne* has ever been in a coma for twenty-six years before. But your House is convinced that the connection is vital. That if *les Femmes Blanches* were to stop their vigil, your mother would die."

She tried to process that. "Do you agree?"

"I don't know." He gestured to the rows of women. "But they've dedicated their lives to maintaining the connection. Some of them are second generation, mother sitting beside daughter."

"They stay in here all the time?" she asked, looking around the room.

"In shifts," he said. "They rotate with two other groups. They even take vacations."

"It's their *job?*"

He shook his head. "Their calling. And one of the arguments the opposition has put forward for choosing a new heir. A generation of Gifted women have spent their lives trying to preserve Marianne's existence. They see that as a waste. Others, as a privilege and an honor."

"And if they…stopped?"

"I don't know. All I know is that they tell me their bond with her has been weakening. She is taking less of the magical energy they offer her. And her physical body is beginning to deteriorate rapidly. Both *les Femmes Blanches* and Marianne's medical support team insisted upon getting you here as quickly as possible."

"And now I'm here," she said.

"And now you're here." He gazed down at her. His gaze was smoldering. "Not many women would have consented to come."

He inclined his head. "No matter what happens next, I'm grateful to you for that."

She narrowed her eyes. "You didn't give me much choice."

"I did. I pushed, but you always had a choice."

"Fair enough."

She raised her chin. Everyone held a collective breath, she included. The next move was hers to make.

She closed her eyes, trying to strip out her fear and anxiety, and to discern what to do.

She had a strong, clear knowing that she needed to be apart from Jean-Marc for this meeting. He was a man, and that mattered, somehow. She didn't want to do this alone, away from her only ally. But it was what must be.

Opening her eyes, she put out a restraining hand and murmured to him, "Stay here."

"As you wish," he replied.

She glided forward on the mist, alone. The woman nearest to Izzy's right began to get to her feet as Izzy came abreast of her. But her companion gently tugged her hand.

Izzy moved on. Her heart was pounding; her hands were damp. She wanted to turn back. She wanted Jean-Marc to come with her.

But this was her walk, her path, not his.

As she passed each veiled face and looked at the pairs of hands tightly entwined with each other, a pulse of energy surged through her like a mild shock. She scrutinized the blank, veiled faces. Were they sending her a message? Greeting her? She didn't know. There was so much she didn't know. No wonder Jean-Marc had been overwhelmed by the idea of teaching her about the world of the Gifted. It was like landing on another planet.

I can't do this, she thought.

Yes, you can, chère, a voice inside her head replied.

Another voice said, *We'll help you do this.*

We are your cousins in blood and in magic. You're one of us.

She didn't want to be one of them. A faceless woman in a room? No thank you.

And yet she became aware that with each movement forward, the surges increased, buoying her. Her anxiety slipped away, very gradually, and her spirits rose to a mild euphoria.

She held out her hands before her and turned them over. Her palms began to faintly glow. And then her fingers and her arms. She was glowing with white light.

A ripple went through the right line of women, answered by the left. The veiled women murmured quietly; she heard a whisper. *Guardienne. We're with you, chère.*

She didn't want them to be with her. She didn't want to be here at all.

Finally she saw what lay before her.

It was the gilt bed she had seen in Jean-Marc's magic mirror, festooned with white lilies from a crystal hanger dangling from the ceiling. Luminous white pillar candles in large filigree candleholders stood like sentinels on either side.

Between the candles, a figure reclined, positioned so that it faced Izzy. It was shrouded in white fabric like the veils of *les Femmes Blanches;* she saw only its silhouette, could only imagine what it looked like. On either side, a veiled woman sat with her hand beneath the cover. White light was streaming from the bed, casting a nimbus around the figure. The light was caught in the mosaics and reflected in the shiny white metal chandeliers. It pulsed; it was as if the room itself breathed in and out, with light.

Banks of hospital machines were piled one on top of another behind the bed. The whooshing sound of a ventilator was like a distant wind. An EKG readout said 108. The setup reminded her of Ma's many hospital stays, and she felt a wave of panic at being around lingering sickness and possible death again—especially so soon after Big Vince's disclosure.

Am I to watch two mothers die?

She began to sweat, her hands to shake.

I can't do it.

Then sweet soprano voices rose in song. Was it the women in the room? She couldn't tell, but she had heard them before: in the tunnel of white light when, apparently, *she* had died.

Is that what magic is about? Death?

The singing buoyed her, as Jean-Marc's magic had so many times previous. She allowed it to affect her; she would take help where she got it, to get through this.

She approached the bed, studying the shrouded figure as the voices caressed her ears. Steeling herself, she glided onward, and the mist evaporated; she walked on the solid floor to the right side of the bed, careful not to jostle the veiled woman who sat vigil beside it.

Ma mère. The French words popped into her head. *My mother.*

Hesitantly, Izzy gathered the fabric from above the head of the body in the bed and lifted it up. The singing cut off abruptly and a collective gasp issued from the women, as if she had done something very wrong—something she should have known not to do. The one closest to her whispered, *"Guardienne."*

Izzy looked down, swaying with shock. She had already seen her face, in Jean-Marc's mirror. But in the flesh, in her coma, looking exactly like Izzy…

"Ma mère," Izzy choked out, burying her face in her hands. Her knees buckled and she sank down into the mist, weeping.

Strong arms seized her. Warmth seeped into her. It was Jean-Marc. He had run the length of the room to come to her.

"I know this is a shock," he said under his breath. "Would you like to stay here awhile? I'll tell Gelineau and the others to come back later."

She'd forgotten about the people waiting to meet her. About the mansion, and the vampires, and the politics, and all of it.

"Oh," she said dully. "Them."

"I'm sorry." He apologized a lot. He didn't mean it, though. He just said it to fill time while she pulled herself together after whatever blow he had just dealt her.

She moved out of his embrace and walked back to the bed.

Below Marianne's chin, at the base of her neck, a plastic tube was inserted into her throat and trailed down the side of the bed. It was the trach tube for her ventilator.

They've kept you alive all this time, because they were looking for your successor. Do you know that? Do you see me? Do you know they brought me here because they think you're dying?

Then her thoughts drifted; she floated as light refracted, bounced off shadows. Then she heard a heartbeat, rushing and surging in her ears, throughout her body, deep into her soul. She heard a voice:

"Ma belle Isabelle. My sweet one. Comme je t'aime, ma douce."

"Maman?" Izzy whispered. Without warning, she reached down and cupped the sides of Marianne's face.

A gale force buffeted her body; wind rushed through her head. Her heartbeat clanged like a gong and a deep, sharp burning sizzled through the center of her head. She swayed and then she fell overboard, down, down, into a well of white light.

"Go forward now." She didn't know if Marianne was whispering the words or if it was the mother she had always loved and always missed, Anna Maria. *"It is your time. Mine is over..."*

Les Femmes Blanches were shouting. Some cheered. Izzy staggered back from Marianne's bed with her left hand wrapped around her wrist. Her hand was smoking. Her palm burned and sizzled.

"*Mais qu'est-ce que tu fais?*" Jean-Marc said, grabbing her hand and examining it.

In the center of her palm, the shape of a flame had been burned into her flesh.

A door opened in the wall and six or seven people in white scrubs raced to Marianne's side. Four of them were wheeling in more hospital equipment. Izzy recognized a defib machine, an oxygen bottle.

They scrambled around Marianne, checking readouts, examining the many tubes and cords streaming from the bed like tentacles.

An Asian woman in scrubs bent over Marianne. She clicked on a penlight and examined first her right eye and then her left. She placed a stethoscope in her ears and pressed the listening end on Marianne's chest. She gazed at the wall of machines, her lips moving soundlessly.

"She's…she's…" The woman looked first at her colleagues, then at Izzy.

"She's *better.*"

As one, the medical team turned and stared at Izzy.

Then they sank to their knees and bowed their heads.

The veiled women knelt, as well, maintaining their chain.

And then Jean-Marc knelt.

Izzy remained standing as she looked down at Marianne.

She could swear that she was smiling.

Izzy knew it was not what anyone had expected. This was not part of Jean-Marc's plan, whatever plan he had.

Izzy had changed things.

The room swirled; she stared at the crown of Jean-Marc's

head. He was the only familiar thing in the room. The only person here she knew.

Except for Marianne.

Surrendering, Izzy took a breath and gazed at Jean-Marc as he raised his head. Their gazes locked and she nodded at him.

He nodded back.

He did not smile.

Minutes later, Izzy and Jean-Marc left Marianne's chamber. Jean-Marc pressed his palm over Izzy's, removing the pain of the burn as effectively as if the wound had never occurred. As she examined the flame-shaped brand, Michel met them in the corridor. There was no white mist this time. The spectral knights had disappeared, as well. Act two of her dramatic arrival in New Orleans was far more mundane—despite the miracle that had occurred in Marianne's room.

"I've asked the governor and the mayor to join us in the great room," Michel told them. Neither Izzy nor Jean-Marc told him what had just happened. If Jean-Marc wanted to play it close to the vest, that was fine with her.

"*D'accord,*" Jean-Marc replied. He said to Michel, "Where's Alain? I expected him to greet us." His voice was tight; Izzy knew him well enough to know that he was worried.

"I don't know. I haven't seen him since breakfast," Michel said.

Jean-Marc frowned, began to say something, and held his tongue.

Michel and Jean-Marc walked on either side of Izzy as they headed deeper into the house. The three stepped into an old-fashioned birdcage elevator. Michel slid the wrought-iron door shut and the cage creaked up two floors, revealing more splendors of the house—Grecian statues, trickling fountains and expansive Victorian-era rooms decorated in white and gold.

They reached the third story. Michel slid the door open and Jean-Marc guided her through a warren of corridors paneled in dark wood and ivory-flocked wallpaper.

Then Michel opened two large, oak-grained double doors and the three swept into the great room of the mansion.

It was octagonal, like the library room back in the safe house in New York. Enormous mosaic windows of flames at least twenty feet tall rose to the top of the ceiling. They were swathed in cream-velvet hangings. A chandelier the size of a sofa glittered and gleamed with crystal teardrops over hundreds of people, milling and talking.

"Isabelle de Bouvard, Maison des Flammes," a voice rang out.

Faces turned expectantly toward Izzy. Men and women— some of them were very old, some young. Others were decked in goth regalia, like Sauvage and Ruthven. Upon seeing Izzy, Sauvage ran to her side and squeezed her hand.

"Freaky, huh?" she whispered.

A group of men looked like monks in black hooded robes. Or maybe Jawas. There were at least two dozen women in white gowns like the women downstairs, except that their veils had been raised off their faces but still covered their hair. They looked like Catholic noviates—nuns who had yet to take their final vows.

Twenty or so other women wore elaborate evening gowns, their male escorts in tuxes. Others were dressed in beautifully tailored street clothes—power suits, dresses created for night-time business functions.

All of them were staring at her.

And not all of them were human.

Three…*creatures* stood off to one side. Their faces were green and leathery, their eyes almond-shaped and yellow. They were vaguely reptilian, wearing purple hooded robes that covered their heads.

A few rows from the back, an extremely pale woman fixed on Izzy with scarlet eyes. She was dressed in a simple black-satin gown and her stark white hair hung in ringlets down to her waist. Rows of fangs were tipped with sparkling gems, which glittered and gleamed as she smiled at the newcomer in their midst.

"Holy crap," Sauvage murmured.

Jean-Marc gently moved Sauvage aside and stood beside Izzy. Sauvage rejoined the little pocket of goths. Her boyfriend Ruthven put his arm around her.

"*Il faut présenter,*" Jean-Marc began, then gave his head a little shake. Switching to English, he said, "I introduce you to Isabelle, Heiress of the Flames."

A sigh of admiration wafted around the room. About half of the onlookers knelt on one knee. A few swept curtsies or bowed from the waist. More than a few looked at her skeptically.

"Is she truly the one?" asked the fanged creature. Her voice was very sexy, very feminine.

Heads swiveled in the woman's direction. Those around her parted to give her room as she moved forward through the group. It was clear that some of the others were afraid of her.

"*Oui,*" Jean-Marc replied. "She truly is."

The creature glided more than literally walked. Out of the corner of her eye, Izzy saw Sauvage and her boyfriend tense. Sauvage's gaze traveled from Izzy to the creature to Jean-Marc and back again.

The fanged woman studied Izzy's neck. Her wide, sharp smile nearly split her face in two as she halted.

"You know more about our world than Jean-Marc led us to believe," she hissed. "What a pretty little crucifix."

"This is Madame Sange," Jean-Marc told Izzy. "She leads a family of vampires allied with us."

Izzy had suspected she was a vampire, but hearing the word out loud made her want to bolt. Izzy felt Jean-Marc's hand tighten around her bicep. Which was good, because her knees had turned to rubber and she could no longer stand.

"I'm a Catholic," Izzy snapped, to hide her fear. "I wear a crucifix all the time."

"Ah," Sange said, affecting a moue of disappointment. "And here I thought my reputation had preceded me."

There were a few more scattered forced chuckles; someone coughed.

"The Regent promised me that I would be shown respect," Izzy said as she forced herself to take a step toward the stat- uesque creature. Jean-Marc released her arm and lowered his to his side. "I'm not here for you to score points off."

"Go, *Guardienne*," Sauvage murmured appreciatively.

Sange turned her bloody gaze on Jean-Marc. "How can we be certain you've located the correct woman?"

"She is the one," Jean-Marc insisted.

"But you were wrong before."

"What?" Izzy look at Jean-Marc, who stared impassively at Sange, appearing calm, but his reddening cheeks betrayed him. Sange was deliberately putting him on the spot.

Sange smiled evilly at Izzy. "Didn't the Regent mention a young woman named Christine? He 'found' her about six months after he took over. He was sure she was Marianne's daughter. And she died under his protection."

"No, the Regent sure as hell didn't mention that," Izzy snapped. There was a murmur throughout the room; she sensed shifting loyalties, new impressions. She reminded

herself that an NYPD precinct house was a hotbed of polit-
icking and fraternization; this gathering was no different, at
least in that respect.

"It's immaterial," he replied. "Isabelle is the one. She destroyed a fabricant without any assistance."

That caused another stir. As if to take advantage of his
momentum, Jean-Marc clutched her wrist and held up her
hand, displaying the fresh brand in her palm.

"And when she touched her mother, this appeared."

Gasps filled the room. Six or seven of the assembled knelt.
Two of *les Femme Blanches* embraced each other and began
to weep. One of the hooded men stepped forward. Izzy
couldn't see his face, and she wondered if he had one.

"That is surely a sign," the man proclaimed. "Marianne has
the same brand."

"She *is* the Heiress," another of the hooded men said. "Our
new *Guardienne*."

"Marianne is still alive," a man in a tuxedo argued. He was
rotund, with blond hair and sideburns. "Isn't she? That means
she's the *Guardienne*. And as for having a specific brand,
Desta's got a tarantula tattooed on her back. But that doesn't
make her Spider-Man."

He looked challengingly Izzy; she knew she had seen his
photograph in the stack of dossiers Michel had shown her, and
she racked her brains. Desta…

He was Mayor Gelineau.

"Well? Is Marianne still alive or not?" Gelineau demanded, hooking thumbs in his cummerbund and rocking
back on his heels.

"Marianne is still alive," Jean-Marc said evenly.

"And we don't have time for this," Gelineau said. "It will
be dark in a couple of hours, and *Le Fils* will be back in business."

Izzy wondered how it could be that Sange was present during daylight hours. Jean-Marc had said the vampire minions couldn't hunt her once dawn rose. Was Sange a different kind of vampire? Or was she protected from the sun because she was indoors?

I know so little. I know practically nothing.

"*Le Fils* is never out of business," grumbled an older man with silver hair and jowls as he moved out from the crowd. Izzy remembered his picture, too. He was the Superintendent of Police. Broussard. "I have informants all over the French Quarter who tell me he's got something going on in that haunted convent on Rue Casconnes."

Izzy blinked, aware of increased scrutiny on herself. She turned her head; about twenty feet away, an older woman stood alone, an intense expression of loathing on her face. Her wild, curly hair was gray, and her face, though lined, was classically beautiful. She was wearing a loose black-velvet top and black wool pants; her jaw was clenched and her hands were tellingly balled at her sides.

Izzy left Jean-Marc's side and walked toward her; people bowed and moved out of Izzy's way as she approached. The elderly woman did neither, simply waited for Izzy to come to her.

Izzy stopped. All eyes were on the two of them.

The woman raised her chin, as if in defiance.

Izzy said, "Madame Mirielle, I'm very sorry for your loss."

Mirielle's eyes slitted; Izzy heard, quite distinctly, a voice inside her head.

I don't want you here. You're an imposter.

That remains to be seen, Izzy replied silently.

The woman blinked. Izzy did not.

As Izzy returned to her original spot, a third man had joined Gelineau and Broussard. Dapper in a tux, he sported a head of snowy-white hair and a white goatee that, frankly, made him look like a skinny version of the Kentucky Fried Chicken guy.

"Governor Jackson," she said. "Superintendent Broussard. Mayor Gelineau."

"I'm glad to see you've done your homework," Governor Jackson said. His voice was cold. "If so, you know that New Orleans is in a state of panic. And your family is falling down on the job."

"Well, if *you've* done *your* homework," Izzy retorted, "you know things are about to change." She had no idea what that meant, exactly. But it sounded good.

Suddenly the room tinkled with silvery bells. A shiny metal knight appeared in the center of the room. Sauvage leaped into Ruthven's arms and Izzy instinctively took hold of Jean-Marc's forearm.

"The meal is served," the knight announced. Then he— it?—vanished.

No one else so much as blinked.

Everyone turned to Izzy. Jean-Marc offered his arm. She took it, and the two led the way into an enormous formal dining room. Izzy had never seen such a long table in her life; it was a very dark, highly polished table laden with gold dishes and lily centerpieces. Rows of gold tableware glittered beneath chandeliers of moonstones and white crystals.

"The food will be New Orleans style," Jean-Marc told her. "Gumbo, jambalaya, beignets. More wine than you can imagine."

"Suddenly I'm not hungry," she confessed.

Jean-Marc said, "I'm here," he reminded her. "This is for show. This is so they can see you. It's been arranged that you will sit at the head of the table. I will sit at your right hand."

"You usually sit at the head," she guessed. "You're making a statement by putting me there."

"Oui."

And with that, they swept into dinner. Jean-Marc was tense. After a while, he called over a man wearing a dark suit and an earpiece, who was standing near the door and spoke to him in rapid French. The man shook his head. Jean-Marc muttered something, and the man returned to his post.

When Izzy looked questioningly at Jean-Marc, he said, "My cousin's missing."

"The one you did the rituals for?"

"Oui. I've sent out security to search for him. So far, no luck."

"Do you want to go?" she asked.

He gazed at her. "That's not an option," he told her.

"But…"

"It's not an option," he said again.

A waiter approached with a golden basket of breadsticks and offered one to Izzy. She took it; then suddenly everything began to whirl, the room to tilt. She laid the bread on her plate as she broke into a sweat.

Jean-Marc saw her distress. He quirked his left eyebrow; she said, "This is too much for me."

He studied her. "You're right. I can see it in your aura." He put his napkin to his lips. "I'll get you out of here."

She considered. "Get me through dinner."

"Agreed." A muscle jumped in his cheek. "But no meeting after. I told Michel not to do it."

"Thank you," she breathed.

Dinner dragged on interminably. People spoke to her, courted her, subtly insulted her. She responded on total autopilot. She was exhausted and beyond stressed.

She was barely aware of the curtsies and bows that accompanied her exit from the dining room as Jean-Marc escorted her out. Sauvage and Ruthven looked cast adrift, but she was too tired to deal with them. She was trembling with fatigue.

Jean-Marc said, "I'll take you to your bedroom. It's on this floor."

"No. Take me to Marianne's chamber." When he hesitated, she placed a hand on his arm. "I need to be there. Please."

He looked down at her hand, then into her eyes. She felt the low-level connection between them and it made her tremble harder.

"I'll take you," he said, and she wondered if he was aware of the double meaning of his words.

He walked beside her as she traversed the length of the hall past *les Femmes Blanches*. She lowered the fabric from Marianne's face again and glanced at the brand on her palm. It had healed into a dark pink scar.

Andre and the others had flown separately from New York, circling above the mansion for most of the dinner. Jean-Marc had asked them to come in, assigning Andre to guard Izzy while he dealt with the fallout of the canceled meeting.

Andre wore what she assumed was his native garb—a buckskin jacket with fringes, military-green parachute pants and heavy boots. He wore a necklace of what looked to be a string of feathers and chicken feet, and when he caught her gazing at it in repulsed fascination, he said, "This is a *gris-gris*. I know Jean-Marc, he don't have no truck with *voudon*, him." He grinned at Jean-Marc. "But I'm a Cajun and I know the *bokors* take good care of Andre."

"They're trash," Jean-Marc huffed.

"Mais non, cher," Andre protested. "You need to be more tolerant. Don't he, Madame?"

"Ah," she said, having no idea what else to say.

He pointed to her rose quartz necklace. "That's a *gris-gris*, same as this. Your cross, too. Just a different magical style. And Cajuns, we got a lot of style." He chuckled. "We'll have you over to our place, have a *fais-do-do* and welcome you to New Orleans the right way!"

"Thank you."

Leaning over Izzy's shoulder, Jean-Marc said, "I've had a room made up for you." He gestured to a petite blond woman in white scrubs, who drew near and gave Izzy a little curtsy.

"This is Annette de Bouvard," Jean-Marc explained. "She is one of your mother's medical nurses. I place Madame in your special care," Jean-Marc told her.

"What an honor," she said sincerely.

"Isabelle," Jean-Marc began. He scratched his chin, as if he didn't have the slightest idea what to say next. He had a heavy five o' clock shadow; she wondered how long he'd been up.

He said, "In New York, magic use was fairly minimal. I wasn't supposed to even be there, and I knew it would be unpredictable. It's that way in New Orleans proper. When we're out in the streets, we stay beneath the radar of the Ungifted. When we're playing by the rules, that is. *Le Fils* and the voodoo *bokors*—" he glanced in Andre's direction "—are pushing the limits. The Ungifted in power don't like that."

"And the Malchances," Andre added. "They don't like it, either. And they're the worst."

"Which we can't prove, and which the Grand Covenate seems to be intent on ignoring," Jean-Marc added, shaking his head.

"But that's another subject. What I am trying to tell you is that out here in the swamps, magic is going to be far more common. More intense. You may find it frightening."

"O-kay," she said slowly.

Jean-Marc kept going. "I sent out a memo before you arrived to keep it down at your first meeting. But they're going to forget. For Gifted, using magic is as common as breathing."

Andre nodded. "Jean-Marc is right, him. You stick close with us, *chère*."

"All right," she said. "Thanks for the warning."

"It *is* a warning." Jean-Marc could not have looked more somber if he was attending a funeral. "Go rest," he ordered, and then he left.

Go rest. Was he kidding?

She was a nervous wreck.

Andre shadowing her, Izzy followed Annette through the door from which Izzy had seen the medical team emerge. She was astonished at what she saw: banks of monitors and equipment, and about half a dozen technicians seated at them. They glanced at her, rising, bowing.

Izzy, Annette and Andre walked on through the room; wrapping her hand around a crystal doorknob, Annette opened another door with a flourish.

Izzy was charmed. There was a white iron daybed made up in white satin sheets. White picture frames displayed paintings of lilies. There was a white wood desk and a white whicker chair. And beyond, a bathroom with a clawfoot tub and a hand shower.

And neatly folded on a graceful stool, a gauzy white nightgown, much like the one she had back home. Izzy felt the tranquility of the room. Savored the sense of solitude.

Annette said, "If you need anything, *anything,* just call me."

"*Merci,*" Izzy said, surprising herself by speaking in French.

"*De rien,*" Annette replied, bobbing another little curtsy.

The two left her in peace. As soon as the door was shut, she filled the tub. She found some rose-scented bubble bath in a cupboard over the toilet, which was in a small alcove set off discreetly from the tub. As the tub ran, she took off her clothes.

With a sigh, she slid into the steamy bath. She picked up a luxurious bar of soap and washed herself. Then she found shampoo and washed her hair. She used the hand shower to rinse. The cares and fears of the last few hours did not slide away entirely, but she felt rejuvenated. Hopeful.

As her lids fluttered, she realized she was about to drift off. Not a good place to sleep, a tub. Reluctantly she pulled out the stopper and let the water down the drain.

She wrapped her body in a thick white towel emblazoned with the letter B in a ring of fire. Then she put on the night-gown, found a matching robe beneath it, and carried it to the bed as she pulled back the covers.

Last night I slept with Pat, she thought. She remembered how he moved inside her; the sensation of him thrusting, the taste of him. She closed her eyes with longing. When would she see him again?

She drowsed. Then all too soon, she heard a soft knock on the door. She groaned.

She sat up, slipped on the bathrobe and padded across the room.

"I'm awake," she said, opening the door. Then she fell forward.

Into the nightmare forest of her recurring dream.

Chapter 18

What's happening? *Izzy thought, as she tumbled onto the boggy earth. Her hands sank into mucky ooze.* How did I get here?

"*Andre!*" *she shouted.*

A whooping, crazed animal cry answered her. Cypress trees stretched and shivered as they reached toward the blood-red moon, then collapsed back into the dank water, as if the vines and moss wrapped around their trunks had suffocated them.

The forest all around her was slithering with shadows.

I'm not really here. I'm having the nightmare, *she reminded herself. It made sense—her high stress level, her exhaustion—everything that was happening—here she was.*

Running.

From monsters: she heard them baying. Something panted as it charged after her. She could smell its breath and feel its heat. She didn't dare turn to look at it as she ducked a glis-

tening vine. She slogged into water again, then back onto mucky ground. Roots threaded between her toes. Then her foot came down on something sharp and she body-slammed a tree trunk, grabbing on to it and clutching her foot.

Four deep slashes across the trunk were fresh.

"Madame Bouvard?"

A tall, brown-haired man trotted into her line of vision. He was wearing a dark blue windbreaker with NOPD written on the back in white, and he was carrying a rifle. He had a holster at his side and she could see a revolver.

He drew up short; he cupped the barrel of the rifle with his left hand as he laid it over his chest.

The wolf howls rose in pitch and frenzy. The man scanned left, right, tense, alert…and frightened.

He said, "Where's your gun?"

About fifteen feet to their right, a shadow glided through the darkness. The whooping rose to a shrill shriek. The trees and vines jittered in a frenzy. Clouds raced across the moon, slicing the bloody sphere in half, fog spilling out like clots.

"Hustle it up! They're dogging you!" the man in the windbreaker shouted.

Then the shadow burst out of the forest with an unholy shriek, and flung her to the forest floor.

Her head cracked hard against the tree trunk; she groaned as explosions of light blotted out her vision. Whatever had landed on her stank like rotten meat.

It raised a limb—serrated, like an insect leg—and swiped at her. Jagged, incisor-like nails sliced her cheek, cutting deeply; she felt scalded, burnt. Shocked, she batted ineffectually at her attacker.

The sharp report of a rifle shot cracked against her eardrum.

The thing swiped at her again. This time she blocked it, panting as the serrations on the limb pierced her arm.

"Let me get a good shot!" he yelled.

Then the thing straddled her. Moonlight fell across it, revealing a triangular face, covered with a wet, purple skin that had no places for eyes, or a nose; but the bottom point of the triangle fell open as a set of bone-white upper and lower jaws extended from it and sprang toward her.

Its teeth clacked; she cried out, jerking her head to the side, and the jaws struck the tree trunk behind her. A handful of its teeth dislodged and showered down on her.

"Shoot it, damn it!" she yelled.

There was no shot, no response from the man.

"Jehanne, Marianne, aidez-moi," she prayed.

She formed her right hand into a palm strike and aimed it at the monster. She willed it to grow hot. It burned and sizzled; it was agony.

She clenched her teeth hard and screamed, "Help me! Now!"

Energy bubbled from her flesh, coagulating into a sphere of platinum-white light. It slammed into the monster's face and threw the thing backward, where it slammed against the trunk and exploded into a supernova of sparks.

Izzy rolled over on her stomach, heaving, retching. Her body convulsed as she got to her hands and knees. Blood dripped from her face. She began to hyperventilate as more adrenaline poured through her system.

She craned her neck up, looking everywhere for the man. Something was dangling from the tree.

It was a man, hung by his neck.

The figure was shrouded in darkness; she could make out only the silhouette. It twisted slowly from one side to another.

She spotted the rifle on the ground and grabbed it, raising it as she looked through the sickly green nightscope.

The scope cast white ghost trails on the crown of Jean-

Marc's wild hair; his eyes were open, but there was no life in them. His mouth hung open, slack. He looked dead.

His clothes were shredded; his chest was a gaping wound and little else....

She threw down the rifle and raced to the tree, grabbing the branches with her hands, searching for footholds with her feet—

—searching for footholds as she climbed the side of the little stone house.

What? *she thought, staring up, down, around.*

Now she was in a graveyard, one of New Orleans' notorious Cities of the Dead. Statues of angels with drooping wings and sad Madonnas dotted the rows of crypts like mourners. Dead flowers drooped in vases set on stone steps. Skeletal trees dripped with Spanish moss. Tombs shaped like houses stretched beyond her range of vision, some with slanted roofs, like the one to which she clung. She was about six feet off the ground—an easy drop down.

I'm dreaming, *she reminded herself.* Jean-Marc wasn't really there. I didn't kill a monster. I'm not here.

But her nightgown was shredded. She was injured, and cold and she tasted blood in her mouth. Her dreams had never been this real before.

I'm not here.

But she was.

Jean-Marc, *she sent out.* I need help.

As if in reply, cruel laughter wafted toward her on a stiff breeze. Footfalls padded on the grass. Someone was coming.

She closed her eyes and prayed for strength. With no effort at all, she scrabbled on top of the tomb, shrinking back as a face met hers.

It was a marble angel, weeping tears of moss. She held on to it and she pulled her ravaged feet beneath her into a crouch, making herself as small and inconspicuous as possible. Then she leaned slightly forward, straining to peer over the canted roof. An icy chill seized her abdomen and she sucked in her breath.

Julius Esposito, the missing new-hire in Prop, strode into view.

Oh, my God. He's the *bokor,* Izzy realized. He helped Cratty kill Yolanda. David was working for him. He could have killed me. Could have killed Big Vince…it was only a matter of time.

A male creature walked beside Julius, statuesque in a black shirt and pants, and as bone-white as Sange. He had long hair that trailed down his back, and his red eyes glowed. Also like Sange, long, sharp fangs tipped with jewels glistened in the moonlight.

As they strolled along together, the vampire tugged on a rope. He said, "Allez, vite," in much the same tone Jean-Marc used when he was impatient.

The rope was secured around the neck of a young girl whose arms were tied behind her back; she was dressed in a long tulle skirt, cowboy boots, and a heavy coat, and she was crying.

"Ferme-la!" The vampire sneered at her, jerking hard, making her stumble forward. Her throat closed on a strangled sob; she sounded like she was choking to death. "Your father will be the one crying, when he finds your body in the gutter."

"It's not a good idea," Esposito said. His voice was thick and raspy, like that of someone who had smoked too much. "We shouldn't antagonize Gelineau."

The vampire laughed. "Maybe we can spare you, little Desta. Take us to your twin and we'll kill her instead. She's the one who always gets you into trouble, oui? She's the one who snuck into the Quarter to drink shots with the college boys tonight."

Izzy lifted up her palm. The moonlight gleamed on the raised welt, no longer ripped and bleeding as it had been in the forest.

I will it, she thought.

Her palm began to warm.

Then more figures emerged from behind other tombs. There was a towering, dark man dressed in a robe and a fancy headdress of feathers and beads. Several women flanked him, also in robes, their hair hidden by kerchiefs. The colors were leeched by the moonlight, but the patterns on them looked like elaborate writing in a foreign language.

Men approached, in white shirts and jeans, with drums and what appeared to be a trash bag slung over the shoulder of the largest one.

And one carried a long, gleaming knife, which he ceremoniously handed to Esposito.

At the sight of it, Desta screamed.

The knife in his right hand, Esposito backhanded her with his left. She fell to her knees, then flopped onto her side. She remained there, unmoving.

Izzy tentatively touched her palm with her fingertips. It was still only lukewarm.

Faster, she thought. Jehanne, help me.

As Izzy huddled on the rooftop, the men planted the drums in the grass. The trash bag yielded large candles, bowls, more knives...and a rooster, its legs tied together.

Two of the women picked up Desta by the wrists and ankles, and carried her as the man in the robe sprinkled ashy powder on her. Then Esposito held out the knife, and the robe man sprinkled the blade.

The drums beat, slowly, rhythmic, hypnotic. They matched her heartbeat. Esposito and the vampire looked on, arms folded.

It was a voodoo ceremony.

Esposito jerked. One arm lifted spastically; then the opposite leg. His head pushed forward, like a chicken's. He raised his knees to his chest as he danced with the knife.

The women lowered Desta to the ground. The one at her head placed her hand beneath Desta's chin and tilted back her head, exposing her neck.

Esposito capered toward her.

The drumbeats played louder, faster, reverberating off the crypts and statues. The earth itself seemed to rumble and jump.

Swaying, Esposito licked his lips and moved his body seductively, sexually. Lightning flashed, crashed; the sky broke open and it began to rain, hard.

Lightning sparked off the knife as the man raised it over his head. He spoke in a language she didn't know; then the doors to the tombs crashed open and shapes emerged, their faces and bodies concealed by the driving rain.

Jehanne! Izzy *pleaded, feeling her palm. Nothing was happening; it wasn't getting any warmer—*

The knife slashed down—

Izzy leaped off the crypt—

And the sky lit up with an enormous ball of purple-black energy as—

—Jean-Marc dangled lifelessly from the treetop above her, his chest gaping open, twisting in the wind.

Izzy threw back her head and screamed at the top of her lungs.

The door to her little bedroom in the de Bouvard mansion burst open and Andre barreled in. Izzy lay on the floor in a fetal position, shrieking.

He dropped down beside her and gathered her up against his chest.

"*Mon Dieu,* what happened? *Au secours!*" he yelled.

Annette raced into the room as Andre hoisted Izzy to her feet. He touched her face, her ruined nightgown, her muddy, matted hair.

"Where did you go? How did you get past me?" he cried.

"Jean-Marc is dead. He's dead!" Izzy sobbed.

"Look at her hand," Annette gasped, examining her palm.

The newly formed scar was a welt. It was bleeding; flaps of skin dangled from it. She was dripping with mud. Her feet were bloody.

Then a thundering explosion shook the room, throwing Annette to her knees. Andre and Izzy crashed into a wall, Andre's weight pushing the air out of Izzy's lungs.

Beyond the door, women began screaming.

"The *Guardienne,*" Annette whispered. She got to her feet and rushed out of the room.

"Team! Stat!" someone yelled. "We have an MI! The *Guardienne*'s throwing VPCs!"

Izzy scrambled to her feet and ran with Andre into Marianne's chamber as people in scrubs surrounded Marianne's bed. Two women were holding Marianne's hands. One of them shouted to the other, "Don't break the chain!"

Annette turned to Izzy. "She's having a heart attack. Touch her. Do it like before!"

Closing her eyes, breathing deeply, Izzy placed her hands on either side of Marianne's face and braced herself.

Nothing happened.

She did it again.

Les Femmes Blanches were huddling in a huge mass. Some of them were crying as they gripped each other's hands.

Andre touched his forehead. "*Ah, mon Dieu,* is she dying? Jean-Marc, where is Jean-Marc?"

Izzy stood with both her hands on Marianne's face as one

of the women grabbed up the paddles on a defibrillator. They had a crash cart. They were prepared for heroic measures to save Marianne's life. Izzy felt the familiar wave of panic: they had done things like this to Anna Maria—forcing her back to life.

"Defib, charge two hundred!" the Asian woman cried.

A short young man pulled down Marianne's sheets as Annette yanked her white nightgown above her waist. Marianne's body was young and thin.

"Clear!" the woman bellowed.

Annette said to Izzy, "You need to move away," wrapping her hand around Izzy's forearm and pulling her away from Marianne's bed.

The Asian woman placed the paddles on Marianne's chest, one to the left and one to the right.

"Clear now!" she shouted.

"Wait!" cried the veiled woman who was holding Marianne's right hand. "We can't break our chain!"

"You'd better, or she's going to die," the woman said grimly. "Right now."

Les Femmes Blanches stirred, stared at each other. The one who had spoken turned to Izzy.

"What do we do?" she asked.

Izzy stared back. She had no idea. None whatsoever.

"Madame, I'm Dr. Janice Bouvard. I'm your mother's physician. And I am out of time," the Asian woman said.

Marianne's face was turning blue.

"Let go," Izzy ordered.

"No!" the woman cried.

"You will. You will *now!*" Izzy said, with no idea if she was doing the right thing.

"No!" the woman yelled back. "It'll kill her!"

Andre took a step toward her. The woman raised her left palm. White energy began to glow in the center.

"Do it," Izzy ordered her. "Step away."

"Please, don't make me do this," the woman pleaded, bursting into tears. "She's the *Guardienne!* I have sat in here for her for five years!"

"I'll make it easy for you," said the woman beside her, the next link in the healing chain. And she let go of the crying woman's hand. At the same time, the woman holding Marianne's other hand let go, bursting into tears as she did so.

"The chain!" the first woman cried. "The connection is broken!"

"Clear!" the Asian woman yelled as she pressed the button on the right paddle. Izzy heard the discharge. Marianne convulsed like a flopping fish.

"Still in defib!" someone shouted.

"Bag her!" Dr. Bouvard yelled.

Izzy looked beyond Marianne's face to the other medical personnel working to save Marianne's life. A coffee-hued woman put a mask over Marianne's face and pumped the squeeze bulb attached to it, forcing air into Marianne's lungs.

"Paddles again, people," Dr. Bouvard announced. "Clear!"

Everyone stood back. Some of *les Femmes Blanches* started chanting. A few fell to their knees. Others held one another. Here and there, they were taking off their veils. They looked like ordinary women, nothing more, nothing less. Some moved their lips in prayer, or whatever it was that Gifted did, and tears ran down the faces of all of them.

The doctor hit the button. Marianne convulsed again. The doctor gazed at a readout.

"It's good!" she announced.

Annette said to Izzy, "She's back in business."

"Oh, thank God, thank God," Izzy said in a rush, stroking Marianne's face. She bent over and kissed her forehead.

Then she straightened. She said to Andre, "I have to find Jean-Marc."

"Leave that to me," Andre insisted. "Stay here with your *maman*."

She couldn't. She knew she had to find him. She had to know if he was alive.

"Take care of her," Izzy said to Annette, who swallowed hard and nodded.

Then Izzy raced out of the chamber and into the hall. Swearing, Andre barreled after her, shouting, "He won't want you to do this!"

Michel came running toward her from the opposite direction. His eyes were enormous; a sheen of perspiration glistened on his forehead, despite the coolness of the corridor.

He grabbed her by the arms. "Go back inside! The mansion is under attack!"

Izzy held her ground, pushing against him.

"Have you seen Jean-Marc?" she demanded.

"No," Michel replied. He looked past her to Andre. "Sange says that it's *Le Fils*."

"But those are magical bursts, *non?*" Andre asked. "He must have Gifted with him."

"Malchances," Michel spat.

"I'm going upstairs," Izzy said.

"No!" Michel said, grabbing her again. "You need to stay out of the line of fire."

She looked at his hands on her arms and raised her chin. "Let me pass."

Michel exhaled, overruled. "I'll check on your mother and then I'll join you." He nodded at Andre. "Take her up the service stairs. It's safer."

She picked up the hem of her filthy, mud-soaked nightgown as Andre led her down the corridor. They ran through a door and onto plain, concrete steps that reminded her of the ones in Tria's building. They shot up the stairs, two at a time, around and around until she was dizzy.

She heard machine gun fire. And were those grenade explosions? The pop of pistols. And swearing, in French. Screaming, in English.

As they reached the top of the landing, Andre pushed through another door and they stumbled out onto the mansion's upper verandah, the wide balcony that surrounded the house. It was bulging with people, many of whom she recognized. The men in the hoods were there, and the leathery creatures.

A curtain of white sparkles jittered from the bottom of the balcony and rocketed into the sky. It jittered and flickered, and in the parts that were thin, balls of purple-black splattered against it, bursting into showers of sparks.

Then a black orb penetrated the field; a chunk of the white curtain disappeared and the black light took out a section of the verandah railing; the floor burst into flames.

Dazzling light from several hands put the fire out as de Bouvards massed together to combine their energy. Then the sparkling barrier began to fade again, revealing a black sky beyond. Night had fallen.

Vampires could walk.

"Our field can't hold much longer!" a woman in an evening gown shouted. "Where's security?"

"On the roof," someone yelled back. "And in the air."

There was more machine gun fire. An explosion nearly knocked Izzy off her feet. She held on to Andre, who growled, his face twitching strangely.

Behind Izzy, a beautifully feminine voice chimed, "If you're really the next *Guardienne,* can't you do something about this?"

It was Madame Sange.

"She doesn't have the power yet," Andre informed her, his voice deep and gravelly. His beard was lusher. His jaw, longer. His eyes had taken on an unearthly glow.

"That's not what I heard," Sange retorted. "I heard that she sucked power from Marianne. And that Marianne has had a heart attack because of it."

"Have you seen Jean-Marc?" Izzy asked, ignoring her accusation.

"No," Sange said coldly. "You should finish the job. Take *all* Marianne's power. Or this family may end today." Her fangs glistened as she exhaled in disgust. "All this because of *Le Fils. Incroyable.* How the mighty are fallen."

Izzy skirted around her. Adrenaline coursed through her; despite her exhaustion she propelled herself forward, searching for Jean-Marc. Her nightmare filled her mind; she had seen him hung and gutted—

—*drawn and quartered, as the English did to the loyal soldiers of Jehanne's army*—

—and silent tears slid down her cheeks as she gasped for breath, seeing him nowhere in the chaos. She smelled smoke, and blood. A man staggered past her with a deep gash in his forehead. A woman sat on the floor, holding her arm, weeping.

Izzy couldn't speak; she sent out her thoughts. *Jean-Marc!*

And in the noise and confusion, a man turned and faced her from across the verandah.

Jean-Marc!

He was glowing; surrounded by a deep indigo cascade of sparks. He looked like a being from another planet. She was both frightened and awed…and relieved beyond the telling.

He was *alive.*

"What are you doing here?" he cried, rushing toward her. "Get out of here!"

"Oh, God, thank you," she rasped, and threw her arms around him. She raised her face to his and he blinked, and kissed her hard. Like a lover.

Energy coursed through her; a low flame burned low and deep, and fanned upward. She answered his kiss, desperately. His body crushed against hers; his flesh burned her.

Then he broke away and said, "You have got to get out of here! *Le Fils* is attacking!"

He pulled on her arm and then—

Something slammed into his chest and threw him back against the wall of the house. Blood gushed from the entry wound. A torrent of it. A river.

Izzy turned to the clusters of men and women ducking the shower of debris to fling white flashes of energy off the ruined balcony.

"Officer down!" she cried, retreating into cop-speak as her mind went on automatic. "MOS!"

She grabbed two men by the arms and gestured to Jean-Marc.

"Pick the Regent up! *Now!*" she ordered them. "Get him out of here *now!*"

One of the men made motions over Jean-Marc and the unconscious man rose into the air.

"Take the Regent to Marianne's chamber," she said, pushing her hands over Jean-Marc's wound. They slipped in his blood *into* his wound. The tangy, copper scent of blood permeated the air. She was certain she could feel his heart pumping against her palm.

Moving in tandem, she and her helpers raced back into the service stairwell. Blood gushed onto the concrete.

"Andre!" she shouted.

There was no answer.

Down the stairs, all the damn stairs, through the corridors

of the House of the Flames, Izzy jogged alongside Jean-Marc, dodging people who were running without any apparent destination; simply running, because they were panicking.

Large sections of the ceiling split apart and rained down on their shoulders. She hunched forward over Jean-Marc to protect him, wincing as heavy chunks battered her, gouging into her back.

Then the door to Marianne's chamber burst open; Izzy was alarmed that it wasn't being guarded.

No time for that now.

"Med team, stat!" she shouted.

The dozens of veiled women had been standing in snaking lines. Some of them had pulled back their face coverings, and they were crying. Medical personnel in white scrubs and surgical masks and caps were huddled around Marianne's bed. Dr. Bouvard had a hypo in her hand, and Annette stood at her side, her arms crossed, her shoulders slumped.

They all turned to look at her. Izzy kept her hands in Jean-Marc's wound as Annette hurried over, took one look at his injury and went white.

"Oh, my God." She gestured to the door where the monitoring equipment and Izzy's bedroom were located. "We have an OR." She said to Izzy's helper, "Take him there." She said to Izzy, "You stay here."

Izzy kept running. "No. I have to compress the wound or he'll bleed out."

"You!" Annette yelled to a clump of veiled women. "Elise! Antoinette! Maria, come here! Help with this." To the men, "Stop!"

Three women hurried over, grouping around Jean-Marc's inert body.

"Stop the blood flow," Annette ordered them. To Izzy, "Move your hands."

"No," Izzy said. "He'll die."

The tallest of the three closed her eyes, concentrating; a blinding glow emanated from her hands and she placed them over Izzy's. The other two put their hands over the tall one's.

The glow intensified. The heat scorched Izzy's hands; shockwaves of pain vibrated over every cell of her skin, but Izzy didn't let go.

"Take your hands away," Annette instructed Izzy. When Izzy didn't, she bellowed, "Madame, do it now or we will lose him! You're creating a barrier!"

Izzy complied, lowering her hands to her side. Blood dripped on the floor.

A halo of white surrounded the women. Their hands glowed as if white-hot.

"Go, go, go!" Annette bellowed, leading the way. The men with Jean-Marc and the three women rushed off with her.

Izzy started to follow, but the doctor caught up with her and put a restraining hand on her shoulder.

"Madame," she said, "I need to talk to you."

Izzy said, "In a minute," and turned on her heel.

The woman kept a firm grip on her shoulder and said, "It's best to stay out of the way for a moment."

"What's going on out here? What's wrong?" Izzy took in the medical team, the weeping women. "What's happened?"

"She had another heart attack," the doctor said carefully. "We couldn't stop the damage. And...she flatlined."

The world spun. Izzy swayed.

"She...died?"

The doctor looked caught, as if she had no idea how to proceed. She said, "Your mother is a Gifted, but she is still flesh and blood. As in other cases like this, machines are keeping her body alive. But her mind..."

The doctor looked stricken; her professional detachment

had completely deserted her. She looked like what she was: a middle-aged woman faced with unacceptable circumstances, called upon to handle a situation that she simply could not respond to.

"Madame, she won't recover." Her voice was barely audible.

"What are you...what?" Izzy's knees buckled. The doctor grabbed her by the upper arm.

"What in the name of the Patroness is going on?" Michel shouted as he burst into the room. A dozen women accosted him; their voices competed with one another in a frenzied babble, frightened and desperate.

One of them grabbed his hand and said, "You have to listen to us! She can't take over! You need to do something!"

"Madame!" Michel cried, yanking his hand away and running to where Izzy was standing. He gaped at her blood-soaked face and hands. "I was told the *Regent* had been injured."

"I'm fine," Izzy said dully.

The doctor took over, stepping around Izzy to face Michel. She said, in her best professional voice, "The *Guardienne* has sustained irrevocable bodily insult. She has flatlined."

All around them, the Gifted Bouvard women sobbed. A wild keening filled the room, punctuated by shrieks and pleas to Jehanne. All for nothing, all to no avail...

"Flatlined," Michel repeated.

"For all intents and purposes, our beloved *Guardienne* is gone," the doctor said brokenly. She began to cry. "She is gone."

Chapter 19

Michel stared at Marianne, who lay still and silent, then at the doctor, and finally at Izzy.

"You're covered in blood," he said, sounding dazed. "What happened to the *Guardienne*?"

"It happened to Jean-Marc," Izzy replied. "Chest wound."

"If she is gone," he said, "and there has been no transfer of power…"

Then I'm safe, Izzy thought. Maybe it was petty, to think of herself in that moment, but it was the thought that came. She looked anxiously at the door where they had taken Jean-Marc. Everything in her wanted to bolt through it.

"Marianne's *body* is being maintained," the doctor said carefully.

"So she *is* still alive," Michel replied. Izzy couldn't read his tone of voice. She didn't know where he stood on the issue of Marianne's survival. She didn't know what he wanted.

She didn't think she could trust him.

"Technically," the doctor told him, drying her tears and composing herself, "she is still alive."

There was a pause. It was a chasm, and Izzy felt herself falling into it. She couldn't make a sound. Her hands were shaking. Her heart was beating out of rhythm, battering her rib cage like a bird trapped inside a chimney.

"Get out of my way," Izzy ordered everyone in a raspy, gravely voice as she moved to the head of the bed.

She closed her eyes and willed heat into her palms. She imagined her magical energy traveling from her body into Marianne's. Saw the white light, the heat; she shut her eyes and concentrated with every ounce of her ability, seeing life-giving magic in her blood, in her bones, in her cells.

She placed her hands on either side of Marianne's face and croaked, "Live!"

But nothing happened. Marianne's skin was cool, and there was no warmth in Izzy's palms, no answering light around Marianne's body. No sense of magic, anywhere. If anything, she felt weaker.

"You people are magical," she said to Michel. "Why can't you do anything?"

"I would ask the same of you. You're her daughter," Michel replied. "Save her."

Izzy leaned forward again, this time pressing her lips against Marianne's, pushing air into her mouth. She cupped her palms over Marianne's heart and compressed. She leaned forward to breathe into her mouth again.

"Stop," the doctor said, placing a restraining hand on Izzy's forearm. "It won't help."

"No," Izzy said. "No."

At that moment Andre loped into the room, shouting,

"Jean-Marc! Where is he? Our barrier is down! *Le Fils* is coming in!"

He stopped in his tracks as he took in his surroundings. He hurried over to Izzy and took her bloody hand in his.

"Eh, bon, jolie?" he said to Izzy, his dark gaze probing her. "What is it?"

Then a head poked out of the door to the monitoring room and a woman in white scrubs shouted, "The Regent is in trouble! We need more help!"

Izzy gazed down at Marianne.

"She's stable," the doctor said. Then translated, "Nothing is going to happen right now."

Released, Izzy ran to the woman who had cried for help, who turned and led her into a fully equipped ER. Light from a huge overhanging fixture pressed down like a weight on an operating table surrounded by medical personnel and the three *Femmes Blanches*. Rows of surgical instruments gleamed beneath the harsh disc of light over the table.

A mask over his face, Jean-Mark lay splayed on the table. There were tubes and machines and wires and half a dozen people or more in masks and scrubs. He was nude, a sheet gathered around his pelvis.

A man in white scrubs—the surgeon?—said, "Jesus, he's bleeding out! Get me some light and some sponges here! Type and crossmatch four units. I can't see shit here—no, no, the pericardium looks okay—aorta is patent, looks like a couple big bleeders, there, and there. Get a hemostat on that, gimme some sutures here!"

Someone said, "Pulse is rapid and thready, one-ten, respirations thirty-two and shallow. BP is eighty over forty."

"He's shocky!" said a new voice.

She and Andre moved closer. Her gaze shot over Jean-Marc's blue-tinged skin, the gaping wound. His chest was an unbelievable ruin. She didn't know a person could be so badly injured and yet be alive.

Izzy put her hands on Jean-Marc's forehead, violating the sterile field. His skin was icy.

"Jehanne, aidez-moi," she whispered, exhaling, inhaling, trying to concentrate. "Please, *please* don't let him die."

She willed warmth into her palms, healing energy into Jean-Marc. But there was nothing. She had never felt more like ordinary Izzy DeMarco than in that moment.

"We're losing him!" one of the team shouted.

"Isabelle! Do it!" Andre cried. He ripped his chicken-feet *gris-gris* from around his neck and draped it around her neck.

She tried again.

Again.

"I can't, I can't," she conceded. "I'm…helpless."

"You are *not*," he insisted. His eyes blazed with fury. His face lengthened and he growled, deep and angry and feral. His eyes caught the light; they were more golden. His teeth were growing before her eyes. "You can have all the power. You know it!"

She looked at him. "What?"

His eyes glittered like hard, smoky topazes. "You *know*. Turn off Marianne's life support and the Kiss of Fire will pass to you."

He looked as shocked by what he said as she did. They stared at each other.

There was one second where it could have been a mistake. But he left it there, spoken out loud.

He wiped his forehead and said, "That's what must be done, *chère*."

"Madame, we're losing him," the surgeon told Izzy. His eyes above his mask were unreadable.

The three women in white stared at her, hushed, anxious, expectant.

"Stay with me," Izzy said to Jean-Marc. She took his hand and squeezed it. If he went, she was alone here. If he went, he would take her heart with him.

He would take everything.

She gave herself the luxury of one last doubt; then she ran back through the double doors, back through the monitoring room, where the techs were hunched over their monitors.

Then back into the room where Marianne lay, lifeless but not dead. Izzy took her limp, unresponsive hand in both of hers, closed her eyes, and bowed her head.

There was a tunnel of white and the angelic sopranos of women singing for joy. A female figure stood at the end of the brilliant light. Her arms were outstretched and filled with lilies.

Izzy couldn't see her face, but she knew who she was.

Her mother.

Lilies and oranges; a life together that they had never had, mother and daughter. A lifetime of learning about the Gift, a lifetime of growing together, savoring the world and all its majesty, and its consequences.

Izzy smelled smoke. She heard the crackle of flames.

She heard her mother's voice, which she would never hear in this life. It was sweet and deep.

"I named you Isabelle. They must have known, somehow, when they found you. They called you Isabella, but I left no records of who you were, or what to call you. No history. No trail.

"But I have loved you all these years, and I prayed to Jehanne to spare you from my burden.

"That is not to be."

The figure shimmered with light. She was unimaginably beautiful.

Then it all started to blur. The figure dimmed. Izzy was losing the connection.

The figure stretched out her hands. The lilies floated out of her arms, tumbling in slow motion end over end.

"Oh, my darling, the other one is coming for you. You desperately need the power of the Patroness to see you through this. So let me go."

She became dimmer, just a shadow, just a whisper...

Clutching Marianne's hand, Izzy came back to herself. She licked her lips; her head was pounding.

She heard screaming in the hall and the women in the room began to panic anew in response, rushing toward the bed. One tripped on her gown; two others grabbed her under her arms and dragged her with them.

My gun.

The image of the Medusa filled her mind. She turned on her heel and ran into the OR, past Jean-Marc, yelling, "Where are his clothes?"

Before anyone could answer, she saw a clear plastic bag against the wall; it contained his tux. She raced over and plunged her hands inside the bag, feeling the bloody, ruined clothing for the shape of her revolver.

There.

She found it, pulled it out and opened the barrel. It contained six rounds.

She closed it and ran back into the chamber.

Andre had changed. Where a man had stood, a hunched, demonic creature covered with glossy black fur roared at *les Femmes Blanches*. Enormous teeth jutted from its elongated jaw as it clacked at the women. Its golden eyes gleamed.

A werewolf.

If she had had time to think about it, she would have been terrified. But it caught her eye and she saw intelligence there. She saw Andre there.

She said to it, *"Allez. Vite."*

The werewolf fell into place beside her as she flew down the length of the chamber, yanked open the door and burst into the hall. It was clogged with smoke, fire and people running in all directions. She was shoved against the wall so hard she bounced back off it.

She grabbed the nearest person—a woman who resembled Annette to an astonishing degree—and said, "How do I get out of here?"

"You mustn't! It's you they're after!" the woman cried, grabbing on to Izzy's arm. "Oh, please, *Guardienne,* go back inside the chamber. We'll try to save you."

Izzy shook herself free and darted down the hall, using the same route she and Andre had taken. The werewolf followed close behind; she could feel the heat of his breath on the nape of her neck.

The service stairwell was jammed. She yelled, "Move it!" to the parade of people racing down the stairs, and when they didn't comply, she hit and kicked and used the butt of her revolver to clear a path. Behind her, Andre howled with rage.

She had no idea how long she struggled; each stair step was a victory. Thick smoke rolled over her, obscuring her vision. Her lungs filled with smoke; her eyes watered and she could no longer see. Still she fought her way up, until she was nothing but a ropy, jangled piece of iron will.

She felt for a door and realized she had gone up one flight. Two more to go.

More people crashed into her. Someone said, "Good God, woman, have you lost your mind?" It was Mayor Gelineau. "Go back!"

She pushed him out of her way. Pushed them all out of her way as she inched her way up.

Where are you going? What are you doing? she asked herself. But she knew.

Then she reached the third floor and burst through the door.

"Your Majesty! Oh, my God, they've got Jesse!"

It was Ruthven, Sauvage's boyfriend, buffeted by Bouvards as he ran toward her. Bouvards were swarming the ruined balcony; some carried conventional weapons—Glocks, Uzi's, SIG-Sauers. White light erupted from their outstretched palms, ammo from their arsenal of technologically advanced death-dealing machines.

Izzy peered at Ruthven through the slits of her burning eyelids. Though his image was blurred, she could see his terror, his eyes huge, his face chalk-white.

"They've got her! Oh, God, save her!"

He grabbed her hand and dragged her to the edge of the verandah, where Bouvards threw spheres of white light at flapping shapes as they flew at the mansion. Vampire minions. As she watched, one of the horrible things glommed onto the chest of a woman in an evening gown, opened its jaws and bit into her face.

Izzy swayed, but she did not fall.

In the sky, the moon glowed scarlet; the clouds were clots.

Below a vast body of water shone damascene-black, silhouetted by broad trees draped with moss. A dozen shapes—three dozen, maybe a hundred—darted behind the trees, then lunged out from their shielding cover to throw brilliant purple-black spheres of energy at the mansion. Some of the shapes were men and some of them were things she couldn't begin to describe. Deformed, misshapen. Some had enormous bald heads and protruding teeth; some were stark-white, like phantoms. The bursts of energy cast a strobe effect, adding to her confusion.

Then a ball of white light emanating from the mansion smashed into one of the trees, setting it ablaze. The shape behind it danced away, reveling in the mayhem; in the crackling black light, it—he—turned and faced Izzy's vantage point square-on; and though she was some distance away, she saw a very familiar face.

Julius Esposito.

He smiled at her broadly and gave her a little wave. Then he snapped his fingers. She couldn't hear the snap and yet it echoed strangely in her mind—as if in a dream.

Let me be dreaming.

The vampire she had seen in the voodoo ceremony in the City of the Dead dragged Sauvage forward by the hair. She struggled, batting at him; she may as well have been a ghost for the effect it had on him.

"Kill him! Save her!" Ruthven pleaded as the vampire thrust Sauvage at Esposito, who grabbed her around the neck and put a blade to her throat. Sauvage stood stock-still, weeping.

And Julius looked up at Izzy with such evil that her blood ran cold.

Izzy held up her palm; it was barely warm. Not even warm; that was just her wishful thinking—she had no magical energy at all.

A jag of lightning cracked the sky. Sudden hard rain sluiced down, pouring in heavy cascades as if from overfilled rain gutters. It was so thick Izzy could barely make out the nightmare tableau below her, as Sauvage remained frozen in the same unearthly position for another second. For two. Three.

Then Izzy remembered that she had another weapon. A powerful one.

She raised her gun, steadying her hand with her left palm, and held her breath. Her reality collapsed to a pinprick as she sighted down on Julius Esposito, her co-worker...and a death-dealing monster. What if the bullet killed Sauvage?

She had another bullet. She had five more.

I can't, she thought.

And then an image filled her mind.

A girl, younger than she, astride a horse as she spoke to her troops in Medieval French. "Some of you will be sacrificed. I cannot help it. I beg your forgiveness now, while you are still alive."

"Sauvage, I'm sorry," she whispered.

She wrapped her finger around the trigger.

At the same instant Andre leaped from the third-story verandah, his werewolf shape arcing into the night sky like a bullet himself. As he fell, he threw back his head and howled.

Through the forest, more howls raised, a chorus of rage and despair.

The movement and the noise startled Esposito. Sauvage took advantage and elbowed her captor hard in the stomach, and she collapsed to the ground and rolled away like a seasoned commando.

Izzy pulled the trigger.

Her bullet found its target, dead-on.

Esposito didn't die the way a person dies. He exploded. In a blinding flash of purple light, he fragmented as if he had stepped on a grenade. Streams of black energy issued from a central point, rocketing in all directions like fireworks lighting up the sky.

Sauvage ran screaming toward the mansion as, everywhere, the white shapes threw back their heads, shrieked and collapsed. Down they went; the deformed things, the pale men; all of them, except the vampire, who somehow melted into the night.

Overwhelmed, Izzy fell forward onto her knees.

Around her, the Bouvards began cheering. They hugged each other, laughed, applauded.

Then hands raised her up above the heads of the survivors of the battle. Fire crackled and smoke rolled as she was carried the length of the verandah, looking down on the carnage that had been the enemy.

"Guardienne!" someone shouted.

It was taken up. *"Guardienne! Guardienne! Isabelle, la Guardienne!"*

"No," she whispered. "Not me."

But no one heard her…except perhaps, her mother.

Epilogue

She wore the white gown.

Lilies in her hands, Izzy stood before her mother's bed and gazed down at the woman who was not alive and not dead. *Les Femmes Blanches* had taken up their positions on their wooden benches, holding hands, willing psychic strength into Marianne.

Marianne, who still held the power of Jehanne within her soul.

In the next room, Jean-Marc lay near death.

Sauvage had been reunited with Ruthven.

And Andre was missing.

Gelineau, Broussard and Jackson were already making plans for a counteroffensive. They were hounding her for data. Who was the man she had shot and what kind of *bokor* magic had he wielded? What should they do now?

She had no idea.

All she knew was that the House of the Flames still stood.

The fires were nearly out. The wounded were being tended; the dead were being mourned. The remaining de Bouvards had strengthened the wards and fresh security forces were stationed all over the grounds.

It was nearly dawn. It was a new day.

Her gun was strapped to her hip.

She moved away and keyed a number into her cell phone.

"Iz?" Pat said. "Hey, darlin'. How's it going?"

Tears welled in her eyes as she said, "Fine, Pat. How's by you?"

"Missing you."

"Same here. Just checking in. I'll call again later."

"Tell me what's wrong," he urged.

"Nothing," she lied. *Everything.*

"When you're ready."

She closed her eyes, grateful for his perception—and his kindness, and his steadiness—and said, "I will."

Then she disconnected. She walked back to her mother's still form and placed the lilies in a white vase beside her hospital bed.

On numb feet, Izzy walked into the OR, where the doctors and Bouvard healers still fought to save Jean-Marc.

Die, and I die with you, she said to him, though she had the terrible feeling that he would never hear her again.

And then…a fluttering, a gentle whisper against her heart.

Never.

Always.

The Daughter of the Flames raised her head, closed her eyes and murmured, *"Merci, Jehanne. Merci."*

At Silhouette Bombshell,
we love to break barriers and astound our readers.
Turn the page for an exclusive sneak peek
at the first book in a groundbreaking new miniseries
THE MADONNA KEY.
Prepare to be enchanted as seven special women
uncover their lost heritage—the legacy
of the Marian priestesses—and unleash the wrath
of a powerful and vengeful enemy.
The excitement begins with

LOST CALLING
by Rita® Award-winning author Evelyn Vaughn
July 2006

Available wherever Silhouette Books are sold.

That first earthquake was not my fault.

Even if God did smite sinners, would He not use the usual thunderbolts? Besides, I am no saint. But even I haven't the conceit to claim an entire natural disaster!

That—the conceit, not the earthquake—echoed my grandmother's. One of her favorite sayings was, "This is your fault, Catrina." Although if anyone could will earthquakes into existence, it was my *Mémé*.... But I digress.

A rush of feathers and coos startled me from self-pity as I strolled from the hospital. Grateful for the distraction, I looked up. Doves burst from the sycamore trees lining the avenue and scattered into the blue Parisian sky. Hmm.

I glanced over my shoulder to see that, *certainement,* the slight, gray-haired figure who'd been following me on and off for more than a week had returned, as well.

I ignored him to look back to the birds.

"What is wrong now?" I whispered—in French, of course, but I will translate for you. I snorted at my understatement. A great deal was wrong. I had gone months without a lover. My job as curator at the prestigious Musée Cluny dissatisfied me of late. That damned old man really was following me, though I had yet to manage a confrontation—I feared he had something to do with a past mistake of which I am not proud. And the grandmother who had raised me, no matter how poorly, lay dying in the nearby *Hôpital Saint-Vincent de Paul*.

But did I mention, months without a lover?

Fine. If you must know, my grandmother was of even greater concern than both my sex life and the mysterious old man, at the moment. *Mémé* disliked me even more than I disliked her, but in a rare attempt at decency, I had just visited her.

Who would have thought so old and sick a woman could shout so loudly or throw flowers with such vehemence? But today, our mutual disdain held a horrible undercurrent of finality.

Far easier to worry about birds.

At first, I thought I heard the rumble of a truck's approach. But I saw only automobiles and scooters darting along the Avenue Denfert Rochereau. A young couple, strolling and cuddling ahead of me, looked about in concern. Springtime in Paris meant music and sunshine and love and flowers and birds—

Fleeing, frightened birds.

My legs trembled, as if the visit with *Mémé* had upset me more than I cared to admit. Unlikely. Finally, I recognized the sensation from my two years in the U.S.A.

In California, to be exact.

Earthquake!

Logic denied my unsteady legs. Surely not. *In Paris?*

Then the sidewalk rolled, buckled. I fell hard against an iron fence circling a sycamore and caught at it, clung to it.

Other pedestrians ran or stumbled, their shouts half lost beneath the earth's alien growl.

So much for logic.

Losing my balance on the pitching pavement, I managed to secure one elbow around an iron bar, trying to take everything in. The old man had caught himself against a lamppost; his stare unnerved me. The young couple stumbled together. Her hand wrenched from his as she fell to the asphalt.

The bastard ran on without her. Over the woman's screams for him—his name, it seems, was Eduard—the very earth began to shriek in protest, like something huge and maddened.

Clinging beside the sycamore, on my knees to lower my center of balance, I watched a crack open and dart across the walkway and into the road, quick, like the run in a nylon, but not as straight. This was worse than I'd seen in California.

It ran right under Eduard's lover's hips.

Her screams choked into horrified whimpers.

The crack widened beneath her. Jagged chunks of concrete crumbled into the fissure, spreading, gaping across the avenue. Dust plumed upward. A smell of tearing cement burned the air. Once-solid ground shifted, sagged. The din crushed my ears.

And that foolish, abandoned girl had to look over her spread arm at me, wide eyes brimming with terror.

I am no saint, but...*merde.*

I tried reaching toward her with one hand, hoping the little fence would hold. "Quick! Come here!"

Since she may have been a tourist, I repeated the command in English. Then exasperated German.

Surely the little fool understood *something!*

All she had to do was to crawl toward me. Instead, as one

of her knees dropped into the widening crevice beneath her, she began to weep.

Better her than me. Lest it escaped you, I am not a very good person. And yet…she looked so very helpless.

With a groan of disgust, I loosened my elbow-hold on the fence and attempted to hang on with one hand, tight and sweaty on the iron. I stretched closer toward the girl. *"Now!"*

She stared at me and trembled. My fingers began to slip on the age-pitted iron. I wanted my elbow-hold back.

"Fine," I screamed at her. "Die, then!"

The motivational ploy, were it one, had no effect. Suddenly the ground heaved harder, surging up, then dropping. The crack stretched wider, now gushing dust. Steel reinforcing bars ripped from the buckling concrete they had once supported. The girl's legs dropped into the opening, as if the earth were swallowing her. Her nails tore on the pavement as she tried to hold on.

Gravity sucked her downward.

And unexpectedly—under some sisterhood impulse?—I let go of the fencing and dove for her. Spread flat across the walkway, I went for her wrists with both hands and actually caught one.

As she dropped deeper into the fissure and my chin slammed into the asphalt, I recognized my mistake. I swore. Loudly.

I was not saving her. She was dragging me down.

This is why I avoid being nice! Now I could not let go even if I tried, not without beating her off. The idiot dug into my wrists with what nails she had left, sweat stinging the wounds she inflicted. Straining to escape as much as to hold her, I tried to bury my face into my own shoulder, to catch even one breath that wasn't thick with debris. I choked instead. I couldn't breathe. I couldn't get my knees beneath me. I couldn't find purchase. My body slid inexorably toward the widening hole.

With a final shriek, the girl vanished into the road's gaping maw. I lurched forward with her, then caught on the edge. Jagged asphalt cut me under my arms as I momentarily held her. She kicked and writhed upward—*now* she struggled to live?

My arms felt pulled from my shoulder sockets as I inched forward. Downward. The lip of torn rock dragged past my breasts. Past my ribs. I was hanging headfirst into depths I could only imagine. For the record? I dislike heights. And then—

Then I dropped into the void.

The Marian priestesses were destroyed long ago,
but their daughters live on. The time has come
for the heiresses to learn of their legacy, to unite
the pieces of a powerful mosaic and bring light to
a secret their ancestors died to protect.

The Madonna Key

Follow their quests each month.

Lost Calling by Evelyn Vaughn,
July 2006

Haunted Echoes by Cindy Dees,
August 2006

Dark Revelations by Lorna Tedder,
September 2006

Shadow Lines by Carol Stephenson,
October 2006

Hidden Sanctuary by Sharron McClellan,
November 2006

Veiled Legacy by Jenna Mills,
December 2006

Seventh Key by Evelyn Vaughn,
January 2007

www.SilhouetteBombshell.com

SBMK1

**Hidden in the secrets of antiquity,
lies the unimagined truth...**

Introducing

a brand-new line filled with mystery
and suspense, action and adventure,
and a fascinating look into history.

And it all begins with DESTINY.

In a sealed crypt in
France, where the
terrifying legend of
the beast of Gevaudan
begins to unravel,
Annja Creed discovers
a stunning artifact
that will seal her destiny.

*Available every other
month starting
July 2006, wherever
you buy books.*

**GOLD
EAGLE** ®

GRA1

Silhouette

SPECIAL EDITION™

Welcome to Danbury Way— where nothing is as it seems...

Megan Schumacher has managed to maintain a low profile on Danbury Way by keeping the huge success of her graphics business a secret. But when a new client turns out to be a neighbor's sexy ex-husband, rumors of their developing romance quickly start to swirl.

THE RELUCTANT CINDERELLA

by CHRISTINE RIMMER

Available July 2006

Don't miss the first book from the Talk of the Neighborhood miniseries.

Visit Silhouette Books at www.eHarlequin.com   SSETRC

If you enjoyed what you just read,
then we've got an offer you can't resist!

Take 2 bestselling love stories FREE!

Plus get a FREE surprise gift!

Clip this page and mail it to Silhouette Reader Service®

IN U.S.A.	IN CANADA
3010 Walden Ave.	P.O. Box 609
P.O. Box 1867	Fort Erie, Ontario
Buffalo, N.Y. 14240-1867	L2A 5X3

YES! Please send me 2 free Silhouette Bombshell™ novels and my free surprise gift. After receiving them, if I don't wish to receive any more, I can return the shipping statement marked cancel. If I don't cancel, I will receive 4 brand-new novels every month, before they're available in stores! In the U.S.A., bill me at the bargain price of $4.69 plus 25¢ shipping & handling per book and applicable sales tax, if any*. In Canada, bill me at the bargain price of $5.24 plus 25¢ shipping & handling per book and applicable taxes**. That's the complete price and a savings of 10% off the cover prices—what a great deal! I understand that accepting the 2 free books and gift places me under no obligation ever to buy any books. I can always return a shipment and cancel at any time. Even if I never buy another book from Silhouettte, the 2 free books and gift are mine to keep forever.

200 HDN D34H
300 HDN D34J

Name	(PLEASE PRINT)	
Address	Apt.#	
City	State/Prov.	Zip/Postal Code

Not valid to current Silhouette Bombshell™ subscribers.
Want to try another series?
Call 1-800-873-8635 or visit www.morefreebooks.com.

* Terms and prices subject to change without notice. Sales tax applicable in N.Y.
** Canadian residents will be charged applicable provincial taxes and GST.
All orders subject to approval. Offer limited to one per household.
® and ™ are registered trademarks owned and used by the trademark owner and or its licensee.

BOMB04   ©2004 Harlequin Enterprises Limited

BOMBSHELL™

COMING NEXT MONTH

#97 LOST CALLING—Evelyn Vaughn
The Madonna Key
When a freak Paris earthquake plunged her into a hidden catacomb, museum curator Catrina Dauvergne made an amazing find—remains of the Sisters of Mary, legendary guardians of the Black Madonna. But this career coup made Catrina a target of powerful men set on destroying any trace of these martyrs. Now, as the suspicious earthquakes continued, could Catrina harness the sacred powers of the past to save the future?

#98 PAWN—Carla Cassidy
Athena Force
After testifying against her criminal father, Lynn White had been put to good use as a government agent. Her assignment to stake out Miami's Stingray Wharf was a cakewalk for someone of her special abilities—until she ran into ex-lover Nick Barnes, working undercover to bust a crystal meth ring. The feelings between them were explosive—only overshadowed by the *real* bomb Lynn discovered when her mission turned deadly.

#99 WHAT STELLA WANTS—Nancy Bartholomew
Between her partner Jake's demands for a special place in her business and her heart, and refereeing the romances of her agonizing aunt and New Age cousin, private investigator Stella Valocchi had way too many distractions. But then her high school chum Bitsy bit the dust in an explosion at the mall. Or did she? As Stella worked the case, she realized one thing—life was short, and it was time for her to focus on what *Stella* wanted....

#100 DEAD RECKONING—Sandra K. Moore
To rescue her sister from a drug-smuggling husband, charter-yacht captain Chris Hampton needed backup—bad. When two DEA agents offered to help, it was a godsend, and all three set sail for her brother-in-law's island hideaway. But then the "accidents" began—and when Chris nearly drowned, it was *no* accident. With a double-crossing killer on board, never mind her sister—could Chris save herself from being lost at sea?

SBCNM0606